BY NIGHT
THE MOUNTAIN BURNS

BY NIGHT
THE MOUNTAIN
BURNS

Juan Tomás Ávila Laurel

Translated by
Jethro Soutar

LONDON · NEW YORK

First published in English translation in 2014 by
And Other Stories
London – New York

www.andotherstories.org

ISBN 9781908276407
eBook ISBN 9781908276414

A catalogue record for this book is available from the British Library.

This book has been selected to receive financial assistance from English
PEN's 'PEN Translates!' programme. English PEN exists to promote
literature and our understanding of it, to uphold writers' freedoms around
the world, to campaign against the persecution and imprisonment of
writers for stating their views, and to promote the friendly co-operation
of writers and the free exchange of ideas. www.englishpen.org

Supported using public funding by
ARTS COUNCIL ENGLAND

BY NIGHT
THE MOUNTAIN BURNS

The song goes like this:

Maestro: *Aaale, toma suguewa,*
All: *Alewa!*
Maestro: *Aaaalee, toma suguewa,*
All: *Alewa!*

The 'toma suguewa' part means 'give it a pull', but it also means 'will you give it a pull', or 'will you all give it a pull', even 'will sir give it a pull'. Know why it can be any of these things? Because in the language the song is sung, my island's language, there is no polite form of address like there is in Spanish. Nevertheless, the maestro treats everyone with respect, as if he's addressing them as 'sir', and because he asks them so respectfully, they pull. He does it all singing, and it's a song that brings back many memories and fills me with nostalgia. As far as I'm concerned, it's the most beautiful song in the world.

Aaale, toma suguewa,
Alewa!
Aaaalee, toma suguewa,
Alewa!

No, there are no other words to the song, no more verses. That's it. The song consists of what the maestro asks, sung in a beautiful voice, and what the people say in reply, as they answer his call: *Alewa!* Then all together, as one, they pull what they've been asked – with due respect – to pull.

Does anybody know what they're pulling? It's something that happens on my island, which is located just below the equator. If I'd studied geography, I'd give degrees of latitude and longitude, so that you might look the island up on a map, or on some other more modern means of looking for things. In any case, I should mention that the island is African and that the people who live on the island are black, every last one of them. And that it's surrounded by the Atlantic Ocean. Totally surrounded. The black people I speak of live on a sliver of land that pokes out of the murky waters.

And what of the simple but meaningful song? The inhabitants of the island live from fishing, a fishing that's done almost entirely by hand out at sea. And in order to get out to sea the fishermen paddle flimsy canoes. These canoes are made out of tree trunks, cut from trees that are known to be good for floating. There are only three types of tree on the island that can be used for making canoes, only three.

Does anyone know how you start when making a canoe? First you select the tree, and if it's not your tree but a tree on a woman's plantation, women being the ones who farm on the island, you go and speak to her. You might be lucky and she's a widow or has no husband, or she has one but he's away. Or you might be unlucky and she has sons who are growing up, and she knows that one day the tree will make a good canoe for those sons, when they're old enough to go out fishing and transport things about the island. Every man on our Atlantic Ocean island has his own canoe, and if he doesn't have one, a new canoe is brought into the world so that he does, so that nobody on the island has to borrow one from anyone else.

If you manage to do a deal with the woman, or if it turns out that your own woman has one of the three types of trees on her farmland, you cut through it until it falls to the ground where you found it. This last part is worth mentioning because if the land happens to be planted, it's going to be very difficult to get the woman to agree to your cutting the tree down, even if you offer her something of equivalent value in exchange.

After chopping off the branches and piling them up to be used as firewood once they're dry, you're ready to call upon whoever you consider the best craftsman, so that he might start work on your canoe. It's important that you pay him a visit and that he accepts the invitation. He, the maestro, won't ask you for anything impossible in return, nothing that will cause you to look to the heavens. Normally he won't ask you for anything at all and it will simply be enough that you show him

9

respect, but if he does ask you for something, it will be something readily to hand. He might ask for a drink, a drink that everyone has or can get hold of, or he might ask for a favour in return. He might say to you, without lifting his voice or showing much concern, that you could clear some land for his wife, for she's found an empty plot where she'd like to plant malanga and plantain. So anyway, you come to an agreement, and as soon as he can the maestro starts work on your canoe. The first job is the hardest job: hollowing out the trunk. This means digging the wood out so there's enough depth and space for you and your wife, your little children and the load you'll be carrying when you paddle from one part of the island to another. The hollowing out of the trunk is done right where the tree falls, the tree that will become your best friend, your right-hand man. The dug-out chunks of wood are gathered up by boys and girls and some older ladies, for they know a big tree gives a lot of itself. They collect the bark too, and when these chunks of wood and strips of bark are dry, they put them to burn in the stone tripod of the fireside, where the pot boils with things to eat, whatever there is.

The job of hollowing out the trunk is a hard one and it's done using the heaviest kind of axe, an axe with a long handle. In truth it's a job any strong young man can do, albeit with the guidance of the maestro, to make sure the youngster doesn't overdo it and leave the canoe with too little walling. The trunk is only half-emptied at the place where the tree is felled, meaning the top side is cut into, the part that will become the inside of the canoe, and the edges are whittled down evenly, for they will become the sides of the canoe. The part that's in contact with the ground is left alone for now. As the tree trunk is often longer than the canoe's required length, another important job is to separate the canoe from the rest of the trunk. This job is a little more delicate than the hollowing out stage because through this process the front and back ends of the canoe emerge, the parts that distinguish the more striking and beautiful canoes, those made with real skill. One part, the front part, will have to break through the sea waters, and it will also be the part that's seen when the charming little thing is beached after a day's fishing. The back part supports whoever's paddling the canoe, the helmsman, and it's where he jumps on when he gets into the canoe and off when he reaches land.

Once these tasks are complete, most of the maestro's work remains to be done and the canoe is still in the bush, where the tree was felled, a long way from the shore. It now has to be transported to the shore, where the maestro can finish his work close enough to the sea to hear the waves break, to taste them, and close enough for men to come and watch the work being done and comment on it. Only once it's on the shore does the canoe really start to take shape, start to become a canoe that will be admired by all men and make the maestro proud. So that shell of a canoe has to be transported to the nearest feasible beach. The nearest and the most feasible. The double condition mustn't be ignored because transporting the thing is hard, heavy work, and not every part of the coastline on our Atlantic Ocean island will welcome a canoe into its waters. Do not be fooled: there are certain shores on our island, some sandy, some stony, where the waves are angry and will not allow anyone into them in any kind of vessel, no matter what offering is made.

Does anyone know how you get the half-formed canoe to the shore from the bush it lies in? Some of you have guessed: by pulling it to its final destination, the bottom part dragging along the ground, which is why it's left as it is, rugged and round. The owner of the canoe, he who asked for it to be built in the first place and who will use it for his needs, speaks to all his friends, and they in turn speak to their friends, and everyone agrees on a date when they will come and help pull the canoe to the shore. The owner knows there can never be too many hands. He also knows nobody will ask for anything in return, absolutely nothing for what is a hard job that takes a long time and uses up a lot of energy. So he also speaks to all the womenfolk he knows, especially the women who are his relatives, and he asks them for something too. He asks them to prepare, for the afternoon of the day of the pulling, a big pot of malanga soup, enough to feed all the people that will be needed to perform such an arduous task. This will be their only compensation and will send them home satisfied, energies restored, and safe in the knowledge that one day it will be their turn to call for the help of all noble men, and to ask their female nearest and dearest to prepare, for a particular hour of a particular afternoon, a restorative malanga soup.

The day arrives and the half-formed canoe is fastened with a long, thick rope, a rope that has been brought along especially by its owner. Indeed that rope is used for one thing and one thing only on our Atlantic Ocean island, and its owner has long felt obliged to let it be used for that purpose. The maestro ties the rope around the trunk in such a way that those pulling can get a good purchase without the canoe coming to any harm and without those pulling the canoe coming to any harm either. Next, those who know about such things chop down a banana tree, or a different tree of similar size, and cut the branches into rollers the canoe can slide along. The paths on our Atlantic Ocean island are rough, the trails are extremely stony and there are many steep inclines. All of which means that pulling a canoe to its final destination involves a lot of hard, dangerous work. And because there are not an infinite number of rollers, or even enough to cover the entire route to the nearest feasible shore, the way it works is this: after each small stretch, once the run of the rollers is used up, strong young men take them from the back and return them to the front, so that the half-hollow trunk can slide over them again, that's to say, so that the process is repeated. Have I mentioned the inclines on our Atlantic Ocean island? Well, this means that the trunk doesn't always slide along the trail as intended, even though the route has been chosen so that those pulling hopefully won't fall off the path. Therefore other men, typically younger men with some experience of canoe pulling, place themselves at the front of the canoe armed with sticks, sticks they've cut and stripped down especially, and they prod the canoe to straighten its course.

The half-made canoe is pulled along by human force, one single force drawn from many different men and women, with many different physical aspects and motivations. The whole thing is done so that lots of individual pulling becomes one united thrust. But how is it done? After all, herein lies the secret of how that shell of a canoe gets from the bush to the nearest feasible shore. It needs someone who knows how to make lots of little energies come together at the right moment and become one giant mass of energy. That someone is the maestro and he does it by singing, which means he has to have the dual qualities of being a boat-carpenter and a singer. To those dual qualities you might also add that he needs to be tough, because sometimes he has to sing and take his turn pulling on the rope at the same time. His is a rare yet essential skill, the ability to orchestrate everyone's efforts through song, uniting the exertions of men and women of different physical aspects around one half-made

canoe. He knows they will heed his call. So let's go back
to the beginning and sing the song once more:

Aaale, toma suguewa,

Alewa!

Aaaalee, toma suguewa,

Alewa!

The wise old man opens his throat and sings, like a
great maestro, the first part of the song. Then the friends
of the owner of what will soon be a canoe, and the friends
of those friends, cry: *Alewa!* This, as you can hear, is a
word with three syllables. The men and women dedicated
to this arduous task answer at the tops of their voices,
for it could hardly be a conversational reply, and they
put the emphasis on the second syllable, in tandem with
the force they apply to the rope. The middle part stands
out – *aLEwa* – and the canoe, which all of them treat as
their own, gains traction:

Aaale, toma suguewa,

Alewa!

Aaaalee, toma suguewa,

Alewa!

So you could say *alewa* is the ho of heave-ho, or you
could make a more literal translation, like this:

'Will you give it a pull?'

'We'll PUll!'

And on the PU comes the unified force that moves
the canoe along another stretch in its journey to the
nearest feasible beach. For short journeys, for example

15

from the wetlands to an area of the beach safe from the waves, there is a shorter version of the song in which no one leads and everyone chants the *Alewa* part over and over again, until the final destination is reached. Or until the next resting point, where there's a pause while the stronger ones reset the rollers, and then everyone starts the chant again, and so on until the final destination. But when what you want to drag lies several miles from the coast, deep inside the bush, and involves navigating difficult paths, dangerous inclines, stony trails and other hazards and perils, the only version of the song that's sung is the one I've been singing. It doesn't matter if there are several resting points over the long journey. When the pulling gets going again, everyone falls back in with the song, though the conductor of the orchestra is eventually changed. Yes, I call it an orchestra, because there are so many men and women, and they all sing at the tops of their voices in order to keep spirits up. Neighbours on nearby malanga plantations, or plantations of cassava, yam or plantain, neighbours who will typically be mothers with little children, hear the song from wherever they are and know right away what's happening. The song is the same everywhere on the island, and there is no other event or activity when it is sung. So they might come across the pulling procession on their way home, but even before that, whether they have been on high ground or low ground, they'll have heard the song making its way through the silent bush:

Aaale, toma suguewa,
Alewa!
Aaaalee, toma suguewa,
Alewa!

If there were too few people on our Atlantic Ocean island, too few strong people, we obviously wouldn't be able to fish in canoes. There would be no need to ask a woman to have a malanga soup ready at a particular hour of a particular afternoon, and nobody would sing to pull a half-made canoe to its final destination.

Has anyone worked out why the canoe is not finished where its mother tree is felled? If it were done there, the effort needed to move it would certainly be reduced. But have I mentioned the number of rocks there are on the island? I said the island lay in the middle of the Atlantic Ocean, but did I mention the unevenness of its terrain? A canoe that left the bush finished and polished would reach the coast snapped in two, no matter how much care was taken. And then all the singing, all the cooking, all the pain and effort put in over so many hours, would have come to nothing. And this would be very upsetting for the owner of the canoe, for the maestro who built it and for everyone who took part in the pulling. And the owner of the rope used to pull the boat, he'd be upset too. And if it were to snap when the malanga soup was already prepared, everyone would sit down disappointed and eat the soup in silence. The song would be left hanging in the air, unaware as to why it had been sung with such vigour and heart:

Aaale, toma suguewa,
Alewa!
Aaaalee, toma suguewa,
Alewa!

Like I said, that little song fills me with nostalgia and makes me think of all the people who lived on the island when I was a boy, and it makes me think of my grandfather.

I can't say for sure whether my grandfather was or wasn't mad. I saw him through a child's eyes and through such eyes it's impossible to tell whether an adult man, who lives in your house and who you've been told is your grandfather, is mad or not. Whether an adult is mad or not is not something easily understood by a little boy, who judges things with the eyes of his age, or doesn't in fact judge them at all. But grandfather didn't go unnoticed by me or by the other children living in the house. What I mean by saying he didn't go unnoticed is that, if it hadn't been for someone I loved and trusted telling me in a reassuring voice that as well as living in the house he was a member of the family, I'd have been very afraid of him and would have avoided him at all costs.

We lived on our Atlantic Ocean island, as I said, and in a house with an upstairs and a downstairs. There were no more than two houses on the whole island that had an upstairs and a downstairs, so I knew that whoever built our house must have been a man of means at some point in his life, at least of more means than most people on our island, the geographical coordinates of which I still don't know. I say this because it was obvious most people were not of means and had never been of means, for they lived in simple houses built around makeshift wooden posts. The walls between posts were filled in with palm-tree branches, the roofs with *jambab'u*, a shrub you cut when green, leave on the ground to dry and then gather up in sheaves to carry home on your head. These sheaves are then used to make a thatch by weaving the *jambab'u* together and tying it at the corners to the palm-tree branches. It makes a secure roof for it doesn't let water in. Nor does it heat up much when the hot sun beams down on it. In fact it hardly heats up at all. But, unlike the house I grew up in, you don't hear the rain when it rains on a *jambab'u* roof. And I like the rain too much for it to happen without my hearing it. I don't know whether I feel this way because I grew up in a house where the rain pounded on the roof, or just because I like the rain and like to be able to hear it.

So my grandfather lived upstairs in our two-storey house, as if living up there was the only thing he knew how to do. Consumed by time, that man never came downstairs, or practically never, and as a child I couldn't understand why he never came down a set of stairs that he himself must have built. The house wasn't far from the shore and at night, when silence took hold of the village, you could hear the waves breaking on the sand. You heard the waves better at night, and I repeat this because we believed that not only could you hear them better at night, but that night was when the waves brought sea beings to the village, beings that might be good, like the sea king, or bad, like strangers who took children away, which the adults warned us about. No activity took place on the beach at night, nor did people go there to meet up with friends and tell stories. Well, actually yes, some men went down to the beach at night to catch crabs in the wet sand. These crabs made their dens in the sand and came out at night to wash themselves in the splash of the waves. The men used the crabs as bait when they went fishing. But there was no other reason to go down to the beach at night, except, actually yes, people also went there to relieve their bellies. The thing was, as most houses consisted of no more than four tree-trunk posts and a *jambab'u* roof, they had no bathrooms, and therefore some people went down to the shore after dinner and made the most of the darkness to relieve their bellies. They went there in groups, albeit small groups. We didn't go because we lived in one of the few houses on the island to have a bathroom.

Apart from the reasons I just mentioned, there were also some people who went to the beach at night to commit a shameful act and they would have fingers pointed at them the next day and be called wicked. These people were always women, usually older women, and when it started to be said that a particular woman went by herself to the beach at night, our grandmother would tell us never to walk past the door of her house, for that woman had acquired the ability to send objects into any child that went naked before her.

I never saw grandfather come downstairs and I never saw him eat, either. I don't know when he ate or even if he ate at all, and I suppose it didn't bother me because I must have thought that grandfathers just didn't eat. We children were given food on individual plates; at night this consisted of a piece of fish with some sauce, though it wasn't really sauce but rather the water the fish had been boiled in. We were also given a hunk of floury cassava bread and we sat eating on benches underneath the eaves of the house. We ate all together, all the children of the house, and we looked at our plates and at everyone else's, comparing to see if anyone had got a bigger piece of fish. If they had, the more sensitive among us might feel hurt and start crying, which meant that one of two things could happen: the person who'd dished out the food would feel guilty and give the crying child an extra bit of fish to console them; or the crying child would get a smack for spoiling the harmony, a smack on the back that made you go gulp. 'Gulp!' was what grandmother used to say to make us hold back the tears, even when the cause of our tears was a slap on the back from her. 'Gulp!' grandmother would say, with her hand raised, for if you didn't 'gulp' down your crocodile tears you got another smack and then you really did have something to cry about.

When nobody complained about the portion they'd been given, we ate 'savouring' our fish, making it last in order to make the others envious, the greedy ones who finished first. If the fish we ate had lots of bones, and especially if one of us ended up with a piece that had sharp, hard bones, after eating, and after properly sucking them clean, we would store the bones in a corner of the house. Those thick bones were what we used for getting ticks out. We knew ticks lived in the sand, in dusty areas and near pigs, but even knowing all this we were never careful enough to avoid catching them. You knew a tick had made a nest in you when you felt a harsh burning in your foot, between the toes. The smallest children in the house would complain of stinging and cry because of it, but they couldn't get the ticks out by themselves. So an adult, a woman, would have to free them of the parasite. Those of us who were a little more grown-up de-ticked ourselves, though we weren't very good at it. The girls and women were best at it. The trick was to get rid of the tick while causing minimal pain, which meant doing it quickly and breaking as little of the skin it had nested under as possible. To manage all this, you had to have a sharp eye and a steady hand. Often older people in the neighbourhood would send a message to our house to ask one of the girls to go and rid them of that disgusting parasite. As these older people could no longer see clearly and had very thick skin on their feet, they couldn't detect the nests very easily. So on one of those elderly people's feet you might find six or seven of the beasties, all of different shapes and sizes, some so old they had beards, beards that stuck out from under the skin. A tiny tick is about the size of the nib on a ballpoint pen but, once under the skin, after sucking on your blood or whatever it feeds on, it can grow to the size of a drawing pin. Adult ticks are ugly and look like eyeballs, but without the shiny, shimmering bits, and with heads: the part that bites into the skin. Often you feel a sting, look down at your foot and see, between your toes, a tiny tick biting its mouth into you. If you don't get it out straight away, it gets under your skin, expands and grows a beard. Ugh! Disgusting things. When you catch a little one trying to burrow into your foot, you pull it out and stick it on the nail of your left thumb and then squash it with the nail of your right thumb, and it goes *splat* as it bursts.

My grandfather was just the sort of person ticks love but, because he lived upstairs, he was hardly ever troubled by the beasties, which attacked like a plague in the dry season.

I've already talked about my house and where it was located. I said how you could hear the waves breaking on the shore at night and that you could sense the dangers that might emerge from the sea. The house was close to the beach, and not any old beach either but the big village beach. Yet despite being so close to the shore, grandfather had built the house with its back to the sea. In fact, in order to look to the horizon, the house would need to have been built on a different street. But on the street where my grandfather built his house, everything faced the mountain. So although it was the tallest house in the neighbourhood, it had its back to the sea. However, it had a good view of the mountain, the Pico. *El Pico de Fuego*, as it was called in Spanish. From upstairs, you could see all that was happening on that great mountain. And when I think of my grandfather, I think of how he spent years and years of his life sitting where he could watch what was happening on the mountain at all hours of the day. And how he stared at it, and how I ended up thinking he must have been waiting for something to happen there, or for something to emerge from up there. And that's why, though he could have chosen to build his house on a plot of land with a sea view, he'd chosen to build it where the main doors and windows gave out on to the mountain. Was he hiding from something by turning his back on the sea? Did he expect something more important to come from the mountain?

I almost always saw grandfather sitting in the same place. I never saw him eat and I never saw him talk, by which I mean what might properly be called talking. He made minimal communications but I myself never had a conversation with him. Nor did I ever hear him say a word to anyone, although I know, from what my brothers and sisters told me, that he did occasionally talk to one of his friends. Of course a long time has passed since then, since the last time I saw my grandfather, and it could be that I did have short conversations with him when I was very little but that I no longer remember them. Yes, that could be so.

You entered the house at ground level and then went up some stairs into a living room. That living room gave on to a balcony where you could see practically the whole village, although we don't call it a village in my language; the word we use is more like town or capital city. Anyway, like I said, you went into the living room and came out on a balcony that looked towards the Pico, and you'd see grandfather sitting there with his back to you, in a chair made out of esparto grass. He positioned the chair a little away from the balcony handrail, as if not wanting to expose himself fully in public. He'd be dressed in a shirt, a V-neck sweater and brown trousers, almost always with a towel draped over his thighs, although he was never seen without his trousers on. The first thing that you noticed about the man was that he'd shaved off half his hair, by which I mean the hair had been deliberately removed, for there was nothing to suggest an accident had caused him to lose half his hair. Well, I suppose it wasn't quite half, but it was the better part of half, and it was shorn right down to the bone. What was this? Why didn't he shave the other half off too, or let the shaved half grow so that it was all uniform? Was it some kind of fashion? And if it was, could someone not have told him it looked awful? That it was really very ugly and didn't suit him at all?

Whenever any of us went out on the balcony, we'd greet him, for he was our granddad, and he'd make a gesture to show us he'd heard. He might briefly look at his feet to check he wasn't being bitten by mosquitoes, but he never turned to look at us and answer. Sometimes one of the younger children of the house would go upstairs because they were learning to talk and they knew that the man up there was their grandfather, so they went up there and leaned on the armrest of his chair and asked him questions or tried to make conversation, but grandfather would do no more than look briefly at the child and then carry on attending to the mosquitoes. He didn't get annoyed, but when he thought the child had said enough he looked inside the house for an adult to come and take the child away, which was what usually happened. Sometimes, if he thought the child was old enough to be left on its own without an adult, he'd get up, for grandfather could walk, and lead the child downstairs. But his leading the child downstairs was actually no more than his placing the child at the top of the stairs and giving the boy or girl a little push to help them on their way.

Any child in the house who was prone to crying already had plenty of reasons to do so and there was no need to make matters worse by visiting that man upstairs who never spoke to you. This was to his advantage, for I can't imagine what would have happened if one of the biggest cry-babies in the house had gone up there and made him angry, even made him shout. Of course it possibly did happen, but I never saw it. I think little children are able to sense an adult's kindness, if not their friendliness, and they avoid adults that seem sullen.

Although men usually represent family security on the island, I always felt more secure and connected to the women in our household. This could have been due to my grandfather's particular nature, but I think it had more to do with my grandmother. Grandfather was always around, yes, but one day it occurred to me that maybe he had nothing to do with the family, that maybe he wasn't even from the island. What if he were an incomer, someone who'd got lost on his way home and had taken shelter on our island but knew nobody? What if he'd arrived by sea, all alone, as we were told the images of the church saints had done, and that was why he didn't know how to talk, just as the images didn't? This was what I thought as a child, and I regret that grandfather never let us know more about him. And I never imagined that one day I'd be telling the story of my childhood.

When our mothers went off to their plantations they left the youngest children in the care of an adult of the house, if there was an adult who wasn't going to the plantations for some reason, or in the care of older children, ideally a girl. Entrusting children to a girl was best, because girls are more responsible, but that way you sacrificed someone capable of doing more work on the farm and bringing back a heavier load than a boy. As a child I never understood why girls had a greater capacity for carrying weights on their heads, but now I suppose boys and girls probably have the same capacity, just we boys used to complain and cry about how heavy the loads were while the girls didn't. This might have been because they were under more pressure to put up with it, because one day they'd become women and they'd be talked about and labelled lazy if they started crying because of the weight of a load. But doubtless they hurt just as much as we did.

Anyway, one day we children were left on our own in the house, and a plane flew over the village. Most of us had never heard or seen a plane so close before, and so it gave us all quite a fright. One of the youngest children in the house was so frightened he climbed the stairs and went crying to grandfather, seeking the comfort of an adult embrace. Grandfather understood and saw that though the plane was long gone, the boy was still afraid and sought refuge in his grandfather's lap, which meant he stuck his head between grandfather's thighs and closed his eyes. The boy thought it the safest place for him, and the old man understood his grandson's fear and comforted him by stroking his back with his hand. It was a very brief show of affection. Or maybe it was such an effective show of affection that the boy immediately felt at ease. Either way, he came back downstairs and played with the rest of us, and though we'd all been frightened by the plane, none of us had thought to seek grandfather's protection.

The house I grew up in was full of women, my grandparents having had only daughters. We children were the offspring those women had brought into the world and, as they were all about the same age, and saw that their mother, our grandmother, was still fit and strong, they had us believe that grandmother was really our mother. We never spoke of our fathers. If we needed a man to comfort us, we went upstairs to talk to the only one we had, he who sat staring at the mountain. I've already said what happened then.

Grandmother had a niece who came to our house a lot. She was chubby, with fat thighs, and she was very smiley; I never saw her get angry about anything. When she came to the house we all competed to throw ourselves into her loving arms. She hugged us each in turn, and after she'd greeted and kissed everyone, and after she'd talked to the other girls her age in the house, she would go upstairs, pull over a chair and sit down next to grandfather, her back to the balcony rail. She went up there to chat to him, to tell him things, tell him about her life. Armed with her cheeriness and her smile, she told grandfather things, she smiled, she laughed, and it was as if they really were chatting. Was that aunt of ours so smart and kind that she knew how to make conversation with him, even though he never replied to anything she said? Did she know how to choose the right words so that he didn't need to respond to them, so that only she had to speak but there was no lack of communication? While she talked to him, she never stopped laughing, as if she were chatting away to a normal person. Did she have some ability we lacked? Did she know how to read grandfather's gestures and communicate with him that way? Did they have a secret they shared?

When she thought it had been enough, she would stand up, put the chair back, say her farewells and come back downstairs, and not with the frowning face of a failed encounter, but more smiley than ever. She must have known something we didn't, we who lived with the man. In any case, grandmother's niece was older than we were, as we were the children her cousins had brought into the world, so she knew more things than we did. But she was the same age as our mothers, so we found it strange that none of them enjoyed the same privileged relationship with him that she had. Or could the answer lie simply in her boldness and not the hidden explanations I looked for?

Like all the inhabitants on our Atlantic Ocean island, we lived in the big village during the rainy season and went to the settlements in the dry season, to eat whatever we could find there. In most families the change of season presented few problems, for the whole family went to the settlements and the house in the big village was locked up for the season, sometimes with keys, more typically with two sticks crossed over the door. But in our family we couldn't all go to the settlements, for there was one family member who never made the journey: grandfather. He never made the journey because of two invalidating reasons, if that makes sense. For a long time I thought grandfather was an invalid, which is why that expression popped out just now. It would have had to have been a totally debilitating invalidity, for he did absolutely nothing. But anyway, the two reasons why grandfather couldn't go with us to the settlements in the south were one, he couldn't walk there, and two, he couldn't paddle a canoe. The fact that he couldn't paddle a canoe was what finally convinced me he was an incomer and that he simply hadn't learned since coming to the island. Because every man and grown-up boy on our Atlantic Ocean island knows how to paddle.

The problem was we couldn't leave grandfather on his own in the big village. And the reason wasn't that he didn't want to be left on his own, for doubtless he would have liked it, but rather that there'd be nobody there to cook for him. So grandmother arranged it for her daughters to take turns staying with him, in three shifts of one month, which was how long the dry season lasted. I didn't think anyone needed to stay behind with him to make him food, for I didn't think the man ate. I only learned of this requirement the year when it was my mother's turn to stay with him, by which I mean the mother who'd brought me into the world and with whom I was very much in love at the time, for I'd only just found out she was my real mother. I missed her, and if it hadn't been for the fact that by being in the big village I'd have missed my brothers and sisters, and missed out on all the fun being had in the settlements, I'd have asked to go with her. But I'd have been on my own, for my brothers and sisters were happy where they were, eating birds that were preserved in salt after they'd been caught by those who'd learned how using traps or a sticky resin from a tree.

Sometimes grandmother's niece invented a reason why she had to stay in the big village during the dry season and said it would be no trouble to take food to grandfather every day. When this happened none of my mothers had to take a turn to stay behind and cook. And I kept thinking: but the man doesn't even eat! What did he eat? Who was he? What was going on with that crazy haircut? In truth there were a great many things that puzzled me about my grandfather. For one thing, why did he not go to the *vidjil*, the recreation hut the men had down by the beach? He never went, maybe because he didn't like it there but more likely because he refused to leave the lookout that was his balcony at home. That a man living on an island in the middle of the Atlantic Ocean should refuse to have anything to do with the sea, and never go to the *vidjil*, was a strange and striking thing. You actually did nothing at all at the *vidjil*, so it was especially strange that he didn't want to go somewhere where you did nothing and where I'd have thought he'd be happier. The men at the *vidjil* were about the same age as him, they would have reminisced about old times and talked about things he knew. Did he not go because he didn't know the others, didn't know about the same things? It was possible, and this reinforced my belief that he was an incomer.

That he didn't go to the *vidjil* because of his views or tastes was of no interest to anybody. That was his business. But it was a great disadvantage to us that he stayed at home. Because, if he had spent long hours at the *vidjil*, as the other men of his age did, he would have come home at the end of the day with a bundle of fish and we would have eaten more fish than we did. That's why I found it so incomprehensible that he stayed at home. Because at the *vidjil* you did nothing and you took home handouts given away by the fishermen when they got back from a day at sea. The thing was, it was customary on the island for the men at the *vidjil* to help pull the canoe in when a fisherman got back from sea, and to show he was a good man as well as a good fisherman, and to keep our island's customs alive, the fisherman would hand out a few fish to the men who helped pull him in. Now some of the men at the *vidjil* were quite old, and some of them no longer could, or no longer would, get up to drag a canoe in. But others, though they too lacked youthful vigour, got up whenever a fisherman came back and, while the strong ones pulled the canoe in, they merely touched it, making sure it was noted that they'd touched it, and with this gesture they qualified for the thank-you handout. It was a kind of begging, a kind of scrounging that was quietly accepted. Or a kind of gentleman's agreement. Which just left those old men who no longer could, or would, get up from where they were seated. But no fisherman ever failed to show his appreciation to them too, be it because he was fond of a particular old man or because the old man had certain qualities that meant he was somehow esteemed. In truth, all men were esteemed once they'd reached a certain age.

But back to my grandfather and his not going to the *vidjil*, nor to any other part of the shore where people fished, and to us, as a consequence, eating so little fish. All of my grandfather's offspring were female, and we, the males, the grandsons, were too young to go out fishing. Was my grandfather not somehow esteemed? Did he not have in him those qualities that meant he'd be given fish even though he'd done nothing? Had he been bad in his youth and that was why he avoided other people, because he'd wronged them and they didn't like him because of his past?

The one person who made sure we didn't go too long without eating fish was my grandmother's lovely niece. From an early age she developed a habit of being charitable towards us, at first giving us fish from her father, then her brothers, and then from the husband she acquired once she'd reached the age of desire. There was never any doubt that girl would find a good husband for she was so lovely.

That we didn't eat fish because the man of our house didn't fish and refused to go where he ought to go was no small thing. Because, on our Atlantic Ocean island, if you didn't fish, or get fish to eat, you didn't eat. And don't ask me why we didn't raise hens, goats or pigs on our island of unknown geographical coordinates. Let's just say that when we did, they were much more likely to be taken away on boats than find their way into grandmother's cooking pot. It was said that all the animals we never saw eaten were taken to where our fathers were. There were many of us in my grandmother's house and all of us had a father in that place you went to by boat, a boat we only ever saw in the distance, from the beach. All of which meant that when we had no fish, grandmother put a hunk of cassava bread in our hands, as dry as a remnant from the fire. And nothing more was said of it. So in order to eat in our house, two adults had jobs to do. It was grandmother's job, aided by her daughters, our mothers, to make sure there was always a hunk of cassava bread to put in our hands or, when there wasn't, a mash of something cooked inside a parcel of green banana leaves. And with this, they could be satisfied they'd done their duty. Then it was the man's turn, and the man of the house could be satisfied he'd done his duty when fish reached the house through his doing, and in sufficient quantity that there was enough to go round. The man of our house refused to have anything to do with the sea; in fact, he built his house turned to face the mountain. Nor could we little men of the house help, as we saw other grandchildren do, grandchildren whose grandfathers took them out to sea to learn how to fish, in exchange for a bit of seasickness and vomiting. Seasickness and vomiting from the grandchildren, I mean.

And how do you think we were left when grandmother's niece didn't send us even a solitary fish's head, which was all she did send some days? We were left holding a hunk of cassava bread and thinking of salt. I've already said how dry the bread was and that it was difficult to swallow on its own. Indeed it was painful to swallow if it wasn't softened by the water the fish had been boiled in, water we liked to call sauce. I think I already mentioned it. You dipped your bread in the water, the leftover water from grandmother's cooking, and that way it went down your throat painlessly and with some sense of taste. So when not even a fish's head reached our house, the more sensitive among us ate nothing and, after biding time beside the kerosene lamp, we went to bed on empty stomachs, feeling terribly sorry for ourselves. That lamp was the only source of light in the house. *Gracias a Dios*, it didn't end up with grandfather upstairs, though maybe he had his own. Anyway, the more enterprising among us held that piece of bread in our hands and thought of salt and chillies. We carried the lamp, or whatever light was available, and groped around outside looking for chillies, tiny chillies that were red when ripe, green otherwise. Then we went back into the house and crushed them up with a bit of salt. As we did so, grandmother and our mothers would warn us about the heat, though sometimes they just left us to it. Emergency preparations made, the next step was to dip your piece of bread into the chilli and salt mix, then stuff it in your mouth. It was our substitute for fish, the fish our grandfather had failed to bring us by shutting himself away at home. You had to blow on your lips as you chewed, to counter the intense heat and burning. For the thing is, the chillies on our Atlantic Ocean island may be small, but boy are they potent. You chewed and *wham!* You blew on your lips and tears came to your eyes, for chillies seem to demand a lot of water. In fact, you blew on your lips only because you couldn't eat and drink at the same time, but as soon as you'd chewed and swallowed, you tipped a whole glass of water down your throat. You finished and then it was bedtime, and ouch for any boy who forgot to wash his hands before putting them in his trousers and taking hold of his organ to pee! And ouch for any girl who carelessly let her unwashed hand touch her slit! Ouch! Ouuuch! I already said how hot the chillies are on our island. And if it was hard enough to get over the heat on your lips, it was harder still to get over a heat that burned inside you, and in such a sensitive area, and all because of a man whom we knew nothing about, our grandfather.

I don't want to say any more about the lack of fish and other animals to eat without mentioning that I knew the island priest because we used to take eggs to him. So surely we could have eaten eggs with the cassava bread! Why did they not cook eggs for us? Grandmother would send us to take eggs to the *Padre*, and we were glad to be sent on such an important assignment. The *Padre* lived at the *Misión*, just above the church, or behind it, in the upstairs of a building joined on to the *Misión*. Someone worked for him and it was this person who opened the door and took the eggs from us. Sometimes we could see the priest whiling away time on the balcony, staring out to sea. From the *Misión* you could see the sea, and also our house. And you could see someone sitting on our balcony, which had to be grandfather. Sometimes we thought our grandmother sent us there just to see grandfather and the house from a different angle. The *Padre* did the opposite to grandfather and stared at the sea, in case a boat passed the island. Grandfather stared at the mountain, every day, and never tired of looking at it, as if he knew that whatever it was he was waiting for would come from up there. Perhaps he was waiting for the king of the mountain, or of the lake, which was, and still is, on the other side of the mountain.

As our bodies grew, so too our curiosity, and one day we got the idea of going into grandfather's sleeping room. He slept alone, or at least I thought he slept alone, though I never knew if grandmother slept with him. I didn't know if his room was really their room, because grandmother always went to bed after everyone else, so I never knew where she slept. But anyway, we wanted to know what was inside grandfather's sleeping room. Although first I should probably explain where we all slept. Our mothers slept with their littlest children and their daughters, even if those daughters were not little but the same age as us, the boys. So it might be that in one bed slept one of my aunts, a child of between two and six, sometimes older, and a girl about the same age as me. They arranged themselves like this: first the mother, then the child in the middle, and the girl by the wall. If there was another little child, a little girl or a boy who wasn't yet as old as we were, he or she slept at the feet of the other three, and nobody complained, and two of them would wet the bed, even if they'd been made to go outside and pee at the door before bedtime. In another bed there might be the same arrangement, assuming the next aunt had the same number of children, by a father who was in another town, somewhere you got to by boat.

All the boys who were a bit more grown-up, of whom there were three in grandmother's house, slept in the same bed, a bed that had evidently been of good quality once upon a time. I was the youngest of the three, so I slept in the middle. All three of us peed in our sleep, that's to say, we all wet the bed. Which is why it ended up ruined. When I started sleeping in it, the base had already begun to rot because of the ferocity of my older brothers' peeing. Wetting the bed was something we just couldn't help and if I were to start telling all the stories born of our torrential peeing, we'd be here for several days. Let's just say that between the three of us we got through that good mattress, which had been a white man's mattress, the grass mattress they gave us afterwards, the bed base, the board they put under the mattress when we first made a hole in it, and so on, until there was nothing left for us to get through. And the cloth we covered ourselves with was turned to rags. Of course the adults sought cures; someone said we'd stop wetting the bed if we ate crab droppings. I ate them, my bedfellows ate them, and still the unstoppable river flowed. Such was life when we decided to explore grandfather's room.

Our chance came when a man we understood to be grandfather's friend came to visit him. He was a man the adults in the house said had only just come to the island, that he'd arrived on the last boat, although we had the impression we already knew him, or had at least seen him around the big village. Maybe we confused him for someone who looked like him, or we never associated him with the arrival of a boat, and therefore we never knew that previously he hadn't lived on the island. Whatever it was, we were told he'd arrived on the last boat and, as he was a good friend of grandfather's, he came over to see him. He waved to grandfather up on the balcony and grandfather went downstairs and out to meet him. We watched them walk away together, towards the north of the village, and it was said that grandfather talked to him and that they talked about things only they knew about. It was even said that from time to time during the conversation my grandfather shook his head and cried out in exclamation, as if incredulous or surprised, as if one of them had said to the other that only in Africa could such things happen. In any case, it was said they talked in low voices, as if exchanging confidences or secrets. We didn't see any of this, but it made sense that if grandfather had gone out with the man, he must have said something to him. Grandfather knew how to speak after all! So why did he never talk to us at home? Anyway, we saw them walk away towards the cemetery. Now that I think about it, somebody had died that day and there'd been a funeral procession.

There was, indeed there still is, only one cemetery on the island and everyone is buried there. Before heading for the cemetery, the priest is called, and he comes dressed in his official garments, assisted by his altar boys, at least two of them, one to carry candles, the other to carry incense. In my youth, back in my grandparents' days, the whole church entourage would come to the house of the deceased and then leave with the coffin, followed by almost every one of the town's inhabitants. And if it wasn't quite every last one of them, it practically was, and it certainly included people who weren't very close to the deceased or the deceased's family. I remember seeing it and I remember there being so many people they wouldn't fit in the church. But before the funeral procession made its way through the town or big village, all the children who lived along the procession route were shut up in their homes, with the windows covered over. It was said that if the funeral air, 'the air of the dead', came into contact with children, it killed them and took them away with whoever was being buried. Of all the terrifying things we were told about in our youth, being touched by the air of the dead was the thing that frightened us most. Children could only open the door again when their mother or another adult of the house told them it was safe to do so.

So that day someone had died, although we didn't know who, and that friend of grandfather's, who'd recently arrived by boat, came to tell him about it, and grandfather left his lookout and went off with him. The funeral procession had already set off but they followed along, slowly, each man walking with his hands clasped behind his back, walking along as if they knew everyone would wait for them, as if whatever had to be done at the cemetery couldn't be done without them. As if everyone were waiting for them to arrive and deliver the final prayers in Latin, though it's highly likely grandfather and his friend were atheists and refused to have anything to do with religion. Didn't I say my grandfather might have been an incomer? That would explain why he wasn't the same religion as us. I knew, from what people had told me, that incomers often didn't go to church and that they ate people. They ate other human beings.

When we knew grandfather was far away, we older boys, and a few of the girls, got rid of the little ones and went up to grandfather's room. We looked at each other and put fingers on lips calling for silence, even though the house was already silent, and then we carefully opened the door, just a bit, and three of us went in, two boys and one girl. We went in and opened our eyes wide. Shit! Grandfather's secrets! The things we saw in that room only confirmed what a strange, disconcerting man he was. After seeing what was in there, we went out again, our hearts pounding, and called for silence. Our other brothers and sisters wanted to see what we'd seen, so we let them go in but, because we were nervous, for we knew we were doing something forbidden, we told them to hurry up and they rushed out wide-eyed. Then we put fingers on lips again and I knew, we all knew, what was meant by that, and we closed the door. Can anyone guess what we saw in that mysterious man's sleeping room?

We knew grandfather would soon be home from the cemetery and so we hurried to put everything back the way we'd found it. What did we see in that room? Before I say, we ought to think for a moment about what a great friend that man who came to see him must have been. I say this because he made something happen that none of us had ever seen happen before, namely that grandfather came down from upstairs. Or did grandfather go out sometimes when we were asleep? Because, to us, grandfather leaving the house really was a big deal. And in our island's culture, it's believed that when something extraordinary is about to happen, there's always a warning sign. In this case, the warning was grandfather going out with his friend to join the funeral procession, although I don't know for sure whether they actually entered the cemetery. What happened after that was something truly extraordinary, one of the most extraordinary things that ever happened on our Atlantic Ocean island. But it wasn't a good thing, it was very tragic, so not extraordinary in a good way. Something momentous. It might be said that we children unleashed an evil by going into grandfather's room. I wouldn't say that, but it is true that the momentous thing began that day, after that funeral. I don't know if I'll be able to remember all the details but I'll try to, and I'll tell you as much as I remember. But I'll do it slowly, like telling a ghost story under a full moon, for it would be wrong to rush the telling of something so momentous.

Afterwards, when things eventually got back to normal, and in light of the visit of that friend of his, we were told that grandfather had once worked on a boat, that he'd been to many countries, even that he'd been the captain of the ship he'd visited those countries on. And that other man, the one I've said was supposed to be a newcomer but who we thought we'd known all our lives, was one of his travel companions, or worked with grandfather on the boat at any rate. Have I not said several times that grandfather might have been an incomer?

The thing was, grandfather was so strange, that's why people thought he was an incomer and were always talking about him, trying to work him out. And as he was our grandfather, we asked our grandmother about him, though not all at once: one at a time and on different days, according to the particular doubts each of us had. But she never told us anything that satisfied us. So we decided that she either didn't like him or didn't know anything about him either. Besides, if she never talked to him, it made sense that she didn't know anything about him. She wasn't annoyed by our questioning, for she didn't scold us; she just didn't answer, and she made gestures to suggest there was nothing to say. Then we tried asking her when she was eating, knowing the best time to catch someone in a good mood is to catch them eating, but she just chewed, sucked on a bone and waved her hand in the air to suggest that maybe there was something to say, but who were we to bother her about it. We were children and we knew there were some things adults couldn't tell children, so we assumed the reason for his strange behaviour, the crazy haircut and the way he didn't want to have anything to do with anyone, was something serious, something children couldn't be told. Grandfather didn't speak to us, but this didn't bother us the way the lack of fish did, and the fact that we suffered that lack because he didn't know any fishermen. And this on an island surrounded by waters overflowing with fish, for the sea around us had so many fish that sometimes they fell out of it onto the beaches, like mangoes falling from a tree. You'd be walking along the beach and suddenly hear a great splashing, and you looked up and saw a big fish jump in the air, chasing a number of smaller fish that jumped in the air to evade their pursuer. And all that movement and jumping told of a great quantity of fish just a few feet from where you were standing. The splashing would continue, the jumping would go on, and then the smaller fish jumped onto the sand to avoid capture. There was no need for a net or bait or a hook: the fish just landed at your feet. The most common type of fish on our shores were sardines, and they sometimes spilled onto the sand by the handful. But it wasn't unusual to come across fish of bigger sizes that way too, like tuna, or fish from the tuna family; not fish that liked rocks and deep waters but ones that moved about in schools searching for whatever it is they search for.

Fish spilling onto the shore was nothing, nothing I tell you, compared to something similar that happened, though on a much larger scale and for reasons nobody understood. It happened less frequently, though it was regular in that it tended to happen around the same time most years, years long ago lost in time. So it was impossible to predict, but it was regular. That's all I can say. If I'd seen it happen as an adult, I'd have tried to find out more about it, that wonder of our island's oceans. What happened was that at a certain time, and without anyone understanding what caused it, there flowed onto all the island's shores, onto every beach on the island, an unquantifiable number of squid. You could see them coming from way out at sea, one by one or in groups, rushing towards the shore and then onto the beach, where they stayed. Watching this curious phenomenon, it looked as if the squid had received a strange order they were determined to obey. After washing up on the beach they showed no sign of wanting to get back in the water, back to where they came from, which must have been very far away, deep out at sea, for squid weren't common or easy to catch. Indeed it was very rare for a fisherman to catch such a specimen and it was generally thought that squid lived in a different part of the ocean, or in its extreme depths. Well that's what we thought until this strange phenomenon occurred, this mass squid exodus, as we called it. Although it was more like a mass suicide or a mass expulsion than a mass exodus, for it surely wasn't something those molluscs would have done voluntarily. What was it? What drew them on such a journey away from wherever they lived – and on a one-way trip at that? Was it because they were chased by predators, as happened on a smaller scale with the sardines? It was something nobody understood, for the quantities involved were truly amazing: hundreds and thousands of squid would wash up on the beaches, stranded in the sand or on rocks, and perish, never to return to the sea. What an incredible thing! What an amazing phenomenon! I've said it once but I'll say it again: what was it?

Whenever it happened, and it always happened in the afternoon, the first people to see it would start yelling to let everyone else know: 'Squid! Squid! Squid!' That was all it took for everyone to come running and for the great squid festival to begin. There were huge piles of squid run aground on the beach in the big village. Piles and piles of them. Then more piles on the next beach, and more on the next beach after that, and so on; hundreds of squid landing on the shores of our island for no apparent reason. And down came men, women and children to harvest the bumper sea crop. And they went on shouting squid squid squid, and no one went without, and no one knew what to do with so much squid. And something needed to be done to provide for times of shortage. So, after the harvest was complete and all the squid that had spilled out from the Atlantic Ocean had been gathered in, decisions had to be made about how to make all that nourishment last for the days and months ahead. But before anything was decided, the island's fishermen had made their preparations and were licking their lips in anticipation. For they knew squid meat was the perfect bait. With squid meat for bait, you could lure any fish onto your hook, even fish that usually only ate plants. And there was one fish in particular that was very fond of squid, a fish that swims in our waters and doesn't have a name in Spanish, only in our language. It's a flat fish and it must be an oily fish, for it has a blueish colour. We call it *pámpan'a*. And so the squid harvest was always eclipsed by the great *pámpan'a* harvest, and we thought we lived by the most bountiful sea in all the world, somewhere so bountiful that fish could just be plucked from the water. For the fishermen caught *pámpan'a* in such huge quantities . . . Amazing, truly amazing quantities. They caught so many that nobody, absolutely nobody, went without fish for several days. Even families with grandfathers who had no friends and refused to go to the beach to fraternise with the fishermen. Widows, single women, disabled men, recluses, men who didn't fish because they had a different job, everyone, everywhere; no one went without a fish to boil in their pot. Fish was smoked, fried, salted, lightly boiled, the water used as the next day's condiment, and everything came accompanied with what was left over from a few days ago, namely squid, boiled and salted. What huge quantities of seafood we ate! Truly amazing quantities! We could never have imagined, without seeing it before our eyes, that there were so many fish in the sea.

We ate the squid, we ate the *pámpan'a,* and later we experienced periods when we hungered for fish again. In truth, the people on the island didn't appreciate the squid itself as much as they appreciated the marvel of its coming. Because the sudden abundance of squid was a mere prelude to that huge fish harvest, to what we considered the sea's fertile season. We saw the sea as our island's larder, the place where we kept the fish assigned to us; any man past adolescence could pick up his fishing tackle and go out to sea at any time, so long as it wasn't stormy. And with such a larder at our disposal, households with men didn't go as hungry as households without them. Or households with one who refused to have anything to do with the sea, even turned his back to it.

The sea's resources seemed so readily available to us that people overlooked the need to make provisions for the times of shortage. Ways might have been found to make that huge quantity of fish last to cover less plentiful times, times when men went out to sea and came back complaining that it was too windy, that it was too calm, that little fish were eating the bait and stopping it reaching the bigger fish, that conditions basically weren't right for fishing . . . Some efforts were made, fish were salted and smoked, the only preserving techniques the adults knew on our island, but the smoked and salted provisions soon ran out and then it was back to eating chillies again.

Wham! Blowing on your lips, and ouch if you touched yourself where you shouldn't.

Fish was for us a product of primary necessity; as I've already said, if there was no fish, you didn't eat. What I didn't realise as a child was that the whole island suffered from disastrous shortages. Yes, they can be described as such. And maybe I didn't realise the island suffered disastrous shortages because I didn't wash my own clothes or light the lamp in our house. Therefore I didn't know there was no soap on the whole island and I didn't realise that kerosene was in such short supply that at a certain time at night we had to switch the lamp off or turn the flame down to preserve what little we had. Reducing the light's intensity was a tricky operation and only grandmother did it well. It seemed like such a simple thing but really it wasn't and if you hadn't mastered it, and we little ones never mastered it, nor did our aunties, it was better not to get involved. Only grandmother did it well, and this was significant, for it might happen that the lamp went out in the middle of the night, leaving the house in total darkness, all because whoever had reduced the flame had not done so with a steady hand. Then grandmother would have to trouble herself with getting out of bed and calling for a neighbour in a low voice, asking if we might relight our lamp from hers. And grandmother did this because she believed that so many children under one roof ought not to spend the night without any light, in case something happened to one of us and some problem needed resolving. And why did she call on the neighbour in such a situation? Because the neighbour shared her sentiments and also kept the light on low all night. And because we didn't have any matches in the house.

When the lamp went out for some reason before we'd gone to sleep, it constituted something of an education for me: I started to learn about our life and started to realise that things weren't the way I'd always seen them. I started to realise that we didn't have it so good. That kerosene, the liquid saviour, was scarce, that we had no matches and possibly no soap either. But how did all the kerosene lamps in our big village get lit? The same way the fires were lit. You took a coconut shell, with its leftover kernel, and went to the neighbour's house, or to the neighbour's neighbour, and asked for some burning embers. And you went back home and got some kindling you kept in the house and added it to the embers and the *cuscús*, which is what we call the kernel when it goes dry after all the oil is pounded out, and you lit the fire. If your neighbour had matches but already had a fire going in the stone tripod, she saved on a match and sent you into the kitchen to light your lamp. You had to kneel over the ashes, and this always betrayed what you'd been doing, though some people were able to squat and avoid getting dirty.

If your immediate neighbour had nothing to make fire with, you went to the next one, and from the next one to the next one, a hundred yards, two hundred, it didn't matter, you might walk two hundred and fifty yards until you found someone with smoke coming out of their kitchen. Often what you did when you were sent out with the lamp was peer over the rooftops looking for smoke. Then you headed straight for where you saw it, avoiding having to go from house to house singing 'Mum says can we have some fire?' That's what you said in our island's language.

What with going from house to house asking for embers, a matchstick or a fireside to kneel over and stain your knees on, I realised that the adults on the island were exasperated by our situation and sought solutions in everything they could lay their hands on. But they could hardly lay their hands on anything, for our island was all alone at sea and there was no other land we could join forces with to combat our lack of everything. It was around then that I realised we islanders had no one to depend on but ourselves. That's to say, we were on our own out in the middle of the Atlantic Ocean. People had given up hope of the boat ever coming back – the boat from the place where our fathers were. And in this great solitude, they stared out at the horizon all day, looking for a boat to appear that we could go and ask for things from. As children we saw how they rushed out to sea whenever they saw a stick on the horizon, thinking it might be a boat full of everything we needed. And they set off chasing after it with such conviction that they persuaded themselves the strength in their arms was equal to the power of the motor on the boat they were trying to catch. In any case, they tried, and they came back looking so disappointed it was as if they'd received confirmation that our situation was hopeless.

In the period I'm talking about, those who had someone to go out fishing ate fish, and those who had nylon and hooks went out fishing. So the lack of fish was considerable in some families. We longed for the big fish to chase the little fish and for them all to fling themselves on the sand, as we'd seen happen so many times before. And we longed for the squid beaching, that it might become a weekly event. And if we longed for such miracles, which is basically what they were, for it's quite something to have fish flung at your feet, it was because our situation had become desperate. And it was during those desperate times that the extraordinary events I mentioned began to occur. All the evil came at once. The worst moments in the history of the island.

With the shortage of everything really squeezing at our throats, a boat appeared off the coast, and it was so close that we could tell it was taking fish from our larder, our sea. And so out we went, for we had something to say about this. But it turned out to be a boat from a friendly nation, stealing fish because it knew our island belonged to no one. Or rather that it belonged to us, but that we had no control over it. And we didn't say anything about what they were doing, for every man's conscience is his own, but we gave them a list of things we needed. This was it: soap, kerosene, matches and food. We didn't ask for clothing because there was no need to say we lacked things to wear. But do you know what those men gave us? Cigarettes and fish. So many they wouldn't fit in the canoes our men had gone out to the boat in. Can you believe it? They gave us cigarettes and fish. It was therefore clear that the owners of the boat from the friendly nation knew the fish were ours and wished to share them with us. And what about the tobacco? Our men had an unhealthy yearning for it, because for a long time they'd been reduced to smoking papaya leaves. So the men came back from the boat and no one can say things weren't shared out evenly: fish for the women, tobacco for the men. In fact hardly any women on the island smoked, though a few of the older ones did something similar, chewing it and stuffing it in their gums. But only a few of them, and they never used it as snuff.

When they saw all that fish and tobacco, some people thought we could maybe have done better, that fish and tobacco wasn't exactly what we needed most. So it was decided it would be a good idea if the women went to ask for themselves, because if the men on the boat saw the women and talked to them, then things would doubtless change for the better. That's right, for the better. The problem was that the women on our island didn't know how to paddle – they still don't – and so they had to be taken out to the boat to talk to the white men. I remember one of the women told me . . . No, nobody told me anything. The result of the deal the women struck with the white men was the arrival on our island – not in the canoes that the women were taken out in, but in the big boat's fishing vessels – of everything the women felt we lacked in that terrible time of shortages: soap, kerosene, salt, clothes, shoes, matches, a variety of things to eat, fish and cigarettes, and alcoholic drinks. There were several containers of soap powder, which was good because it meant people could take a handful for themselves and everyone left happy. The same thing with the salt, because most of it was unrefined. The alcohol and tobacco caused a great furore among the men, and one or two of the women too, it has to be said. A few people were lucky enough to get a shirt; others made do with seeing someone they knew take one away. The products that stretched the furthest were the fish, the salt and various things for making fire. And the alcohol, which spreads fast. Perhaps due to its flammable nature.

The time came for the boat to up anchor. Months went by and the things we got from the friendly nation's fishing boat ran out. One of the women who had been to talk to the white men was the goddaughter of that man we thought had always been on the island and who was friendly with our grandfather. It so happened that this man, who I'm not sure we didn't confuse with somebody else, had been not to the place where our fathers were – the place you went to in a boat full of hens and cockerels and other edible things, donated by our grandmother and other women from the island – but somewhere else: Calabar. And there were Igbos in Calabar and they were people who ate other people. We were told you had to be very careful with Calabarians. Well, that friend of grandfather's was a bit of a joker, among other things, and he let it be understood by everyone on the island that he'd been to Calabar and knew things about the people who lived there. In fact he sometimes talked the way people from Calabar talked and he founded an association of people who danced at Christmas dressed the way Calabarians dress, and talked the way men who liked eating other men talked. Anyway, his goddaughter took part in the expedition to the boat, where the women went to see those white men and talked to them so well they reached an understanding. And the fruit of that understanding was the growth of that girl's belly, a growth that remained even when everything else from that expedition of understanding had run out. In fact not everyone knew that her belly was growing, nor did they know that the growth was a result of her having talked to, or with, the white men on the boat. But her belly went on growing and people gradually found out that she was expecting a child and that the child would be the son of a white man, and that only she knew who he was because the liaison on the boat had taken place out of sight of everyone else in the village. She was a goddaughter, it's true, but she lived with her sister, the person she was closest to in life. Her parents had died a long time ago, back when nobody could imagine that one day we'd find ourselves in this situation.

The days went by and the island gradually went back to being gripped by shortages, and then something happened that frightened everybody. In fact all the wicked things started to happen, as if they'd been lining up, waiting their turn. The first thing was that a woman and her sister set off up the Pico carrying a piece of smoking kindling. They were going to their plantations in the mountain's foothills, next to a lake – Lake Nosopay. The lake and the mountain look like they're side by side when viewed from a certain angle, but really they lie on different planes and are not that close together at all. The mountain, the Pico, or *el Pico de Fuego*, to give it its full Spanish name, looks down on everything else, defiant and proud, and at its feet, as if asleep, lies Nosopay, the lake. Nosopay is also the name given to the flat plateau above, from where you catch a sudden glimpse of the lake down below when the plateau breaks off into a sharp precipice. You look out into a void and see the lake in a vast bowl at the bottom, its water disturbed only by a gentle breeze.

So the two sisters set off towards Nosopay carrying a piece of smoking kindling, for they planned to make a fire up there, at the base of a dried-out tree they wanted to fell and use as firewood. If they'd been more agile, or if they'd been born men rather than women, they'd have climbed the dried-out tree with axes and chopped it down, bit by bit, branch by branch, for a tree gives firewood for many months, many, many months. But they didn't have axes, or they didn't have the dexterity to use them, and they'd been born women. And back then there weren't enough men on the island for all the undexterous women. Which was why the two sisters resorted to fire, burning through the base of the tree instead of cutting through it. Furthermore, by making a fire on that plantation of theirs, they could pull a yam from the ground and leave it to cook in the embers, giving them something to fill their stomachs with while they worked. So they made the fire and got stuck into their tasks. They worked from the moment the sun poked its nose over the horizon until they felt they'd done enough, when they stopped and straightened their backs; it was time to go round the plantation with the basket to collect all the yam and cassava they'd pulled up, the fruits of their labour of a few months ago, plus any bits of cane they'd cut down while searching for the yam and cassava. On that Atlantic Ocean island, harvesting was something you did day in, day out, for no one had an area of land large enough to harvest everything all at once, at least not a harvest big enough to keep the whole family from hardship. When those two sisters finally straightened their backs, it was just a few hours until sunset, but the king of stars was nowhere to be seen due to the thick clouds of smoke.

'*Dios mío*, we got distracted,' said the older sister.

'We're in trouble! We're in big trouble . . . ' added the younger one, putting her hands on her head, tears already surfacing.

What had happened? Well, while they were busy at work, bent at the waist, eyes glued to the ground, they'd not once stood up, and so they hadn't realised that the fire they'd made around the base of that dried-out tree had spread, that it had burned through the dry leaves, dry twigs and dry grass under the tree and reached the next field, a field full of shrubs about three feet tall that were of no use to anybody but that were also dry at that time of year. The women's eyes bulged and they started to scream. They knew they had to get out of there fast, not because they were in danger of getting burned, for they could still escape on foot, but because they knew they had set a calamity in motion. The ground in the field where the shrubs were was so stony that nobody on the island ever risked planting there, despite the fact that it was an area four or five times the size of any plot of farmland the women owned, farmland they inherited from their parents, specifically their mothers. Whenever anyone looked at that large area and thought about planting on it, they remembered that anything they raised above their heads, a hoe or a pick, or whatever name they gave to the tool they had, would meet stone as soon as it hit the ground, that in fact that whole area covered in shrubs was one giant rock. But the awful thing was that if that area caught fire, the flames would spread through it fast, skirt around the Pico and advance on the big village itself. And before that happened, assuming it didn't go out for some lucky reason, the fire would raze all the neighbouring farmland for, as it made its way down towards sea level, it would meet pockets of earth where a few trees grew, and in among those trees were plots where women had planted to make the most of what opportunities there were in that oasis of rock. Too much effort had gone into tending those little plots for a fire to consume them before the women had reaped their rewards. So the two sisters would earn the wrath of all the women whose plots had been destroyed – and this before the worst of it for, after raging through the plantations, the fire would advance and seek lower ground, sea level. And sea level, in the direction the fire was travelling, meant the big village and everyone's homes.

There was nothing those two sisters could do about the fire other than pray to the *Señor* on high that the wind didn't pick up and fan the flames. The water in the lake below twinkled before their eyes. Water to put the fire out. But it was an optical illusion: what the naked eye couldn't see was the impassable precipice. And if the precipice was impassable, carrying buckets of water out on people's heads was simply unfeasible. Besides, there were no buckets anywhere on the mountain.

The sisters rushed to gather up what they'd harvested, loaded it on their heads and ran to get home. But the fire had already reached the edge of the path, so that if they tried to go back the way they'd come, they risked becoming surrounded. They probably wouldn't have been surrounded and, even if they had, they probably wouldn't have been incinerated, but the chance of it happening frightened them and it's easy to imagine how, under the circumstances, without being able to see properly in the smoke, they weren't thinking straight. Anyone in their position would have been afraid of the wind making matters worse by blowing in from the right, stoking the fire and forcing them to move off the path to the left. And with loads on their heads, panicked and unable to see properly, they didn't know what lay off the path to the left – which in fact was nothing much – and they feared losing their footing and falling off the precipice, delivering their hard but young lives to *Dios*, and whoever else, down on the muddy banks of the lake.

So they retraced their steps in search of a different route. The safest option was a path on the edge of the precipice that skirted round the lake before descending on the other side, via countless steep steps, coming out by the main access point to the lake, the waters of which were useless to them. From there, the path ran in an almost straight line all the way to the big village. This was the path the sisters took, but it was a long journey. Therefore, by the time they reached the village, our village, the big village, their family had become very worried. Having seen the fire, they feared something terrible had happened and some of them had gone off in search of the two sisters, for on our island everybody knows how long it ought to take anyone to get anywhere. When they then saw the two sisters approaching from a totally different direction, they realised the situation could be about to get worse. However they were a long way from imagining how much worse: that in a few days' time they'd experience the most significant and distressing moment of their lives. Nor could I imagine I was about to experience, albeit in someone else's skin, the most significant and distressing moment of my life, my life on our quiet Atlantic Ocean island. And it wasn't just significant and distressing, but an evil that wrapped its tentacles around so many people, including me. Around our lives.

The sun turned crimson, ready to take itself away to wherever it went at that time of day, and by now everyone's eyes were fixed on the mountain. Everything else paled into insignificance as we watched the fire spread, a fire whose cause we still didn't know. We had eyes only for that advancing fire, ears only for its crackle. And the fire went on advancing. The sun set and night awoke but we didn't notice the stars in the sky, nor any other jewels up in the great canopy: our eyes were transfixed by the fire, our ears by the crackle of the dry branches as they burned. Many plantations were at risk but, as the fire spread, the real risk was to our lives. If it went on advancing as it was doing, there was a strong chance it would reach the houses on the edge of the big village, and from there it would rage through the village, a village where most of the houses were made of dry wood and *jambab'u*. Everything would burn to satisfy the fire. Whenever I'd seen fires before, fires nobody had provoked but that were impossible to put out, I'd been struck by how many things had to burn to satisfy the fire, to make it happy. And so we were all unhappy. Everyone was on tenterhooks. The mountain would burn, the fire would spread, our houses would burn to the ground and there was nothing we could do about it other than paddle out to sea in canoes and wait until everything had been consumed. And our family had it particularly bad because it was hard to imagine grandfather, the only man of the house, managing to find us a canoe and paddle us to safety. He didn't have a canoe. I was only a child at the time but I could tell we couldn't put the fire out by turning on all the street taps in the village and fetching buckets and buckets of water, and fetching buckets and buckets from the sea if there was no water in the taps. Child's eyes they may have been, but I could tell the fire was big, really big, too big for us to fight, too big for us to extinguish and save ourselves from incineration. So the fire would push us out into the immensity of the deep blue sea, and it was night and we wouldn't know what to do . . . Well, I just couldn't see how we could all go out to sea in the middle of the night and not come to any harm so, as far as I was concerned, the fire had to burn itself out up there, on the slopes of the Pico, where it had started.

Night advanced and the fire advanced and we went upstairs to grandfather's balcony. And there we saw that he was very worried too. So much so that the doors to the balcony were wide open and grandfather was on his feet the whole time we were up there. He watched the fire with a worried look on his face and he made no attempt to hide it. Maybe he thought the same as me: that if the fire penned us in, he wouldn't be able to save us and we'd be the only ones in the whole village to perish. Doubtless I wasn't thinking about the business of going out in canoes very clearly, for I'd always been nervous of the sea. But anyway, grandfather made frantic, worried gestures and, of course, seeing him so affected made us worry all the more. If he'd appeared calm before us, we'd probably have thought the whole thing was serious but nothing the adults couldn't handle, the adults who weren't like him.

Night advanced, the fire went on advancing and grandfather remained where he was, standing up, perhaps cursing his lack of paddling expertise, and we noticed that he was crying, and, what's more, we noticed that the chair he usually sat on, which was empty right then, had a round hole in the seat, where the middle part of his backside would go. But it wasn't a hole made by accident: it was a special chair with a hole that had been put there deliberately. This discovery, big though it was, couldn't distract us from our fear, a fear grandfather made worse with his crying. We were crying too and so his tears added to our tears, although only one or two of us actually saw the tears on his cheeks. As night was well advanced and the whole thing was shaping up to be very distressing, grandmother sent us to bed. It was impossible to tell what she thought about the whole situation, but she thought it was time we went to bed, even though she must have known we wouldn't be able to sleep with a fire breathing down our necks, with our lives hanging by a thread that might be singed at any moment. We could tell she was afraid, but she hid her emotions from us and so we didn't know whether she thought the same way we did about grandfather's attitude, the feelings he'd openly shown, or whether she felt the same way he did. We knew she was afraid but it was impossible to gauge how afraid she was. Nevertheless, when she sent us to bed we obeyed, and we did so because we needed someone to give us an order, as an indication of the gravity of the situation if nothing else. An order from an adult, a person we loved and trusted, and who we knew loved us. If she'd told us to go down to the beach and paddle aimlessly out into the deep blue sea, we'd have obeyed, understanding that it was our only hope given the grave danger we faced. But she told us to go to bed, so we went to bed, a bed we typically woke up in several times during the night because it was sopping wet. And do you know why it was sopping wet? Yes, you know. Oh, the stink of stale urine! Anyway, there we were, lying in bed, while outside, up on the Pico, a fire burned that threatened to raze the big village to the ground. We'd left grandfather up on his feet, rather than sitting in his chair, a chair that had a hole in the middle of the seat, a hole he usually hid by covering it with a cloth, or a rag, or some kind of fabric at any rate, that he draped over his knees and tucked his hands beneath. We left him there unable to hold back the tears, even if they were only two little trickles that ran down his face. The way we saw it, those tears were revealing, because he was an adult. If an adult was crying, it was because the situation was a lost cause. Why did the man cry? Did the fire remind him of something that had happened to him before he knew us? What did it remind him of? Or maybe he cried because he wasn't an adult but a child?

That could have been it, that would have explained a lot, because on our island the only people who didn't fish or paddle canoes and who cried about things they didn't understand were children. Nor could children enter the *vidjil* to talk to the adults there. Didn't I begin by saying I never knew whether my grandfather was mad? Didn't I say I never quite knew what he was? Well, we discovered part of what he was that day, on the balcony, and when we went into his room. Which I'll tell you about later.

That night was one of the most restless nights of our young lives and we woke up in a soaking wet bed, the unstoppable river having flowed with such vigour it might have been used to put the fire out. The mattress was sodden, from head to toe, sodden with something that seemed to gush out of you the moment you were about to wake. Those morning pees were the worst, the ones that happened when the adults had already left the house. They were the worst because they made you think that if you'd only woken up a minute earlier, you'd have done so with a full bladder and been able to open the front door and aim your stream in the sand. You wouldn't bother writing your name or drawing a house or anything so early in the morning, you'd stretch and yawn as you peed, eyes half-closed. Peeing outside was the best; we always peed outside, even though we had a bathroom in the house. So when you woke to find the bed freshly wet with the spray of your own pee, you were angry with yourself because you'd been so near to waking up a hero, returning triumphant from war. I say war, but whatever really, anything you can return from triumphant. Or undefeated, at least. Not having been struck down by stones, witchcraft or evil.

We got out of the wet bed and went to look at the mountain that had put the fear of death in us the previous night. Everything was bare and black. Bare because all the vegetation on the mountain had burned, leaving only the rock itself, the immense rock that was the mountain. And black because it was all scorched, that greedy fire having raged through everything in its path: bushes, shrubs, lizards, centipedes, snakes, the nests of hens that ran wild on the island and laid their eggs up there. All the rats had died, rats that were the scourge of the plantations. But the worst of the inventory was the total destruction of the plantations. We didn't see the damage for ourselves, for we didn't go up there, but from the house we saw women come back from the plantations in tears. The look of despondency on their faces told of what they had seen. Mango trees, that belonged to nobody and everybody, their leaves and fruit burned along with their seeds, the seeds which were the fruits of the future. Cassava plants with stems and leaves burned, though the cassavas themselves had been saved, protected as they were underground. Banana and plantain trees with everything burned, and only those yet to bear fruit would ever grow back. Yam plants with the overground parts burned, the leaves and stalks that tangle up with neighbouring trees as they climb, though the yams, like the cassavas, had survived, meaning the owner of the plantation would have to have a very good memory to remember where she'd planted everything. Malanga plants weren't so affected because they didn't really grow on the Pico; they needed the moister ground of the southern plantations. All the snakes, crabs, lizards and lizards' eggs burned. And I mustn't forget the rats, all of them destroyed by the fire, all those rats and mice that were such a scourge of the women's plantations. Maybe I already mentioned the rats, but it's worth mentioning them again, because of the terrible damage they used to cause. The eggs of all the snakes also burned. Can you imagine the job the women now faced to resurrect their farms, to revive them from the state I've just described? They cried over the catastrophe that had befallen them. They'd already cried the night before, when the fire was raging, but out of fear that the flames would devour us. Now they cried for their wasted labour. They left the yams as they were, for the overground parts would sprout again with the first rains. They recovered what plantains and bananas they could, those that had reached a certain ripeness and hadn't been totally scorched. As for the cassava, the cornerstone of our island diet, they pulled them from the ground and rescued what they could. The cassava plant can't survive the death of its stalk, and the stalks had surrendered their sap to the all-consuming fire. It was such a terrible pity, but, more than a pity, it meant a lot of hard work, hard work wasted and hard work to come, to make use of so many cassavas, large and small, cassavas that should have remained underground and sustained the family for several years. Of course the women put them to good use, making breads and flour, but the plots were left moribund, as if they'd never been planted in, so the women would have to start again from scratch at the beginning of the rainy season, plant everything all over again and then wait almost a year before gathering the first fruits. It was such a pity to have lost so many years of effort, and all because of a fire whose cause still nobody knew. Given what I know now, and all that happened afterwards, I can say with some conviction that it was for the best that nobody ever knew exactly how the fire started. For I know now that all people are not treated equally when it comes to apportioning blame for bad things that happen in communities. I know that, in this world of ours, how facts are judged depends on who's doing the judging. I learned all this later, after seeing what happened on our Atlantic Ocean island.

Time passed, the tide came in and went back out, big fish were caught, octopus was eaten. There were rains and storms, the sun rose and set, and when it rose once more the woman's pregnancy had grown big enough for all to see, the woman who'd talked to the sailors from the friendly nation. By the way, does anyone know why we say that boat belonged to a friendly nation? For it certainly wasn't the only nation whose boats came to take our fish. Boats from many different places came to our waters, our shores, but when our men saw them and took to the sea to go and ask them for a handout, the sailors of those boats must have thought the people in the flimsy canoes were going to accuse them of stealing, for they quickly hauled in their nets, wound in their reels and disappeared over the horizon. Isn't that disgraceful? They made it obvious that they were thieves, and what's more, thieves who couldn't care less about us, every man for himself, each to his own suffering. Sometimes the boats from nations we didn't know even waited until our canoes were right up beside their boats and then they fired jets of dirty water, or hot water, at our men, to show us they were prepared to play ugly. They tried to sink our canoes, or maybe poison our men with toxic water. *Gracias a Dios*, our canoes didn't sink. They capsized, but thankfully all the men on our Atlantic Ocean island can swim, although there was no one to teach us in our house. The arrival of these boats on our shores was fairly frequent and so we soon learned to differentiate the friendly nation's flag from the flags of other nations. There were all kinds of flags: three bright horizontal stripes, one of them blue; three vertical stripes, one of them black; a single dark colour with a white sun in the middle; a single dark colour with a picture of something curved, the colour of mango. No one knew what nation this last flag belonged to, but it had, along with one of the tricolours, the fastest engine driver: as soon as a canoe left our shore, the boat set off at full pelt, as if the driver had heard there were witches on our island that had to be avoided at all costs.

Do you know what colour the friendly nation's flag was? I doubt the woman who dealt with the sailors on the boat knew. Back then, the women who were old enough to go and talk to the sailors didn't know much about the flags of nations. Did the woman even know for sure which sailor she'd had the liaison with when she fell pregnant? She wouldn't have recognised the flag and I doubt she'd have recognised the sailor. For one thing, white people all look alike, even those who live under different flags, never mind those who live under the same one.

Coloured flags, men who had to be liaised with, women who were taken out to the boat of the friendly nation by other men. Flags that had to be distinguished beforehand, paddles put at rest if the boat with its nets cast was from a nation that liked to play ugly. If the men on our island had trouble recognising the flags, how could the women be expected to recognise them? As I've already said, the women didn't know the flags and it's unlikely they'd ever even noticed them. And that's because in order to see them you had to be quite close to the boats, those thieving boats, friendly or otherwise. But the women on our island went about on foot until the need arose to go somewhere by canoe, when they would find a man to transport them. But even then, they would sit in the canoe facing the man doing the paddling, the canoeman they'd asked to take them wherever they needed to go. So to get to the meeting with the men on the boat, the canoemen paddled with their backs to the little village, meaning the women sat with their backs to the horizon and, with their backs turned, they wouldn't have seen the flag of the nation of the men they were about to reach an understanding with, in order to help ease the desperate situation the island found itself in. And once the canoe was moored at the side of the boat, you could no longer see the flag. The women therefore liaised with the men oblivious to their nation or flag. *Gracias a Dios,* those boats were from a friendly nation and didn't flee as soon as our canoes took to the water.

The pregnancy grew and that woman gave birth to a pretty little child they wrapped in rags, for by then there was nothing left of what had been brought back from the boat. And nobody had known at the time that visiting the boat would result in the birth of a child who'd require clean clothes. Anyway, the baby was born. Time passed and by now those white men knew when our waters were most full of fish and so they came back the following season, after a particular length of time had passed. They came back in the same boat, with the same name painted on the back and the same flag, but with different people who answered to different names. For example, the one who might have been the father of the newborn child didn't come. However, I doubt that woman could have pointed to any one man and said he was the father of that pretty child. Unless something had happened on the boat and only one man . . . No, there was no way of telling; she wouldn't be able to tell.

They cast out their nets, which is why they'd come, stole our fish and then looked to the shore, and when they saw us coming in our canoes they were pleased to see us. And they listened to the story of the white child being born in our big village, and they held their hands up and said no, the child's father was not with them, but yes, they ought to do something for the boy, who was still then only a baby. And so they gave us fish, they gave us salt, soap, matches, cigarettes, clothing for the baby boy and for other children, kerosene to light our houses on dark nights and many different types of things to eat, for they had lots of food on the boat to keep them going for several months away from home, away from their nation. They also gave us fish hooks and nylon, which we'd really struggled without since the boat from the place where our fathers were had stopped coming to the island. And they held the boy in their hands and they danced with him gleefully and they said he reminded them of the father, who could not, for whatever reason, be with them. And, because he reminded them of the father, they said that child of theirs should be called Luis Mari.

They came ashore and visited the house where their boy lived, met all his brothers and sisters, and realised they probably ought to do more for him. But they had a busy job sailing the seas and stealing other people's fish, and they couldn't afford to worry too much about a boy growing up without a specific father, for who knows what really happened out on that boat. So the sailors from the boat with the flag of the friendly nation decided their duty was done and they bid us farewell, their boat's storerooms overflowing with fish taken from our waters. The men from the island who went out to the boat saw this for themselves. Goodbye Atlantic Ocean island, goodbye Luis Mari. Goodbye sister-in-law. We'll be back to steal your fish again at a particular time in the future, and we hope to find the boy has grown and the mother is well. But given what we've just seen, it wouldn't surprise us at all if we came back and were told the boy had gone to fill his place in the cemetery, which incidentally doesn't seem to have too many places left. You really do have a large cemetery for an island of so few inhabitants. Bye.

Months passed and everything returned to the way it had been before. Those inhabitants who weren't so well connected to the white men from the boat went back to living with outstretched hands. The first thing to run out was the tobacco, the island's supply of cigarettes. Men were soon forced to return to old ways, smoking papaya leaves, or else they wandered the streets with bundles of fish in search of a cigarette or half a tobacco leaf. Women kept tobacco stored away like gold, real gold, and they called their tobacco leaves their 'husband'. Tobacco became the husband of any woman who didn't have a

flesh-and-bone husband. Tobacco in all its forms, including snuff. The women pounded tobacco into snuff and
added the powder of a stone only known to people who
liked sniffing it. I've already said how some older women
stuffed tobacco in their gums, which I never understood,
but that wasn't why tobacco became a woman's husband.
Tobacco was like a husband because it enabled single
women to get things they usually needed a man for.
They kept their tobacco in a strongbox and turned to it
whenever the need arose. And when a man yearned for
tobacco more than he yearned for anything else, he took
to the streets with his fishing bundle and offered fish in
exchange for tobacco, doing so with the following cry:
'Fish, tobacco! Fish, tobacco!' If he needed palm oil, it
was: 'Fish, palm oil! Fish, palm oil!' If a single woman
had a 'husband' in a strongbox, she could do deals to
satisfy her needs: if she needed a man to clear a plot of
land she wanted to plant on, if she needed a canoeman
to transport her and her children to the settlements, if
she needed a tapper to give her a pot of palm wine to
take to a *Misa* for the dead, etc, etc . . . I speak only of the
needs a woman might satisfy by keeping her 'husband'
safe in a strongbox. Tobacco was a sort of life insurance
to them. Even so, the time inevitably came when there
was no longer a scrap of tobacco anywhere on the island.
And the men, driven on by their craving, made their
bundles larger, the fish in their offerings more colourful,
and they headed out into the street with the same cry

on their lips: 'Fish, tobacco! Fish, tobacco!' And they covered every street, the entire village, and found nothing. All that was left in the strongbox was the smell, a smell that lingered in the houses, clinging to clothes hung up for some special occasion. 'Ahhh!' sighed the smokers as they breathed in the air from the strongbox, trying to satisfy their craving with the smell.

Yes, tobacco life insurance, and I think the tobacco husband was actually more useful than the flesh-and-bone one, because the tobacco husband could fish, clear land and transport a woman and her load wherever she needed to go, which was all real husbands did back then anyway. And if there was no fishing line in the strongbox for the flesh-and-bone husband to use, nor any tobacco or cigarettes, soap or kerosene, he probably wouldn't have been able to satisfy the needs of the household. Furthermore, a flesh-and-bone husband might lose his strength for clearing small plots of land. So tobacco always trumped them as husbands. Ah, yes, and brandy too. I could never understand why men on our island went to such great lengths to get products that provided enjoyment for such a short amount of time. It made me think that maybe we had more than just material needs on the island. But what could be made of a man who spent his whole day sitting in a canoe on the choppy sea and then prowled the streets looking for tobacco and brandy as soon as he set foot on land? As a child, I thought tobacco and brandy must be the most powerful substances known to man. It's easy to see why youngsters desire cigarettes and brandy when they see the strongest men in their communities making superhuman efforts to get them. Youngsters look up to such men and think the quickest way to be like them is to get tobacco and alcohol for themselves.

My grandfather, the house, his room, that hair, which I think he groomed in the privacy of his sleeping room. I've said it before, but I'll say it again now he's come back to mind: what was it with that haircut? I know some people make deals and pacts with dangerous beings and if their deals turn sour they have to honour whatever they agreed to, which might mean doing strange things in public. But although we suffered terrible hardship on the island, we did have mirrors. As a man who'd once been a sailor, the captain of a ship even, grandfather must have had a mirror and he must have looked at himself and seen that his haircut looked ridiculous. And though it's true he never left the house, people still saw him, and they must all have thought that crazy haircut really didn't suit him. How could that man he went to the cemetery with, a man who was supposed to be his friend, not have said anything about such an awful haircut? What were they hiding? What secrets did they share? What mysterious things were they mixed up in for something that everyone saw and thought ugly to be of no consequence to them? They who were adults, older men even! I mention his haircut again because we found nothing in his room to explain it. Whatever his reasons were for having that haircut, they weren't reasons of a tangible or material nature, just as the reasons for his overall behaviour lay beyond our grasp. We saw things in his room, but nothing to explain why an adult man would shave the hair off one side of his head and act like it was perfectly normal, indeed act like it was the only hairstyle to have.

Furthermore, why did he cry on the night of the fire? I ask this now, when I'm no longer a child, for, looking back, I see how inconsiderate it was of him to shed those tears in front of us, that he had no appreciation of how we'd react to seeing him cry. I think he either didn't know how to act like an adult or basically wasn't an adult, and all the people who cared for him, or gave him food, must have thought the same. Grandmother and our mothers, and even our fathers who were away in that place you went to by boat, all treated grandfather like a child who needed looking after. And why did he never speak when there were so many children around him who were anxious to hear what he had to say? Had something happened to him when he was younger that caused him to lose his voice? And what secret did my grandmother's niece know that enabled her to chat to him, or at least to seem satisfied by their conversations? If I'm asking all these questions again, it's because I still don't know the answers. And like I said, I'll talk about what was in his room later, when it's time to talk about him again.

Several days after the Pico burned, we were in the square playing billiards when what I've described as the most significant and distressing thing in the island's history occurred. Did I say billiards? As kids we had a set of see-through plastic balls with coloured pictures inside them, pictures of flowers and things like that. We liked those balls a lot, so much that one day, out of curiosity, we broke into them to find out what the pictures really were. But as soon as we broke into them, the pictures disappeared, so we stopped doing it pretty quickly. It's always sad when you break something pretty but it's especially sad when you do it deliberately and it proves to be pointless. Anyway, we used to play a game with those balls, a game we called billiards. The game consisted of throwing your ball to try and hit your opponent's ball, while proving your skill at laying traps, exploiting openings and speaking in the special jargon of the game. Part of the tactics involved drawing lines in the sand with your hands while saying the names of the positions and moves in the special jargon. But, just as there were shortages of everything on the island, so we ran out of the balls, which were white people's balls, and then we couldn't play any more. But we couldn't just stop playing billiards, so we found a solution. Back then there was an unusual plant that had very thin branches. These branches didn't grow upwards but rather in circles, coiling round the plant's stalk to create an impenetrable barrier that no human could get through. And the barrier became all the more impenetrable when the outside branches dried out and grew spikes, tiny little spikes that pricked your skin and held on to your clothes. It was a very self-protective plant and anyone who went anywhere near it risked getting tangled up in its thin, spiky branches, or pricking their feet on the dead spikes that dropped to the ground. Anyway, this plant, which really was quite something, had little capsules in spiky shells, and the shells opened when ripe to reveal a ball, the billiard balls of our island. Admittedly they weren't perfectly round, like the white people's ones, nor did they have pictures inside them, but for the purposes of the game they proved a good replacement for the real billiard balls. What's more, it meant we had lots of billiard balls to play with, although to get lots you did have to suffer a few scratches and pricks scrambling about under the plant's tangled web of branches. It's a plant everyone ought to see, especially when its branches are dry. Very few living things could get through its spiky branches. Some soldiers came to the island from the place where our fathers were, or possibly from somewhere else, and we named the soldiers after the plant. The soldiers were black, but they never learned our language and they didn't know how to swim or paddle a canoe, despite the fact that they were adults. As I said, they never learned our language. How did they expect to do a good job of being a soldier in a place where they knew nobody, didn't speak the language and couldn't swim or paddle? I don't know whether that's why they were named after a plant you couldn't pass without getting a sharp reminder it was there. We islanders never learned their language either. Nor did we make friends with them, though we didn't treat them badly. The only thing we learned about them was that when they opened their mouths to start a conversation, to call someone over or stop a passerby, they said something in their language that can be translated as 'Me say'. Imagine that! You don't know someone, you've never spoken to them before in your life, you can't even see their face from where you're standing, and when you want to speak to them for the very first time, you begin with 'Me say'. That 'Me' thing must be very important to them. I personally think that anyone who uses 'Me' as the first thing he says to a stranger is rather strange himself. Especially if the person you don't know but want to talk to isn't even looking at you. Is that why they tried to be soldiers without knowing how to swim, fish or paddle a canoe?

Well anyway, those men were sometimes called the 'Me-says' and sometimes called the name of that spiky plant, the plant that provided us with the billiard balls we were playing with when the significant and distressing thing happened. We were near the square, though not actually in the square itself, because billiards is better played on sand and the square is paved. So that afternoon we were happily playing when we saw a great many people come running down from the upper part of the big village, running and shouting. They ran through the square and went off in the direction of the beach. We thought something had happened down on the beach or at the *vidjil*, which was also in that direction. Had the sea dumped fish on the shore? Was it the squid beaching? We got up and followed the uproar and, as we ran through a clearing, we noticed that some people were carrying sticks and seemed angry. We thought it might have been a dog sacrifice. On our island, whenever a dog was to be sacrificed for some reason, a dog or a bitch, it was tied to a tree and all the kids threw stones at it until it died. They were dogs said no longer to serve their purpose, whatever their purpose was, for in truth dogs didn't really do anything. They were sometimes used for hunting wild cats, which we used for their skins. We made drums out of their skins, drums we played in times of need to remind ourselves that we were from our island and that we had our ways and our customs to protect. The cats were skinned and the meat was thrown away, until some people on the island started to eat cat meat. Well, not just any people but specifically a group of young men who gathered together and formed a sort of club to cook cat meat. They formed the club there and then and drew up rules, the main one being that you had to cry before eating the food that was prepared. You couldn't eat unless you cried. As for the dogs, I don't recall anybody ever eating dog meat, but we did use their skins, which were bigger than cat skins and made more than one drum. It wouldn't be right for me to have mentioned the thing about the cat meat without adding that the people who ate cats acquired the habit elsewhere, somewhere they'd met people with bad customs.

We realised the crowd hadn't gathered to sacrifice a dog, for the people running with sticks were adults, who didn't usually participate in dog sacrifices. And sticks were hardly ever used to kill dogs, those said no longer to serve their purpose. So we didn't know what was happening, but we ran along, following the crowd. And the whole throng stopped outside the *vidjil* and waited for a while, until the object of everyone's anger came running out and then the crowd gave chase, waving their sticks in the air. We still weren't really sure what was going on, but we ran after the angry mob. We ran after them and we ran like them, and maybe we even shouted with them and we saw clearly how they raised their sticks and struck a person, the person they'd chased all over the big village. What was this? We were only children and we got left behind and didn't see everything, but we saw that a person was being beaten furiously. So furiously that the person fell to the ground, then managed to get up and start running again, despite blows continuing to rain down from everyone's sticks. Well not everyone's: like me, not everyone giving chase was carrying a stick or beating the person; some of us were there out of curiosity, to witness something we'd never seen before. But what was it? The person being struck, who we later saw was a woman, found strength from who knows where and ran ahead of everyone, right through the whole village, and made for the *Misión*. The path to the *Misión* was steep, and it's amazing that she had the energy to reach the church door, given the beating she'd received. By the time she reached the *Misión*, she was practically naked, for the sticks had torn her clothes off, or maybe the people chasing her had pulled them off before we started following them. She was panting heavily when she reached the church door and went inside. The people chasing her showed their respect for the *Misión*, for they were *católicos*, and they waited outside with their sticks, panting also, making the most of a chance to rest. And we rested too, those of us who were witnessing the barbarity. After a while, the crowd stirred. The woman came out of the church and the crowd went back to beating her relentlessly. She didn't come out as naked as she'd gone in: she was now wrapped in a sheet that someone in the church must have given her. A sheet or an altar cloth, it wasn't exactly clear, but a white cloth of some sort in any case. She came out of the church wrapped in that white cloth, ready to meet her destiny, a destiny to be dictated by those who'd pursued her with such rage. I ought to say that those of us witnessing the events were no longer merely spectating, for by now we were all crying, we, the women and children who were there to witness something we'd never seen before, which was proving to be an unspeakably horrible thing.

With the strength she'd recovered while inside the church, the woman ran, but she soon fell, and what we witnessed next was not only sticks raining down on her but also that a man thrust a stick into her naked femininity. He thrust a stick inside that woman and then pulled it out again, as if thrusting it in had somehow not been enough. Isn't that an act of such wickedness it stands out even amid something so inconceivably awful? Thrusting a stick inside the nakedness of a woman you were beating to death. All the children nearby saw it clearly, and I was nearby, tears streaming down my face, although I never stopped following them, never stopped myself from witnessing the inhumanity. The women who had made it up the hill to the *Misión* held their heads in their hands. After that ultimate act of wickedness, the woman managed to run on for a few more yards and then fell, never to get up again. She'd no strength left. It was only then, when she couldn't get up, that we fully realised what was happening: they were going to kill her. And when we realised this, and saw the sticks coming down on her again, we knew we'd entered a new phase of our young lives. And we couldn't bear that woman's agony. We didn't want to witness it. We, the women and children, did not want to witness the end, now that we understood what was happening. Maybe we'd run after the mob wanting to see a beating, driven on by morbid curiosity, without thinking how it would end. And now events had overtaken us. But the woman's pursuers had no such qualms and they carried their plan through to the end. The end?

Can anyone understand what happened between her coming out of the church and having a stick thrust into her nakedness? That mob acted as one and so that infernal act was carried out by all of them, women included, and maybe they'd even sworn to do it beforehand, come what may. They weren't satisfied with just beating her, they had to go further. They seemed intent on reminding the woman of her motherhood. But why, if they were going to kill her – were, in fact, killing her? What did they mean by reminding her she'd had children, if that is what they meant to do?

I'll tell you what happened in the church: the woman thought she was going to die, so she went to see the *Padre*, so that he would hear her confession. She knew there was no way of escaping her pursuers. She was received by the *Padre*, who, offended by her nudity, gave her a sheet to cover herself with. It was almost certainly the same sheet they used to cover the altar. So the woman covered herself and was then received by the *Padre* in the confessional. She confessed, was given her penance and absolved. Then she took Communion and the priest told her to go in peace. I'd like to think that's what happened, for we saw the woman come out and her persecution continue. But I often ask myself whether that priest did enough. Could he really not have done more? Could he not have come out and admonished the crowd, threatened them with damnation if they carried on with what they'd set out to do? I know the *Padre*'s word has always been accepted on our island, and the faithful on the island have always feared damnation. Or he could have told the woman to stay in the church until her pursuers had gone. I firmly believe he should have gone out to speak to them, to reason with them, pacify them, and that, if he did not do so, it was because he was governed by the same evil spirit that governed the mob. For he let her go back outside, and what did he do with himself then, after he'd heard her confession and given her Communion? Did he do some meditating? Some praying perhaps? Some crying for the sins of the faithful? What would have happened if he'd told the mob that if they wanted to carry on beating that woman they'd have to kill him first, and then taken her in his arms? I doubt very much – but very, very much indeed – whether those wicked people would have dared touch the *Padre*. And if they didn't touch him, it would have shown they weren't actually evil.

But the *Padre* told her to go in peace and those wicked people showed her no mercy. Even watching her leave the church to face the crowd didn't soften the *Padre*'s heart, and so the mob decided to see things through to the end. I've already said what happened when we realised those men, and women, and children, planned to see things through to the end: we decided not to witness it. For most people, beating a woman to death was no small thing. But it was what they wanted, perhaps what they'd sworn to do beforehand, come what may. And they became increasingly hard-hearted and they saw it through to the end. And what if they thought the *Padre* had given them permission to do so by letting the woman out to face their sticks? To face the end? They went on beating her until she died at their hands. It was something we had never seen before on the island, nor heard an adult tell of ever happening before. They killed that woman.

Such a terrible thing could not have happened in sunlight, although the sun had been shining earlier on in the day. Terrible things tend to happen in the late afternoon, when the sky turns gloomy in the absence of the sun. They chased that woman all around town until she was dead, killed before everyone's eyes! They killed her running right through the big village, and so the evil took hold of the big village and entered everyone's spirit. It was the first time such a thing had happened and nobody knew what to do about it. *Dios mío*, they killed that woman, they beat her with sticks until she died at their hands! Before that, they thrust a stick into her nakedness, as if to remind her that she had children, two daughters in fact. And do you know who those two daughters were? The two sisters who'd gone up to the plantations and accidentally set fire to the Pico. That fire had been a terrible accident, but all the adults, and maybe even the sisters themselves, knew that it was also a terrible omen. Which was why they'd cried not so much for the fire itself but for what they thought would come next.

That woman was killed and a sense of foreboding spread through the big village, as if the evil was spreading. As if what had happened hung in the atmosphere and was breathed in, though never talked about. Such an awful thing should have been talked about everywhere in the village, but it couldn't be, at least not on the day it happened, and not in the days that followed. Nobody knew what to say. And before we'd had a chance to fix what had happened in our minds, the evil spread throughout the island and death spread its wings over the village. For weeks, indeed for months, the spirits of death and evil had our Atlantic Ocean island in their grip. In fact it was one evil after another. First there was the fire, seen by many as an omen of more evil to come. Then the killing of that woman, something that had never happened before on our island, and seen by the adults as a warning that untold pain and misery were on their way. And no ordinary adults either but certain adults who had special powers and could see into the future. These people saw everything. And they walked the streets in tears saying that they wouldn't tell, that their 'leaders' were pounding them to make them tell, but they wouldn't tell of what terrible future lay ahead of us. That's what the adults who talked to my grandmother said. Something was going to happen, something was going to happen, and the women who saw things from the future, because they talked to the departed, were supposed to inform everybody of what this terrible thing was, but they refused because it was so bad. But something terrible already had happened! Surely not more? Yet if the clairvoyants said it would happen, it would happen, it was inevitable. What fear I felt during those days! And before I'd had time to think about the terrible thing that had already happened, to try and understand why the whole village had stood by and watched as the Devil ran amok among us, the air turned thick and the skies darkened over everyone as we waited, waited for something we didn't want to come. And I was very, very afraid.

What came next began when a man who was strong and healthy one day dropped down dead the next. He'd seemed perfectly well, chatting contentedly with numerous people, and then, when night came, he asked someone to accompany him to the beach so he could relieve his belly. He asked his wife, who was the only person who could be expected to accompany him to the beach at such an untimely hour. This was because it wasn't just a matter of going to the beach, any old part of it, but of going to a bit beyond the *vidjil*, where the men beached their canoes. The man felt a desperate need to go and he left home accompanied by his wife. They made their way through the darkness and reached the section of the shore where people from that part of the big village went to satisfy their needs, and the man pulled his trousers down and squatted. Time passed, sufficient time for him to have satisfied his need, but he remained squatting.

'You nearly finished?' his wife asked.

'No,' he answered, and although it was only a mono-syllable, the way he pronounced it was enough for his wife to know her husband wasn't well.

'Everything all right?' she said, from where she was waiting a few steps away.

But the man gave no answer, other than a series of groans, groans that suggested all was not right with the relieving of his belly. *Ay! ay! aaay!* Emptying his belly brought sharp pangs of pain, and each pang made him groan. He was getting cramps. *Ay! huy! huy!* And he held his hands to his gut, a gesture his wife couldn't make out, for the moon had not been seen for several weeks and the beach was in total darkness. The pain continued, until finally he summoned up the strength to make his way over to where the sea washed onto the sand, and there he performed the basic ablutions; that's to say, he washed himself in the splash of the waves . . . He still felt pangs of pain but he thought he ought to go back to the house, so he set off home, preceded by his wife. As they turned onto the road that led to their house, the man had another attack of cramps and he had to stop. He leaned on a rail outside a house and bent over, holding his stomach with his free hand. *Aay! huy!* he wailed in pain. Then he had a sudden, desperate need to go, and he tried to hurry back down to the shore to satisfy the need, but he only made it halfway along the path before he had to pull his trousers down and squat. This was totally unacceptable behaviour; he and his wife both knew this. A person couldn't just do his business anywhere, certainly not somewhere that wasn't set aside or used for such a purpose, no matter what the time of day or circumstances. And especially if that person was an adult. It was simply unacceptable. And because they both knew this, his wife knew something was seriously wrong with her husband. And she caught up with him and asked him if the cramps were persisting. But the man no longer had the strength to answer. He suddenly felt a great need to sleep and, without even washing himself, he pulled up his trousers, whimpering in pain. He could no longer walk, at least not without great difficulty.

'I'm dying,' he said.

So his wife leaned forward to offer him her back and she carried him on it, despite her frailty. With considerable trouble, they made it back to the house and laid him down on the communal bed. He started to get cold sweats and suffered wave after wave of cramps, cramps connected to a constant need to relieve his belly. But he could no longer get outside to satisfy the need and so he had to do it right there, in the confined space of the sleeping room. With all the noise, the neighbours realised something was going on and they came round to find out what the problem was. The man was periodically forced to make use of a chamber pot, which his wife took outside at daybreak. Personal business, very personal business, is best dealt with before anyone is out on the streets. So the woman went out of the house carrying the chamber pot, covering it partially, or hiding it under a length of cloth she usually wrapped around her head and back. She emptied the chamber pot wherever she could and went down the path to the shore to clean up the physiological remains her husband had left behind the previous night, and as she bent over she felt a slight cramp, but soon recovered. When she got home, she found her husband with white, sunken eyes, dry lips and only the thinnest thread of breath. And not a single part of the bed was dry, because her husband had suffered multiple attacks of diarrhoea while she'd been away. The woman called the neighbours because, being an adult, she knew what those white eyes might mean. The man no longer had anything to say for himself, or if he did he was no longer able to say it. He no longer knew where he was. His wife sensed his condition deteriorating and she called out to tell him to hang on in there. But the man made only the slightest of gestures, just enough to show he'd heard his dear wife, that he wanted to remain in this world. Remain with her. It was his final gesture. A few minutes later he was still lying on the bed, but nobody in the house could say for sure whether he was still in this world or whether he'd gone over to the other. His wife had already peered into the gloom and allowed a few furtive tears to escape. The neighbours told her not to despair, that there was still hope. And some of them went out to call for the doctor. They called for the doctor because they thought he'd be able to tell them what was happening, not because they thought he'd have anything at the hospital he could treat the man with. For if the island's hospital had any medicine at all, it was unlikely to be of any use for this case. They called him, he came, he saw the state of the bed, looked at the sick man, felt him, opened his eyes, opened his mouth and said nothing. Or rather he said that the man should be taken to the hospital. Perhaps the doctor had something there to be used in emergencies. The question was how to get the man to the hospital, because on our island the seriously ill are usually taken to hospital first by canoe, then on someone's back, but that man had one foot in the other world and was in no state to be put in a canoe or carried on anyone's back. And besides, he was not a young man. But everyone could see life escaping from him, so they summoned four men and those four men took hold of the four sides of the sheet he lay on and they carried him all the way through the village to the hospital. During the journey, the first rays of the sun that would shine that day beamed down on the man's face and he made an attempt to open his eyes. The four men carrying him, on a sheet where he'd done his business, saw this and had a vague sense of hope that their efforts would not be in vain. And they reached the hospital. They passed the *Padre* en route, who had already been informed of the man's spiritual needs and told that he looked set to leave this life for the next unless *Dios* intervened, and if *Dios* didn't intervene, it would be better if he was received by *Providencia* with his last rights administered. The *Padre* followed the procession to the hospital and there he made the sign of the cross on the soles of the man's feet and rubbed *Santo Óleo* into their skin. The man's wife and the people who'd accompanied her saw this. And they saw that the soles of the feet receiving the holy unction were very pale. But had they really seen enough soles of feet to know that these ones were especially pale?

A few minutes later, there was not much left to be said about that man's life. He didn't expire the way many people expire, the soul ripping out of the body in a transcendental moment everyone present is very much aware of. Those present simply realised he was no longer with them, he was no longer alive. So they called the doctor and he certified the death, the end of the man's life on the island. Then they closed his eyes and arranged his hands to show he was no longer going to use them. He would be taken home and preparations would be made for his funeral. The hospital lent its only stretcher and he was carried back to the house he'd lived in and put in the only place there was room for him, the bed. The same bed where he'd had painful cramps, succumbed to his needs and begun to die. Now it was time to prepare his coffin. On our island, coffins are made out of old canoes. And if there isn't an old one available, though there usually is, a canoe is sacrificed, even if it's still fit for the purpose it was built for, in order to provide a last resting place for the deceased. And if the canoe that's sacrificed to make the coffin is the canoe that used to belong to the dead man, all the better. I guess the custom of making the coffin out of the dead man's canoe comes from the idea that once a man is dead, he no longer has use for the canoe that survived him. It was unusual for someone to inherit someone else's canoe. Our village's custom was that when a man died, his canoe died with him, that it felt the weight of earth thrown down on its back at its owner's burial. Besides, our village wasn't so full of trees that one could be chopped down every time someone died. There weren't enough trees for such a ritual.

I've been talking about canoes being turned into coffins to bury their dead owners, but what about the women, who on our island never owned canoes? Well, their coffins were made from the leftovers of other people's canoes. Luckily, there were plenty of big canoes on the island, made from three indigenous trees, or tree trunks from elsewhere that washed up on our beaches, brought by the sea from foreign oceans and shores. And when the canoes got old and had so many holes in them they could no longer be used for paddling, they were abandoned upturned on the shore, and we children always asked what they were for and whom they belonged to. Because we knew nothing about what happened to the dead. But we soon began to learn.

They made the dead man a coffin and in the afternoon they went to bury him, following the procedure I described earlier. All the children who lived on the streets of the funeral procession were shut up in their homes with the windows covered up, forbidden from going outside until the adults got back. The dead man was cried for, his wife cried a lot, his relatives cried too. And finally the man was buried. But the following day, his wife had further cramps, and she thought it was because she had cried so much for her husband, and because she'd not eaten since he'd fallen ill. The cramps continued and at night she had to ask someone to accompany her to the beach. She asked one of her relatives, for they were sleeping in the house awaiting the return of the dead man, as is our custom. When somebody dies, relatives sleep in the deceased's house for a week and it's said that on the third day they feel the return of the departed, by the noise it makes, even the objects it touches. But three days hadn't yet passed and the dead man's wife asked one of the relatives to accompany her to the shore, for her needs were urgent and painful. She wasn't alone in the house and so she couldn't resort to using the chamber pot. She went down to the shore and her belly ached a lot, a belly that had been fed practically nothing since the terrible episode with her husband began. She was now widowed from that man and there were external signs of this, for she'd shaved her hair off and wore black. She was in a lot of pain, she clenched her teeth and held her belly with her hands and she was dripping with sweat. It was said that her sweating alone was cause for alarm, for it was no ordinary outpouring of sweat. The pains continued, but she straightened herself up and made her way home.

She went back to bed, but when the next wave of cramps came she no longer had the strength to ask anyone to accompany her anywhere. She went into the sleeping room, where no one was sleeping, for everyone, including herself, slept in the living room while awaiting the return of the departed, and there she resorted to the chamber pot. She no longer had the will to protect her modesty and hold back the groans of the strained removal of the nothing that filled her intestines. Those groans startled the neighbours and some of the women started to cry. They knew it was something serious, knew it might be the same thing that had happened to her husband, and they went to get help. They went to knock on the doctor's door and he got up, got dressed and followed them, and he told them to do as he instructed. There was nothing he could do to stop the propulsions that were so painfully churning her intestines, but he saw what was coming and so he told them to take the woman to the hospital, even though it was closed at that time, because it wasn't properly speaking a hospital, the sort of place you could go to day and night and be attended to. And in any case, there was no medicine anywhere on the island that could be given to anyone for any kind of ailment.

Hours went by, the woman's eyes went blank and her soul ripped out of her body, to the general disbelief of everyone present, who'd expected her to make a recovery. Her death was a dramatic transcendental moment. Those present screamed to the heavens and cried as if the life had been ripped out of their own bodies. They were not mere tears of lament. They took the woman home, made the usual funeral arrangements and a coffin out of the wood left over from her dead husband's canoe. Then they called the priest and the funeral procession set off all over again: the priest and the altar boys carrying incense and candles, followed by the men bearing the coffin and the women crying behind them, tears that were not, as I said, mere tears of lament, rather something much, much more.

The woman was buried and the house was shut up, for that man and woman hadn't any children, or if they had, they were elsewhere and nobody mentioned them or knew anything about them. After those two deaths the sky closed in over the island and the sun stopped shining on it. And death drew strength from this. In the days that followed, everyone who'd helped try to save that husband and wife started to die, one by one, struck down by the same affliction that had beset the dead man and woman. And so, rather than burying one old person over the course of a year, the island was now burying someone every day. What was this? people asked themselves. And they asked the doctor the same thing and he, along with others who knew about such matters, concluded that what was threatening to wipe out every inhabitant on the island was a sickness called the cholera. But that was as far as the doctor's knowledge went. There was nothing on the island that could be given to people to treat or combat the disease, nothing in the hospital cupboards that could stop the great loss of life.

This all took place at a time when the church was marking the death of *Nuestro Señor*. On the days that preceded the *Resurrección*, special songs were sung to commemorate the date. And women in mourning dress opened their throats and sang, in our language, the bit about 'they put a crown of thorns on him and then nailed him to the cross, and then he died and they buried him to save sinners'. I've just said it all at once, run together, but when said in our language, when sung in our language by the women, it had a different rhythm, a rhythm that was deadly slow, and I knew they were singing it for what was happening on our island and not for what happened to *Cristo*. Back then I'd already taken my first Communion but I didn't know the story of the *Señor* they put a crown of thorns on and nailed to a cross. This was because the '*doctrina cristiana*' was taught to me in Spanish, a language that was not my own, and so I understood practically nothing of what I was supposed to learn before taking my first Communion. All I knew was that to take my first Communion I had to know the *doctrina* off by heart. 'And he suffered, and he suffered, and he was nailed to the cross', and I thought, *Dios mío*, we're all going to die, seeing so many people buried because of that sickness we'd never heard of before. The cholera. The doctor and the others then realised that the death was contagious and so everyone who declared themselves sick had to be taken out of their homes, so as not to pass death on to other members of the family. We shut ourselves away in the house the same way we did when a funeral was taking place, when we had to hide from the air of the dead. Near the *Misión* there was a big house that had no rooms in it, as if it had also been built as a church, though one without any kind of adornments and much, much smaller. They opened it up and from then on anyone suffering from the deadly sickness of the cholera was put in there. But as it had never been a hospital, it had no beds, and so the people who were taken there, people who knew they were going to die, were laid out on the floor itself, covered in the sheets or drapes they'd been carried from their houses in. As there was nothing anywhere on the island to give them, they were given nothing, unless their family had something they thought might keep them going, at least for a few days until they inevitably died. And throughout that month, people kept singing 'they put a crown of thorns on him, then nailed him to the cross'. But in my language it's more graphic than it is in Spanish, and the nails themselves get mentioned, which made it seem all the more painful. In my language you say 'they drove nails into him on the cross, then he died', and our people kept on dying and I knew that song was being sung for them.

As we children couldn't expose ourselves to the air of the dead and had to be shut up at home whenever there was a funeral procession, we spent almost the entire month in the house. For there was a death every single day and it wasn't unusual for one person to be buried in the morning and another to be buried in the afternoon. And every new coffin meant one less canoe in the island's fishing fleet. Every day, a man or a woman's corpse was taken out of that quarantine near the church with a sheet or length of cloth draped over it. It meant they would never be seen again, but nobody cried in there. Corpses were taken out discreetly, with their faces covered, as if they were being taken somewhere for treatment, so that the rest of the infirm didn't lose hope. There was no conversation, everyone in there was silent, probably in agony. It wasn't a hospital, it was a place you went to when you had the air of the dead in you.

A month went by and everyone still alive feared desperately for his or her life. Digestive matters became tremendously important. Everyone knew that the sickness began with a small stomach cramp and ended in a box made of floating wood under a mound of earth after some Latin from the *Padre*. Hearing that Latin was to experience something no one should have to experience. For after the priest's Latin song-orations came the descent into the grave and the shovelling of earth, and everyone at the funeral, the deceased's family and anyone able to come from the village, knew that was the moment you let out all the pain that had built up in your heart and said a final farewell to your loved one. Laments filled the air and the earth shook. Indeed you couldn't witness it without shaking yourself. And this was the moment the women really opened their throats, which were connected to their hearts, the human centre of sadness, and released their tears of lament, which as I've already said, were more than mere tears of lament. They were something else. These laments had tears and words and might be mistaken for a song, but a song wailed with such feeling that it was truly heartrending to hear. And at the same time that the women wailed, they cried so much they drowned themselves in a sea of tears and mucus. Sometimes they even had to interrupt the lament to blow their noses, before carrying on. Someone should have put a stop to the whole practice, for everyone's sake. Hearing people cry so deeply was a very striking thing, at least it was for me. Hearing it was devastating. Never in the history of the island had there been a sadder moment than the moment that immediately followed the *Padre*'s Latin. It was a sadness that was supercharged, magnified to excess, to what might be called monumental levels. And the echoes of that monumental sadness were heard all the way home, all the way to the house of the deceased, where relatives gathered to offer their condolences. And the women thought they had to cry like that, and they thought it their duty to back up anyone else who cried like that. They thought it was a way of showing solidarity in grief.

The days of the 'crown of thorns' passed and our cemetery filled up. And he suffered 'under the cross', and they threw earth on someone else, and he had 'nails driven into him', and they buried others still, until the situation had reached truly alarming proportions. Alarming proportions beyond what were already considered alarming proportions. As there was absolutely nothing to give the sick, people turned to their ways and customs, uncovering special formulas that might protect against the tremendous loss of life. You had to take such and such a thing, tie the image of a saint to your body, boil up the leaves of a particular plant, hang a blessed cloth over all the village taps. It was thought that the ministrants should do something. That the ministrants should carry the *Maté Jachín* around the village to drive away the shadow of evil that was hovering over the village and killing its children. Anything anyone thought of or dreamed up was tried out as a possible prevention or cure for the terrible disease. But one thing was tried more than anything else and that was the drinking of a decoction of leaves from the guava tree. Someone told someone that someone they knew had been told that someone they'd met had heard it said . . . until everyone in the big village knew that boiled guava leaves were the best cure for the evil that was threatening to wipe out the whole population of the island. This medicine was said to *tanjer* the belly – *tanjer* being a word in our language – meaning that it worked as a plug and stopped that never-ending torrent from pouring out of your body, a torrent that left you dry and drained you of life.

That month of the crown of thorns saw entire families buried, the last one to perish having to be buried by neighbours out of charity, for there were no kin left to perform the burial. Some parents lost all their children, children who were adults themselves. Some households had two coffins taken to the village graveyard at once, two loved ones dying on the same day. It wasn't just horrible. It was horrendous. It scarcely needs saying how hard the men who dug the graves had to work. Scores of women died, scores of boys, scores of girls, and men who thought the disease couldn't touch them paid for their ignorance with their lives. People who fished, people who planted on farms, men who were practised in the building of canoes, children who had learned to swim: all of them surrendered to the soil. 'And he suffered, and he suffered under the weight of the cross. Then they put a crown of thorns on him and drove nails into him . . . ' I don't know what would have happened on the island if that loss of life had been accompanied by a different song, a happier song. Or, if it had not coincided with a time of year when the church required sorrowful singing that brought tears to your eyes. What I do know is that I think we should not have gone on singing that song, for everyone already felt abandoned, already felt they had no one to turn to. Think how our people must have felt being told that *Cristo* himself had 'nails driven into him and then he descended into the abyss'. When we sang this, it wasn't as if the abyss was something we didn't know about or hadn't seen. We thought the mournful song referred to us, to the countless brothers and sisters we'd buried with our own hands, to the graves dug by the few healthy men left on our island.

Many people died that month, and on our list of the departed we must include the doctor, who had no medicine to give himself. There was nothing in the hospital and he probably didn't believe in the effectiveness of the decoction of guava tree leaves. Indeed it would have been hard for him to believe in the homemade remedy even if he'd wanted to, for, as the man who certified the dead, he'd seen too many souls rip out of bodies right before his eyes. And besides, he wasn't trained to believe in things that weren't written in books. So the doctor himself died, taken by the air of the dead of those who'd died before his eyes. Our people went to the shore and found a canoe that was no longer fit for paddling and built a coffin for the doctor. With his death, our island was left orphaned, for although he could offer no cure, he'd still been the first person we turned to whenever someone was touched by that evil. And we islanders didn't view his death as just one more death, rather that his passing had left us to face the evil alone, an evil that was decimating the population. Our new solitude meant the evil could take an unexpected turn and no one on the island would know what was happening, no one would know what to do. Our island was all alone with that thing, a thing that had a name, yes, but a name that in no way suggested how lethal it was.

'Goodbye mothers, goodbye children, *Dios* will know where to find you down in the abyss, and he'll guide you to his bosom, or to a place without suffering, for you have died a painful death,' said a woman, and, as she said it, she recalled she'd just heard the *Padre*'s Latin, and she opened her throat to launch into that song that was not really a song but something that made the spirit shake. Something which was no mere lament. And, faced with so much death, there was no reason for her to stop crying. So she cried, and cried, and cried . . .

I don't know for sure how the sickness ended. What basically happened was that we waited for whoever was in charge of our destiny to decide what to do with us. The islanders knew there was nothing they could do by themselves to get out of the hole, so who can blame them for not doing anything? In fact, because that evil had a name, the cholera, and because it was a name we hadn't heard before, it was treated as something new. I know that to try and combat the cholera we didn't just drink water made from boiling guava tree leaves, and I know the adults thought the mass death was being caused by something that came from the sea. So people talked to the ministrants and they took the *Maté Jachín* and went round the island with it three times in a canoe. I never knew what the *Maté Jachín* was but, at the same time, I knew that it was the centre of our strength, the most pure, sacred and powerful thing on the island. The ministrants, and only the ministrants, knew what it was. All I knew was that the *Maté Jachín* was wrapped in a cloth and seemed to be the shape of a cross. And I also know that anything that had to do with the ministrants' science and beliefs was shrouded in mystery and fear. Which is why their songs had such an effect on me. If the song about the cross and the crown of thorns brought tears to our eyes, the ministrants' songs reminded us that they, the ministrants, were our sole protection from the evil powers that hovered over our island. I understood, from what I'd been told, that only the ministrants' orations could save us from the worst dangers our island faced. Therefore, whenever I saw the ministrants praying, I thought the island must be in grave danger, that we were confronting the threat and magic of a very evil and powerful enemy. So I really didn't like it when we had to appeal to the ministrants and I wished we never had to. Was I afraid of the ministrants because I lacked faith? Or did I lack faith because my fear of danger was greater than my belief in the ministrants' ability to combat the danger? Whichever it was, I was afraid of the ministrants; their activities and their songs frightened me terribly.

That axe hanging over us left the whole village exhausted. And while the evil was with us, no one could go to the southern plantations to plant and harvest. Practically none of the women went any further than their nearest plantations, between the big village and

the Pico. And the men didn't stray far from the big village when fishing. No one gathered or sowed anything
of significance. People in the big village simply waited
for the heavy hammer of unrelenting death to strike its
next random blow. So for all that time we either didn't
eat or hardly ate, and when we did eat the food tasted
bitter, because of all the crying, the bitter taste of tears.
As children, we lived in constant fear, all the time expecting to be shut up at home so that the air of the dead
couldn't touch us, and when we had succulent chunks
of yam and boiled banana placed before us, which were
the daily food staples of our island, we stared at them
as if we'd never seen them before, as if we didn't know
what to do with them. With so many of our adults crying,
we lost the will to eat. With so many of our adults not
only crying but disappearing, for back then we didn't
go to the cemetery and so we didn't know where they'd
gone, where they'd been taken. And also because there
was so little fish, for although the yam and banana were
succulent, we preferred to eat fish. We always did. But
we put those chunks of yam and banana in our mouths
and they tasted bitter, especially if in the corner of the
house or the kitchen our adults were crying for that day's
death, or deaths.

The weight of that axe left us exhausted because we
lived with fear in our bodies, and because we didn't know
when the evil would end; the adults were exhausted not
from work but from the tension of constantly expecting

bad news, bad news that unfailingly came. Nobody ate, either because there was nothing to eat or because everything tasted bitter from the tears that ran down everyone's faces in furrows from their eyes. It was a terrible time, truly the worst time in the history of the island. If witnessing the hounding of that woman was the singular thing that made the biggest impression on me, the cholera was what caused me the most tears. Because it took so many of our people . . . If it had taken one hundred people it would have made a huge dent in the island's population. But it took a lot more than that. A lot more than one hundred girls and boys, men and women, were taken from their homes, put in a floating wooden box, buried in the graveyard and given a little cross. In total there were †, † corresponding to the people who died of that violent disease. Some crosses were accompanied by handwriting done by those who knew how to write. Excluding the doctor, there was Mené Jachiga, Mamentu Lavana, Pudu Kenente, Maguntín Jambab'u, Toiñ Yaya, Pudu Toñía, Madalam'u Tómene, Pudu Gadjin'a, Masamentu Áveve, Jodán Tómbôbô, Majosán Ánjala Pet'u, Fidel Tompet'u,

Madosel Menfoi, Chit'e Zete Doix, Nando Guesa Ngaiñ, Mápudu Chipa Longo, Saan'e Sámene, Xancus'u Menenov, Menembo Jalafund'u, Ximá Dancut and his three sons; Manel'a Vepanu, Saana Tábôbô, Mafidel Ménkichi, Mené Ze Palm'a, Pilinguitu Menfoi, Masantu Jadôl'o, Magutín Bichil, Menembofi Dadot, Santo Dadot, Mafidel Dadot, Másamentu Fadoliga, Mal'e Púluv, Menesamentu Guesagaiñ, Fidel Dadalán, Zetoiñ Padjil, Mafide'l Padjil, Yahií Padjil, Ndeza Liguilía, Rosal Tombal'b, Nando Lem'u Bass'u, Tusantu Dosal'u, Mámentu Jonofund'u, Majosán Zanja Gôôd'ô, Chigol Zampet'u, Mal'é Bojô Longô, Gutín Pendê Mozso, Chiit'e Masamentu, Joodán Pendê, Magutín Pendé, Ximé Jambuk'u, Doszal Sámpete, Fiip'a Tonchiip'a, Gutín Tonfiip'a, Madozee Menfoi, Majolé Ntelacul, Menembô Fídiligu'i, Gutín Lamabas'u, Jodán Menpix'i, Yahií Jázuga, Pudul Legaváan, Madalam'u Maapendê, Toiñ Babadjí'an, Mené Jandjía, Mápudu'l Jandjía, Madalam'u Awacul'u, Quilit'u Menedoix, Menembofi Japiz'a, Fidel Sana Jodán, Tayayô Meendjing'u, Nguzal'u Tómene, Mámentu Chipafend'e, Szebel'u Teszalicu, Ndêêsa Jonoxinc'u, Jodán Chiipagaiñ, Menembofi Límapeet'u. All were lowered into the ground to the *Padre*'s Latin. All were of adult age. Boys and girls died too, some without even having names, for on our island children don't tend to have names until they get a little older. Little children have short names their families use in the home, but the real naming process happens later, out on the street; that's where you acquire your real name, the name you'll be known by for the rest of your life. The unnamed dead slain by the furious axe of the cholera were taken to the square in front of the church and splashed with holy water in the form of the cross, then carried to the cemetery and buried. By the end, there could be no wasting time with funerals, for the deaths came too thick and fast. Children even ended up being buried without a cross. A small mound of earth was left atop the grave to remind everyone that here lay a child too young to know its own innocence, a tiny being snatched away from its parents by the vagaries of nature.

Did we count the doctor as separate? Did he not have a name? Why have I not listed him? All I can say is that back then it was normal for a doctor not to have a canoe because, working all day in the hospital, he wouldn't have had time to go fishing. Furthermore, he'd have had to learn how to be a doctor elsewhere, somewhere where people didn't understand the sea. So as an islander, he'd have needed initiation into such matters before he could have his own canoe. But the thing was, a doctor didn't have to go out fishing in order to eat fish. Nor did he have to go to the *vidjil*. Every afternoon, those who knew he was a busy man would send a bundle of fish to his house and he would thank them with a smile. Everybody greeted the doctor because he was the only person who knew the cures for our sicknesses. He was therefore allowed to live like an incomer – in exchange for his charity, and also for his name. Such was his life when that devastating wave of death came to our island and he went to where he worked, to his hospital, the big village's hospital. And when he learned what the disease might be, he opened all the drawers, all the boxes, all the cupboards and glass cabinets in the hospital, but he found nothing, nothing he knew or thought might combat that terrible evil. He went on searching, for the island's need was desperate, and the only thing he did find he administered generously. Know what it was? The sick screamed out in pain from those awful cramps, writhed in agony on the ground and groaned aahs that rolled out to sea, out to the furthermost parts of the deep blue ocean; they sweated and they felt they were dying. So the doctor gave them something to take away the pain, and they closed their eyes and went to sleep, and they slept, and slept, and slept; and so they remained, asleep forever. What happened was that he gave them pills that put them to sleep, yes, but that didn't stop the torrents from pouring out of them and taking their lives away. So those people moved into the other world without waking from their sleep, a sleep they'd entered into after taking the only thing the doctor could find in all the cupboards and glass cabinets of the hospital, the big village's hospital. This only became known afterwards, when everyone could finally talk about what the island had lived through. And people wondered why those pills had been brought to the island in the first place, and in such great quantities that so many people could be put to sleep, in this case without knowing they'd never wake up again because life was pouring out of them and they were left with no water in their insides. You slept, you slept and you slept, in order to forget that before you'd gone to sleep you'd been screaming in pain and even found your cold sweats painful, really very painful. You went on sleeping, but you wet your trousers, your shirt, the mattress, the rest of your clothes, until you no longer had the strength to get up and tell the doctor that you still had pains, or to ask for the chamber pot. If you slept, the person who sat with you let you rest, or they cried in the corner for those who'd gone to the other world that day, or since the previous afternoon.

And in that sleep, the sick rested in everlasting peace, confirmed a few hours later by a brief Latin prayer from the *Padre* at the door to the church. Right where the whole catastrophe had first been unleashed. Right there at the church door where that ominous incident had taken place, where the woman had come out of the church after meeting the *Padre* to surrender her life to those who showed no mercy to her, nor fear of anyone or anything. That incident that took place in broad daylight and about which no one wished or was able to speak. That incident that I saw with my own eyes, though I closed them when I realised they were planning to take the woman's life, and I went running home, albeit having already witnessed an act of such wickedness it stood out even amidst something so awful: when I saw a stick thrust inside her female organ. I just couldn't understand why they had to thrust a stick inside her as they beat her. If someone had told me right then that we'd all die because of that incident, I'd have said it stood to reason. Today, looking back, I see, or understand, that the incident and the cholera were part of the same sickness. And the cure for that sickness was beyond the reach of our adults for it was a sickness that was greater than them, and so it was able to dominate them. And on that island out in the middle of the Atlantic Ocean, nasty episodes unfortunately had to be explained somehow; something had to satisfy people's need for a cause. Living so far away from everything else gave us a particular way of feeling. Of seeing, of thinking.

Our house was on a street that passed through the town square. If you followed it all the way in one direction – north-east – you reached the sea, via the beach area where people went to attend to their physiological needs at night. Going in the other direction, the street ran parallel with the sea before bearing off to the right and reaching the cemetery. Therefore, when grandfather went to the cemetery with that friend of his, we could see him from the house, walking along with his arms behind his back. We could see the back of his head and even make out that haircut of his, so very lacking in taste. Our house had its back to the sea, presumably because grandfather wanted nothing to do with the shore or the ocean. And with that attitude, he presumably wanted nothing to do with what came from the shore and the ocean either, meaning we regularly had no fish to eat. And as I've already said, if you didn't have fish to eat on our island, you didn't put your pot to boil on the stone tripod of the fireside. And if you didn't put your pot on to boil, you had a bad night, or a hot night if you resorted to chillies, that oh-so-painful alternative. Of this I have also already spoken. And our house had its back to the sea because it was located where it was and not on the next street, the one nearest the sea. That street had the same layout as ours, with the cemetery at one end and the beach where people satisfied their physiological needs at the other. But before reaching the beach by that street you came upon a clearing that might have been a town square but wasn't. We played football there some afternoons, but it was an area of town that didn't really correspond to me; if the people who thought it belonged to them were there, those of us who weren't from that neighbourhood weren't allowed to play. That place, that wasn't a square or even a football pitch, always flooded when there was a lot of rain on the island. And even though the flooding only happened once or twice a year, that was the reason there were no houses there. It flooded so badly you could paddle a canoe across it and, as the water made its way to the sea, threatening nearby houses or actually damaging them, it dug a trench in the ground. When you looked at that trench you thought you were looking at the mouth of a river, albeit a river that was dry for most of the year. Any house built nearby had to be made out of cement or, if that wasn't possible, reinforced with a cement base to protect it from what could be four feet of water. I've seen the devastation caused by rising water levels in the mini-lagoon, which was what we called it, or at least a name in our language that sounded like the Spanish for mini-lagoon: Lagunita.

Anyway, I speak of the particulars of the neighbourhood and the Lagunita because on that street, the one that wasn't mine but was the next one along, nearest to the sea, there was a house that you had to avoid walking past, or else hurry past very quickly. I hurried past just as I was told, but I always did so very curiously, very, very curiously. I'd say that along with my grandfather's room, which I'll talk about later, that house aroused more curiosity in me than anything else on the island. From my house, heading in the direction of the cemetery, there was a street that crossed ours, and at the end of that street, if you walked towards the mountain that burned, the Pico, there was another house that you had to avoid or hurry past quickly. That one was far from the beach and not somewhere we tended to go very often, so we didn't have to worry too much about it, but whenever I did pass it, I did so curiously. But it was a curiosity I only felt by day. If for some reason I had to pass by one of those houses at night, I would run past if I was on my own, which was very unusual, or I would position myself on the far side of my companion so that he or she was exposed to the danger emanating from that house. Why were we warned about those houses? Why did they fill us with such fear? Well, in both of them there lived an adult, a woman in each case, and in other houses too, houses I haven't mentioned because they were quite far from my house and so less relevant, and those women were imprisoned in their houses by the governors of the island. They were imprisoned not because they were sick, as with the cholera, but because of what was known about them. They were old, but they weren't so old they couldn't walk to their plantations and perform their farming activities, but they were not allowed to do so by the governors. They had to stay inside, at home. They satisfied their needs in chamber pots and one of their relatives had to come and empty the pot outside. Or if the woman lived alone, she emptied the pot outside herself, when nobody was looking, which was essentially the point of their being confined to their houses: nobody was supposed to look at them.

Those female adults were obliged by the governors to remain in their homes and never come out. They were not allowed to go to their plantations and nobody sent their children to ask them for a burning coal to make a fire or to borrow some bananas, as is our custom. The woman might sometimes ask others for such things if she was desperate, but people would usually not answer the door to her, denying her the right to practise those customs of ours. And this was because the adults were afraid of these women too. In fact it was the adults who agreed to their being confined to their houses. Why? It's a question worth asking again. They were confined to their houses because of their secret knowledge. Women like them lived like normal people, but at a certain hour of the night they started to feel hot, very hot – so hot that if they didn't immediately splash themselves with water they'd fall ill. That's what the adults said, and there had to be some truth to the matter for it had been talked of on the island for so long. Overcome with heat, they secretly left their houses in the middle of the night and went down to the beach to bathe. As I've already said, no activity took place on the beach at night. It was a dark place where all that could be heard was the breaking of the waves on the sand, a sound that was amplified because everything else was silent. What's more, in our village it is very unusual for an old lady to go to the beach to bathe, even during the day. In fact, no woman of marrying age ever does so. Nor is it common for men of the same age to do so. Therefore, was it not rather strange that a female adult would leave her house in the middle of the night to go and bathe? Furthermore, seemingly a confirmation of the secret nature of the thing, she bathed completely naked. This was unthinkable for a woman beyond marrying age. The beach was not somewhere a woman tended to go to by day, unless she needed to send something to the south village, or collect a load brought from there, so what led them to go to such a dark and solitary place at night? Well, it was because of the heats that invaded them. The heats became unbearable after midnight, which in actual fact was not a time when it was particularly hot on our island. And when it was hot, during the daytime, those same women went around with lengths of cloth draped over their clothes, covering their heads and their backs. In any case, they were invaded by the heats, and it was said, the adults said, that it was because they'd been visited by someone. This someone didn't visit just anyone, and not at just any time either, and that's why those women were considered special. If any woman was discovered bathing on the beach at night it was treated as proof that she'd been visited by someone at night, a mysterious being that transmitted the unbearable heats. And because such things always required explanations on our island, it was understood that whoever visited the women at night was a powerful being, because the heats they felt were no ordinary heats. It was therefore understood that it was an evil being, a being that brought evil. A being, therefore, connected to the Devil.

No matter who the woman was, once she'd been discovered bathing on the beach she was judged to be connected to the Devil and became someone you had to avoid. She could no longer share anything with anyone, absolutely nothing at all. Of course it was possible some women were visited by that mysterious being at night and nobody ever found out. But it would have been unusual. It was more common for traces of the terrible heats to show up on their bodies. What's more, it was common knowledge that after being visited by the being, the woman acquired powers she didn't have before. And because the powers were connected to the Devil, they were powers she would use to evil ends. That's why she was feared, and that's why the governors ordered her confinement. And they were indeed special powers. For example, if a child passed by naked before the woman's house, and she was seated at the door and saw the child, she could use her powers to send a piece of wood from the ground into the child's body, or a piece of metal from the street. And from that day forth the child would complain of a pain in his or her side, or chest, or back, or wherever the old woman had sent the stick, the scrap of metal, the saucepan, whatever she'd had to hand when the child passed by. In the language of our Atlantic Ocean island there is a word we use for such women, a word that in Spanish would be witch or sorceress or she-devil, but that in our language means all three things. I'll just pick one and say that those women were she-devils. Well those women could not only send objects into children, they could also poison their food or kill them with witchcraft. What's more, and by some method only they knew about, those women could pass on the condition of being a she-devil. They could choose to pass the condition on to whomever they wanted, though only to women, or someone would be chosen for them by being visited with bad luck. And once a woman had been chosen, she'd be called upon by the mysterious being of the unbearable heats, and she became a she-devil too.

The adults on our island have always recognised she-devils from their bathing naked in the middle of the night and sending objects into children with the intention of killing them, and also from their penetrating stare. If a she-devil thought nobody was watching her, she could often be caught staring at someone with unusual intensity. Or she'd be caught doing the sort of thing nobody would ever admit to, things no adult of sound mind would ever do if they knew there was a chance of being caught. Things that were obviously of evil intent. After being visited by the being that brought the heats, the woman seemed to have a constant need to cause harm to the rest of mankind. A normal person, normal in the sense of being a woman of adult age, would not spit in someone else's bucket of water, for example, unless that someone else was her sworn enemy, and even then she'd only do it when she knew she wouldn't be caught doing something so repulsive. And the she-devils did things like that, or so the adults said. I remember being told to avoid she-devils at all costs, but if I did catch one staring at me with unusual intensity, I was to hold her stare, because if you looked away, she'd send something into you, and then woe betide you. Can you imagine that? Hold the stare of a woman who everyone said was a she-devil and was therefore extremely dangerous. I understand very well why they had to be shut away in their houses. It was so that they couldn't stare at you in such a dangerous way, and to avoid accusations of their sending pieces of stone or lumps of metal into children, for the she-devils were unable to resist the temptation. I heard cases of mothers taking their children to the house of a she-devil to demand that she remove the saucepan, the water cup or the whatever it was she'd sent into the child, because the child was dying from having it inside them. Yes, I've heard it talked about as if it were the most normal thing in the world.

Did the she-devils ever leave their houses even though it was forbidden to do so? Yes, they did. The nature of life on our Atlantic Ocean island meant that most things were done outside. But, for example, any child would run home if a she-devil asked them to go and fetch a pail of water from the public tap, a request that no child could ordinarily refuse from an old person. But with the she-devil, you might take her the pail of water and then, overcome by the evil inside her, she might send the pail into you, and then woe betide you. Or a she-devil might ask you to bring her a bit of smoking kindling from your house, and then send it into your chest and you'd feel your innards burning from the fire inside you. Or you might perform the favour and she'd do nothing, but to thank you she'd give you a piece of yam, and you couldn't eat the yam because the evil caused by her night heats made her put an invisible drop of poison in the yam, a potent poison that only she knew about. And because of all of this, they sometimes left their houses when they needed something, even though they knew they were not supposed to, and when they did they were targeted by children, children who remained innocent but who had heard about the evils of she-devils. All we did was throw stones at them and run away and hide, to avoid their curses or however else they might react.

I've already said that the she-devils were what I most feared on the island. Yes, I was greatly curious about them during the day, when I hoped to see one, if only out of the corner of my eye, standing in the doorway of her house, or even just moving about inside, for I wanted to be able to think about what daily tasks a she-devil busied herself with. But that great curiosity disappeared as soon as night set in, and if I had cause to walk down a street where one of them lived when it was dark, I avoided that street and went down a different one. In fact I avoided the adjacent streets too, even if this meant having to go a very long way round.

Any old lady might be a she-devil, and they filled us with great fear; they got the heats at night and became so tremendously hot that without thinking twice, or if they did think twice nobody knew about it, they took off their clothes and went to the beach, because they knew there would be nobody there, and they would go into the water, into the sea, into the darkness, in strict solitude. What nobody knew for sure, not even the adults, was what triggered the heats. What were the women doing when the heats invaded them? What did the mysterious being that visited them at night say? What did they talk about? Whether anyone knew the answers to these questions or not, it was considered bad luck for any man to catch a woman with the heats in the act of bathing. It was something best avoided. It can't have been easy to ignore, for everyone knew that night bathing was the one sure sign that the island had a new she-devil in its midst. But those who witnessed such a thing didn't always like anyone to know what they'd seen, for if you caught a woman in the act of bathing at night you had to weigh up the risks against you. That new she-devil, or newly discovered she-devil, for she might have long been one but nobody knew about it, would do everything in her power to make your life a misery if you denounced her. She would lay traps for you at every opportunity, traps to inconvenience you and ultimately to ruin your life. Being a witness to the incriminating night bath was, therefore, an uncomfortable and dangerous position to be in.

First came the song about *Nuestro Señor*, the one they put a crown of thorns on, drove nails into and killed to save sinners. Back then I didn't really understand who the sinners were. What's more, in our island's language, the language that very sad song was sung in, the word 'sinners' sounded very like 'people' or 'folk', and so in my innocence, I heard the words wrong. So what I understood was that the man who'd had nails driven into him on the cross had died to save us, us being the people of our island. I knew there were people in other places, but I only actually knew the ones on our island. And as we had so many needs, it seemed obvious to me that the man had died to save us. He had nails driven into him and he died to save us from the she-devils, from all the evils that could befall us, from the bad spirits of the land and the sea, from all the sickness, all the wickedness. But the saviour had died! That's why the song sounded so sad to me. For at the time, whether because I hadn't heard the song properly or didn't understand the *doctrina*, I didn't know about the promise that the saviour, who'd had nails driven into him after suffering so, would be resurrected. As far as I was aware, he was dead, and if he was dead he couldn't save us from anything, least of all the terrible evils that afflicted us: the she-devils, the lack of soap kerosene matches clothes medicine, the terrible diseases, the lack of a man who was strong and tall and had a powerful voice to caution against anyone doing wicked things on the island. Know what the problem was with the *doctrina*? I only realised it many years later, as an adult. The problem was that every time anyone began preaching, they went back to the beginning and started the story from scratch. Nobody ever told the part about the saviour overcoming obstacles and saving us, it was always from the beginning, and then the nails, the thorns, the cross and death. And so those of us who were not familiar with the whole story and did not know the man was resurrected were left to wallow in a swamp of sorrow. Yes, I have seen a swamp before: there's a village in the south of the island where it's extremely swampy.

Anyway, if I'd known the story was not about the *Señor*'s death but his triumph, I'd have known my worst fears wouldn't come true. But the problem was, it was impossible to speak of triumph on our Atlantic Ocean island, given the conditions we found ourselves in. What we feared most was succumbing to our hardship, losing ourselves, disappearing, and then of course we heard our mothers sing the story of the *Señor* who had experienced the same hardships as us and died for his troubles. How could we imagine triumphing without anyone else's help? I think I might already have mentioned it, but if it had been up to me, that song would not have been sung on the island at that time, though who knows whether it would have made any difference. For the thing was that everything happened in sequence, a chain of events, one thing after another: first, the Pico burned. Then they committed that act of awful wickedness with that woman, an unspeakable, truly awful act. Thrusting a stick into that woman's femininity was a very big deal on our island. But it couldn't be spoken of, not in normal conversation, though everyone agreed it should never have happened. And the moment it happened I knew everything would turn out for the worse. Then came the plague of death that brought the island to its knees. Throughout all this, I would have liked to hear what the *Padre* had to say for himself, to have heard him speak. He was a respected man, a venerated man even, and it would have been interesting to hear what he made of it all. But he was a man who spoke a language I didn't understand – not because it was Spanish but because he didn't know how to express himself properly. He was a terrible speaker, at least when not speaking in Latin, the Latin that released such an outpouring of pain and pity in the womenfolk of our island whenever a coffin was lowered into a grave. As the *Padre* was an incomer, I'd have liked to hear his explanations for the events I'm speaking of. The adults on the island did try to understand what was happening, otherwise they wouldn't have gone around the island three times with the *Maté Jachín*. I see now that going round the island with the *Maté Jachín*, taking it to every accessible corner of the island, was more a matter of asking questions about what was happening than providing any kind of answer. For we died in droves, we suffered like the condemned, as if those thorns had been nailed to our heads, and then we lowered hundreds of coffins into hundreds of graves, graves dug by men to provide a final resting place for the dead. That thing about the departed coming home and making noise, I never saw it myself. In fact, I can't imagine why the departed would come back to the house, if indeed they ever really did. It was said the deads could help the alives, and that was why they came back, but if that were the case, surely they'd have come to our aid during that terrible period. Although what was the point of a dead coming to the aid of an alive if the alive's very problem was that the dead had died? Or that the alive's own death was imminent? It would have made much more sense for the dead not to have died, or for the alive's life not to have been in danger.

So why did these catastrophes occur? There will never be an answer. The ministrants didn't know the answer, and back then I thought they knew everything. There will never be an answer. What people sometimes know is how a story began, or rather they manage to work their way back to the origin of a catastrophe. Some draw comfort from the origin, from the first apparent cause, which is enough to satisfy their need for an explanation. Others curl their lips and frown when they get to the origin, the first apparent cause. And people routinely spoke of things that were not food and drink on our island, by which I mean things that were not necessarily tangible. I say all this in case anybody thinks I'm being too philosophical.

By the time the sun pokes its nose over the horizon of a morning, life on our Atlantic Ocean island is already well under way. Most men will already have their paddles in hand and be gliding out into the waves. The many early risers among the women will already be on their way to the plantations. The women set off early if they're going far, to the south of the island or to the mid part, and also if their journeys involve going up mountains into misty areas, places where the trees sit in the clouds. On our island, it's said that if you get up with the sun, your feet are lighter, or your hands are lighter, depending on whether you're a man or a woman, and travel by canoe or by foot.

On our island, the birds fly when the sun comes up. I don't mean nocturnal birds, which we pay little attention to and in fact curse. Life on our Atlantic Ocean island therefore starts early. Early morning is the time when everyone sees each other and greets each other, when people are full of hope that the day ahead will treat them well. That the fishing will be bountiful, that fully grown tubers will be found under the cassava plants. That the bunches of dates on the palm tree will be ripe, that the plantain will be ready to be cut. In the mornings, those heading in the same direction see each other, greet each other, cross paths. But sometimes there are people you don't wish to greet, people you try to avoid if they're taking the same route as you. Sometimes you might even change your plans if you bump into someone you don't wish to greet, be it because you don't like them or are afraid of them. And that's what happened with the incident we all now know about, that horrible thing, the worst thing to ever happen to us, the most wicked thing we've ever done.

A man who was father to many children and known to many people left home one morning to cut the ripe dates from a palm tree. Cutting the dates from a palm tree is a job only men do, at least when the palm tree is tall and its branches are high, rather than close to the ground where women might reach them. But this palm tree was tall and so the man set off with his axe and his machete, and the intention of making palm oil. The man left the house early, not knowing what the day would bring, and although people of all ages lived in his house, for he was father to many sons and daughters, cutting down the dates was a task only he could perform. Men on our island climb palm trees by making a special harness out of vines. The man makes a weave of thick vines and feeds it round the back of the tree. Then he pulls the two ends towards him and ties them together behind his back, so that he and the tree stand inside the loop of the harness. To climb the tree he leans back and lets the harness take his weight, then he transfers some weight to his feet, which support themselves in holds he cuts into the tree trunk with his axe. It's an exercise I've seen done many times and a technique that's taught to all males on the island, once they've reached a certain age. So the man leans back in the loop of his harness, sticks his feet in the holds he excavates in the trunk and walks up the tree two steps at a time. And of course he carries his machete and his axe, for he isn't climbing the tree just to prove he was taught to climb palm trees as a boy, he's doing it to gather dates for his wife, or any other woman who might have asked the favour of him. Or he might be doing it to extract palm wine, the succulent juice found inside palm trees. For on our Atlantic Ocean island, you don't chop a palm tree down and kill it to extract the wine: you climb the tree and tap it. Not a drop of wine would reach a single throat if it weren't for men proving their skills with harness, axe and feet. And with body and eyes too, for it's an artisan's job, a job that would be done anywhere else in the world, anywhere other than an island that had nothing, using some kind of eye and face protection, because all manner of things can fall from above.

Anyway, the man left his house and reached wherever it was he was going. He saw the palm tree, he saw the ripe palm dates at the top, and he prepared the harness, all very calmly. He made a quick sign of the cross, stood in the loop of the harness and fastened himself in. The boy passed him his axe . . . We forgot about the boy. I was talking as if the man had gone there on his own, which would have been very unusual. For one thing, who would have shown the man where the tree was, for men hardly ever went to the plantations on our island? And who would have carried the dates once the bunch had been cut? True, the man himself could have carried them for, though he had a slight limp, he could still walk. But it was more typical for a boy from his house to go with him and for the boy to carry the load on his head. And, before that, the boy would pass the man his axe, and before that he would fasten the man into his harness. The boy did all this, but that's where the story ends, the story of the man climbing the palm tree, the story of his life. We were never told whether the man did or didn't cut any dates, whether he reached the top of the tree or not; all we were told was that the man, father to many sons and daughters, fell from the palm tree and landed with the full force of his weight on the ground. Such a tremendous blow shook him to the core and, though his soul wasn't ripped out of his body there and then, very little life was left in him. It's said he lived just long enough to utter his dying words to his family. The boy ran to get help and the man was carried home, a man who was at death's door but for now remained father to many children. And then, as I've said, what little life there was left in him expired. And everyone was informed, and everyone went to his house for the wake, for he wasn't just a father to many children, he was also one of the main ministrants of the island. His death was similar to the death of the doctor: we had lost a man with the power to heal us and we felt orphaned without him, without his care. Yes, I remember now, he was the senior ministrant. Other senior ministrants had died before him and passed the responsibility on to him. So he was no ordinary old man. The wake at his house, 'his deathplace', as we call it in our language, was a sight to behold, or rather not to behold, something that was best avoided. At least so I was told. I did pass by the house and I saw a lot of people there, and I heard the laments, though I didn't know at the time whether the man was alive and injured or already dead, for nobody told me. But I imagine he was already dead. I only passed the house very briefly, for I wasn't supposed to go because of my age. I went because

I was looking for my grandmother, seeking her comfort, and she was there because she knew how to do some of the things the ministrants did. I didn't really understand why the whole village was there at the time but there were a number of reasons: first and foremost, he was an important figure, because he was the senior ministrant, but there was also the fact that his death had been a tragedy. Looking back I see there was a major barrier between adults and children, and that barrier meant, for example, that I never knew what injuries he died of. The adults never told us. Whether his head was smashed in, or his feet and hands, or his entire body, I couldn't say; we children never knew. Nor does it matter particularly: the fact is he died. He was buried, and I know nothing about his funeral either, for only the adults went.

Days passed, though only a few, and then we saw the man's many relatives come running down from the upper part of the big village, down towards the shore. What they claimed had happened I will tell you now, though whether that man ever did utter his dying words I don't know. They said he did, and they said his dying words concerned what he'd seen on the morning of his death. The members of his household kept his dying words in their hearts and they waited until he was buried before acting on them. What were those dying words the relatives kept in their hearts? What did the man with so many sons and daughters say before his soul was ripped out of his body?

The ministrants sang things in a language that was not our own, and they therefore said things we didn't understand. And given who that man was, the ministrants must have sung for hours and hours when he died and, I should imagine, they also took measures to elect the next senior ministrant. His funeral was a sight to behold, or not to. After the *Padre*'s Latin, the laments drowned out the murmur of the waves breaking on the shore. And if it had been day, night would have fallen, for on an island where we had nothing to combat the eternal darkness, we felt particularly vulnerable at night. Then again, on moonlight nights we felt exposed, for the moon lit up the whole village and advertised our helplessness. I always felt that moonlight nights revealed our skeletons, our defects. In fact the moon illuminated more than the sun did, for night was not meant for seeing as much as we saw on moonlight nights on the island. You could see from one extreme of the beach to the other, and if you saw someone standing at the other end you felt unnerved, for perhaps that someone had evil intentions. I'm not saying I preferred the dark exactly, but moonlight nights were frightening. They exposed our privacy to the world. Night is a time for privacy, for doing little things alone, and moonlight nights upset all that and cause misunderstandings. I remember the story of some older boys who were part of my family, although they lived in a different house rather than with us. Once, they got up in the early hours to gather mangoes, but on a moonlight night. Several cocks had crowed and they thought this singing clock meant it was dawn, or that dawn was at least around the corner. So they got up and they called for one another and they set off walking. Mangoes grow in great abundance on the island but you always go to get them in the early hours, so as not to have to climb any trees. If you get there before anyone else, you can fill your basket gathering mangoes from the ground, mangoes that have fallen from their branches because they are ripe. So those boys went and filled their baskets, but they waited for day to break before heading back home. Everything has its ways and its rules on our island. If they'd set off home right away, when the sun was poking over the blue horizon, they would have crossed paths with the women on their way to the plantations, and this might have led to a scene whereby they had to bend down to let a lady pluck a handful of mangoes from their baskets. The lady might be an aunt, a godmother, a neighbour or the mother of a friend, and it was rude not to offer her mangoes from your basket. She would need a mango to help her digest the hunk of cassava bread she'd taken with her to eat while she was working. And she might not have time to go looking for her own mangoes, if indeed she had a mango tree on her plantation.

So those boys filled their baskets and waited for day to break, to avoid such an eventuality. But what happened? They'd let themselves be tricked by the brightness of the moon, believing it to be dawn when it wasn't, and so they'd got up and set off in the middle of the night. When they realised their mistake, they huddled together, laid their lengths of cloth on the ground and tried to sleep, waiting for the sun to appear and re-establish normality. And it was cold, as it always was at night. And when the moon withdrew behind the clouds, they became afraid, for darkness took hold of the bush and this was something they'd not experienced before. Being in the bush at night. They had never been in the bush at night, it was not something anyone chose to do, and indeed there was no reason for doing it. If, on the other hand, they'd gone straight home, ignoring their fear, it would have meant they'd left and gone back to the house in the middle of the night, and this would have been very suspicious behaviour. And their return would have been noted. And collecting mangoes wouldn't have been a good enough explanation for coming and going at night, especially not given the rules of courtesy involved in gathering mangoes. Why should women waste precious time and energy searching their plantations for mangoes when they could be given a handful by children? What would the men have taken with them to wet their throats whilst out fishing if they hadn't crossed paths with the boys and their baskets of mangoes on the way to the beach?

But anyway, it wasn't mango season when the senior ministrant died, or, if it was, they weren't ripe yet, for neither the man nor the boy accompanying him saw anyone carrying a basket of mangoes on their head. What they would have seen were women going to the plantations to harvest daily food staples. And given all that followed, we also know that they saw someone going to the plantations with evil intentions, or rather someone whose intentions were governed by an evil being. The ministrant said something along those lines before his soul was ripped out of his body. And what he said led to everything that followed, with his relatives charging down from the upper part of the big village. And what that man said was that he'd been followed that morning as he made his way to the palm tree, followed by someone with evil intentions, and it had been that someone who'd thrown him out of the palm tree with such great force that his body had hit the ground and had the life squeezed out of it. Those were the dying words his relatives kept in their hearts. Until the day they acted upon them. What they'd kept in their hearts moved their feet, made them come running from the upper part of the big village to the lower part.

It was the afternoon. They'd kept the words in their hearts for several days and they thought it was time everyone knew what those words were. Well, everyone as in everyone on the island. So what they did, acting as one, was go to the house of the woman I mentioned earlier, the one who lived at the end of a street that began at the shore, crossed our street and ran all the way to the upper part of the village. That woman had two daughters, only two, and lived with a man who was quite well known. He was a man who spoke in a very soft voice, in a woman's voice, or practically a woman's voice, and he also sometimes did women's jobs, although he fished too. All the children knew him because adults had to answer us when we greeted them. And so we knew that man because of his woman's voice, or child's or sick person's voice, and also for his hesitant walk. He was called Toiñ. And his voice was the voice of a man who had little to say. Why did he speak in such a soft voice? What was he afraid of? What was he hiding?

They went to the house where they knew Toiñ's wife would be, and they called her to the door and told her what they'd kept in their hearts, or maybe they didn't, and they started to beat her with sticks. Her two daughters tried to intervene, tried to save their mother, but they were violently pushed aside. The quarrel wasn't with them, they needn't be afraid. They took stock and saw there was nothing they could do, not when faced with so many furious people, furious people full of wicked intent. Later I realised the furious people had been quite calculating. Those two daughters were defenceless, for they hadn't any male siblings. And there were not many of them, only two. There were no male children in the family, no strong men to defend them. That's partly why the ministrant's family members were so bold, and also because of the words they'd kept in their hearts, the words that had given them the strength to act in the first place.

The woman could not fend them off, nor could her two daughters, and the ministrant's family saw there was nothing to stop them from doing exactly as they pleased. And they started to beat the woman out of her house. The woman didn't know what was happening and so she ran out of the house, down the hill that separated the upper part of town from the lower part and into the cluster of streets that led to the beach. She received blows all over her body and she cried out, pleading for them not to kill her, but whatever it was her pursuers carried in their hearts, it was strong, stronger than her pleas and appeals. Don't kill me, what have I done to deserve this, what have I ever done to hurt you? But they weren't interested. They went on beating her with all their might and all over her body, wherever they happened to strike. She carried on running, she was knocked to the ground by the blows, and she wasn't young, but she got up, and took further blows; she had long been bleeding, and she lost her balance again, but her enemies went on beating her on the ground; she got back on her feet and carried on running, although her strength was dwindling, and she ran right through the centre of the village and reached the *vidjil* where her husband was, Toiñ. She thought because he was a man and her husband he'd be able to defend her. And besides, there were always other men at the *vidjil*, men who went there to relax, and they would intervene, they would show the good sense expected of the sort of man who went to the *vidjil*, and they would call an end to the beating. So she got to the *vidjil* and she saw her husband and, with that voice of his, that made him speak so slowly and softly, he tried to say something, to find out what was going on and bring the whole brutal act to an end; our island had never seen anything like it. But the men with sticks attacked Toiñ and in no time at all they'd broken one of his arms and were ready to go much further. The other men in the *vidjil* read the danger but they didn't say anything and they didn't intervene, rather they expelled the woman from their building. They did not come to her defence. That's right: she'd taken refuge in the *vidjil*, sought the protection of her husband and his colleagues, but the men expelled her and left her to face the evil of her pursuers alone, totally alone. First she'd been denied the help of her daughters, then her husband had been unable to defend her and now she'd been thrown out by the men of the *vidjil*. This latest blow made her realise she'd reached a decisive moment in her life and had to make an important decision, one that nobody could make for her. And if she didn't make it right away, a hail of sticks would come down on her and mean there were no more decisions to make. She was half-naked when she came out of the *vidjil* that had turned her away, and she directed her tears and her tottering steps towards the upper part of the big village, towards the *Misión*. What she decided to do, nobody could do for her, and she knew she had little time left to do it. She was bleeding profusely and she could hardly see, but one thing kept her going, made her keep her grip on life. With what little energy she had, she covered the distance from the *vidjil* to the *Misión*. She fell several times, each fall an opportunity that was made the most of by her pursuers, the senior ministrant's family, who paused to select where best to strike her, where would cause her the most harm. She bled profusely. From all parts. With tremendous effort, she reached the church and went inside. When she came out and they did what I've already talked about, with the sticks and her nakedness, I became overwhelmed with the terrible feeling that what I was witnessing was something quite extraordinary. I was not old enough to see such a thing, nor will anyone ever be old enough. They beat her with sticks until she died; that's right, they beat her to death, out in the open, after chasing her through the streets of the big village, after she'd gone to the *vidjil* and been turned away, after she'd been into church and confessed and taken Communion. She died out in the open, after her two daughters were unable to save her, after her husband, Toiñ, whose arm had been broken, was unable to save her, after the men in the *vidjil* were unable to save her. I am still amazed by the fact that her pursuers waited for her outside the door of the church to finish her off. I am still amazed that the priest didn't come out to defend her, to speak to those men, women and children who were so possessed with wicked fury. But what the people of our village, of our island, don't seem to understand is that we all participated in her death, that there will never be another event at which every islander participates as much as we did that day, with that brutal slaying, for it took place out in the open, on the streets, at the *vidjil*, in the church. That woman gave up her soul out in the open, as if she'd died in a tragic accident, as if the only reason she didn't die in bed, at home or in the hospital was because her death was a tragic accident. Oh! Now I see what the ministrant's family perhaps wanted: they wanted her death to echo the death of their father, the senior ministrant, and come like a tragic accident out in the open. Never can an entire village have been so implicated in a single incident as with this. Because everyone took part, even those who thought they didn't. Seeing is a form of taking part, and nobody can claim they didn't see it. And maybe they didn't intervene because deep down, when it really came to it, they thought those people had their reasons for doing what they did. And this is what they did – I'll describe it for what I hope will be the very last time:

They went with sticks to knock on the woman's door. She was there with her daughters. The ministrant's relatives accused her, said the words they'd kept in their hearts, then started to beat her. They did so full of rage, full of fury, and they perhaps intended to finish the matter right there, for they didn't want the whole world to see what they were up to, something that had never been done on the island before. But the woman didn't want to die, so she ran out of the house, a house in which she'd had no sons, nor daughters who'd married, but rather two daughters who'd had children with men who lived elsewhere. She went out to seek protection from Toiñ, who was relaxing at the *vidjil*. By the time she got to the *vidjil*, she was bleeding profusely, and she left trails of blood in the streets where she ran, chased like a dog that had jumped from the tree at the first stone thrown by a child. She cried, she begged to be pardoned, she pleaded for mercy from everyone in the village, from her pursuers, the ministrant's entire family. After fending off so many blows, her fingers must have been broken. But she could still run. If she managed to reach the *vidjil* it was only because the blows hadn't yet ruined her feet. She panted, sweated, bled profusely. And she entered a place that women rarely entered. She saw that she was going to die and she thought her husband, Toiñ, would be able to defend her. What's more, the *vidjil* was a place where important things on the island were judged. It was a place where there were always lots of men during the day and those men would ask what the whole thing was about, for chasing and killing a woman, in fact chasing and killing anyone at all, had never happened on the island before. And she would make the most of the men asking questions and establishing facts in order to rest, to wipe the blood from her face, rub the bumps on her head and hope the men in the *vidjil* would manage to convince that family that the matter should be discussed and resolved in a different fashion. She ran bleeding into the *vidjil*. But the men there didn't know what she expected them to do, and when they saw the blows that cracked the bones of her companion, Toiñ, they realised the situation was more serious than they'd first thought. And they expelled the woman from their *vidjil*, and they told Toiñ that he must trust in *Dios*, for they themselves could do nothing. Although they didn't say as much in words, rather with their actions. Who knows what they really thought. She bled a lot but, with great effort, she accepted the double blow of discovering Toiñ's weakness and the *vidjil*'s cowardice. I think that, of the whole business of running through the streets trying to escape death, being turned away from the *vidjil* must have been some kind of nadir. If things had worked out differently, it could have led to a powerful sense of relief. Salvation from death's shadow. But instead it led to her surrender. Can it not be said that by going into the church she was handing over responsibility for her life to whoever was in there? Yes, I know she was given Communion after she confessed, but I can't ignore the fact that the priest was a man with great authority on the island. Someone with a voice. Then came what I could not bear to watch. She went on bleeding and she died, all the strength having run out of her. Her soul ripped out of her body as it was beaten with sticks by members of the senior ministrant's family. The ground was covered in blood, and I know it wasn't the people who beat her who carried her dead body back to the house to prepare her for burial. That's how this was different from killing a dog when it becomes a burden: the dead dog's killers don't leave the body on the ground for someone else to deal with.

What motivated them to do what they did? I've already said. It was what the family members kept in their hearts, which were the dying words of the ministrant. The morning he died, that woman, the wife of Toiñ, a man who spoke so slowly and softly, that woman, who was a she-devil, left her house and followed the ministrant; when she saw him climb the palm tree, she made him fall using the black magic she'd learned from the being that visited her at night. She was a she-devil, so when everyone else slept in their beds at night, she started to feel suffocating heats, she took off her clothes, opened the door to her house and ran down to the beach to bathe in the sea. And if neither her husband nor her two daughters, the two sisters who caused the fire on the Pico, had ever seen her do this, or were even aware that it happened, how could they be blamed for what she did? The daughters had never noticed the terrible thing that happened to their mother at night. They were totally unaware of it. They weren't she-devils themselves and they were oblivious to her having been one. And maybe that's why they didn't believe in the reasons the ministrant's family had for doing what they did. They were not she-devils and they could not understand how a woman who had not gone up the palm tree and grabbed hold of the harness and thrown the man out of the tree could be said to have caused the accident. But they did not know what someone visited by a strange being in the night is capable of. When did she take her clothes off? Before the visit? Afterwards? As far as the senior ministrant's sons and daughters were concerned, their father had been followed by the she-devil and, if she hadn't been seen there in person, it was because she'd caused the accident that killed him by using her black magic. If the senior ministrant had seen her in person before he climbed that palm tree, he wouldn't have climbed it. He'd have gone home and waited for another day. But she-devils don't always let themselves be seen, and it's possible the man didn't even know he'd been followed that morning, for he might never have looked over his shoulder. On our island, any woman being followed by a she-devil would have realised it, for she would have felt a 'weighing' at her back and she would have stepped aside to allow the she-devil to pass. This I know from my grandmother. She was once on her way to the plantations with one of her grandsons when she felt someone staring at her with great intensity. She looked over her shoulder and saw a woman coming, a woman who people talked about on account of her suspicious behaviour. So my grandmother stepped aside to let the woman pass, but the woman refused to go on ahead and stepped off the path herself, as if to pee. She remained standing but she lifted up her clothes, put her hand between her legs and let out her stream, or at least it's

assumed she did. Everything on the paths to the plantations is governed by rules of courtesy, so my grandmother
didn't wait and watch, rather she went on walking, with
the boy out in front. What a cheek that woman had. For
this behaviour alone she deserved a reprimand; it truly
was suspiciously she-devilish behaviour. They went on
walking and my grandmother felt the weighing at her
back again but, whenever she stopped, the other woman
refused to pass. When they reached a fork in the path, my
grandmother called the boy back, for he'd gone on ahead
as he knew where they were going. But my grandmother
decided to take another route and follow a path that led to
a place where there were no plantations. She'd therefore
never been down that path before. She was only taking
it to escape the other woman's harassment. As the path
forked, my grandmother veered off to the right, while
the other woman went straight on. But after a certain
time had passed, my grandmother felt the weighing and
the harassment again, very strongly, and she knew that
other woman had evil intentions. Not wanting the day
to be spoiled, my grandmother told the boy to stop, and
they turned round and headed in the opposite direction,
to a totally different plantation, one she hadn't thought
of going to that morning.

But the men, who were not at all acquainted with the
paths to the plantations and what might be encountered
on them, felt only the weight of the harnesses on their
shoulders and the axes slung over their backs.

Why am I recounting all this? That woman was buried as if nobody knew her. Only a handful of men dug the grave, with her husband unable to help due to his broken arm, and two men made the coffin. It was a struggle to carry, for those sisters had no husbands on whose shoulders it could be hoisted. The two men who made the coffin found two others to help, and for those four men that funeral would live long in their memories. Four men was the bare minimum for carrying a coffin, so there was no opportunity to swap shoulders, no respite, and the dead are said to weigh heavy. I can picture the scene, for I know they did at least bury her in a coffin. But I don't know any more than that. I think she was buried without anyone wanting or choosing to be there, and that Toiñ and her two daughters went to the cemetery as if they were visiting her tomb, dressed in black and with their heads shaved. They didn't cry much, neither in the house nor out on the street, for although their hearts were full of lament, they held back their tears, knowing nobody would help them cry like the women usually did, with singing. No one would accompany them in their grief, even though their mother's death had been the saddest event the island had ever known. And no one would accompany the sisters in their grief because the dead woman was a she-devil, and anyone who cried for a she-devil in public would have to justify themselves. *Why are you crying for a she-devil? Why are you crying for a she-devil you weren't even related to? What are you crying for? The rest of us turned our backs on her long ago.*

I've never stopped thinking about that woman. As I've already said, the incident affected me a great deal. It's something I'll never forget, something I'll always think about and reflect upon. I'll always have my views on what happened. And I ought to add that my views are the same now as they were then, when it happened: my views haven't changed. For example, even as a child, I thought there was no way that woman could have been responsible for the accident that caused the ministrant's death. Not because I felt particularly inclined to defend that woman, or didn't think she was a she-devil or that she-devils were capable of doing such things. No, the reason I didn't believe that woman was responsible was that I believed a ministrant's powers were greater than a she-devil's. I couldn't believe a she-devil could follow a ministrant to the plantations with the intention of making an attempt on his life and the ministrant wouldn't find out and defend himself from whatever trap she laid. With the *Maté Jachín*, the white tunics they wore, their mysterious songs and all their followers, which was basically the whole island whenever there was danger – I couldn't believe that, with all that, he couldn't defend himself against a she-devil, couldn't use eyes in the back of his head to see her coming, see her following him, scheming to use her evil to make him slip out of the harness or lose his footing and fall to the ground.

Therefore I thought that woman was innocent, though not for one moment did I stop thinking she was a she-devil

151

and therefore dangerous. In fact, I was very afraid of going down her street. When news first reached us that the ministrant had died and that a she-devil was implicated, I immediately thought she must have secretly followed him to the palm tree, waited until he'd climbed to the top, sneaked over, shrieked at the top of her voice, a deafening voice she-devils are capable of producing, and given the man such a fright that he fell from the tree to his death. But I was told later that it didn't happen like that, that her arts had been darker, more silent. More like when she sent a piece of wood into a child. It was then that I thought it couldn't have been her.

I am a *cristiano*, a practising one, and the only reason I haven't been married to my wife by the church is that in the traditions of the island, marriage is a couple's final act. First they do everything else, then they get the wedding suit and talk to the *Padre* about marriage. I continue to believe in *Dios*, in my faith and in the *doctrina*. But in spite of all this, and think of me what you will, I don't believe that woman, the she-devil I've been talking about, went to heaven. She didn't go to heaven, nor is she ever going to go, if indeed it's true that some chosen ones go there later, rather than immediately after their death. And what I believe is hard to explain and justify. But it's got nothing to do with her being a she-devil, or my belief that she-devils don't go to heaven because of their wickedness and night visits. That's to say, I don't think she didn't go to heaven because of what she was. If it were just a matter of what she was, there'd be no doubt in my mind: I've never thought for a second that she-devils go to heaven; none of them do, not a single one. The reason I don't think she went to heaven, wasn't granted salvation by *Dios* even though she confessed and received Communion, has to do with the way she died. That woman died having been abandoned by the entire village, having run naked before us, having pleaded for help that didn't come, having bled profusely. Died out in the open. And no one went to her funeral. When she was alive, she only ate food given to her by her daughters, and only those two daughters and her husband could accept food from her. Food or drink. Practically nobody ever greeted her, nor did she greet anybody, for she knew people were afraid of her and fled from her wherever she went. She was beaten to death and, if nobody tried to save her, it was because they wouldn't forgive her. And she would have needed the island's forgiveness in order to go to heaven. Yes, I know *Dios* forgave her, through the priest, but she didn't receive our forgiveness and she therefore couldn't have gone to our heaven. Or she could have gone, but she'd have had to go alone. A woman who dies hated by her people can't go to heaven. Where would they put her? Not in the same place as us, we who condemned, mistreated and refused to help her, for I can't see how friendships can be rebuilt after the Final Judgement. And although I believe she would cease to be a she-devil in heaven, the way people acted towards her on the island was not wholly down to her being a she-devil. What I mean is that the island's attitude towards her cannot solely be explained by her having been a she-devil. Therefore people were not suddenly going to start laughing and joking with her in heaven, going round to her house and eating her food, not after what they'd done to her. And if reconciliation was an impossibility, she couldn't go to heaven. On one side of heaven you'd have everyone from the island, including the senior ministrant, for there was no doubting he went to heaven, for he was a senior ministrant, and on the other side you'd have her, the she-devil. A she-devil can't go to the same place as a ministrant. And anyway, if anyone deserves damnation it's a she-devil. That's to say, I can't see how we, everyone else on the island, including the senior ministrant, could be damned so that a she-devil might be saved. So I've never believed that woman went to heaven, even though she confessed and received Communion.

I don't know if I have these convictions and feelings about the she-devil's salvation, or lack thereof, because of the *Padre*'s attitude and the way it became engraved on my memory. What I mean is, if I don't think the woman went to heaven, it's because of feelings I still have about that day, feelings I'm not always aware of or able to express. Not believing she was granted salvation is my way of suffering for what the *Padre* failed to do, my way of saying I don't agree with him or what he did; that despite the fact that he took her confession and gave her Communion, I don't believe she went to heaven. It could of course be argued that deep down it's my way of fighting the *Misión* or the *doctrina*. The events of that day affected me a lot, so it's possible that something changed in me beyond my control. I accept this, and I'm conscious that I always thought the situation should have been handled differently, that the *Padre* should have acted differently. If there was any sinning involved, the only person who suffered from it was the she-devil. And *Dios me perdone*, but if that woman had been my mother, I'd have preferred it if she hadn't confessed or received Communion, but had been saved from death. Especially that death. That was no ordinary way to die. The way I see it, the *Padre* considered only the fact that he had a woman before him who needed confession and Communion; he ignored the fact that she was about to die, and how it was going to happen. I believe, and *Dios me perdone* again, that the *Padre* would have done a great deal more by prevent-ing her death. And I know he could have prevented it. And on a personal level, if that woman, that she-devil, had died without confessing and taking Communion, it would have made no difference to me, so long as she hadn't died the way she did. If it was only a matter of the woman's spiritual needs then fine, that's her business, but it wasn't only that: those events affected everyone. What would the priest have done if the woman had been his sister? Or his brother? Yes, the *Padre* was a white man, but even white priests have brothers and sisters. What happened on our island that day was a sin committed by many people at once. It should therefore have been resolved in a way that implicated everybody. As I see it, by hearing her confession the *Padre* left the matter only half resolved. And I refer solely to the confession. When a wicked thing happens in a village, its negative consequences scatter into the air and are left hanging until a ceremony of purification is performed. That's why I say the *Padre* only half resolved things. If I'd had the learning of a priest, or if I'd been an adult at the time, I'd have ended up arguing with the *Padre*. If a man lets his own house burn, or lets the village he lives in burn because of a fire started by his neighbours, I don't believe that man goes to heaven. I don't believe such a man can be admitted into heaven.

After death had called a ceasefire on the island, a friend of my grandmother's came to the house to ask for a boy to accompany her to the south village, for she didn't want to go there alone. The woman was a distant relative of my grandmother and had no children of her own, or if she had them, they were in the same place as the fathers of all the children in our house. It seemed a lot of fathers of children on our island were in that place that you went to by boat. My grandmother could not deny the woman such a favour, so she told me to go with her. I was to live with that woman for as long as she stayed in the south village, I was to accompany her to her plantations and give her someone to talk to. The time of year was approaching when most families moved to the settlements to spend a few months there, planting and harvesting, but that year many families chose not to go. They preferred to stay in the big village and cry for their dead. Therefore, anyone who went to the southern settlements on their own, without company, would have a miserable time, especially a woman. The bush was a lonely place, its atmosphere thick with the sorrow that had spread throughout the island. And in such an atmosphere, it wasn't uncommon for the spirits of the dead to make their presence felt. In such circumstances, a woman was easily frightened on the plantations. Whenever she heard a sound, especially the cry of the bird with the black and yellow feathers, she'd see it as a sign that the spirits of the dead were present, and this would unnerve her. But if she had a boy to accompany her, she'd mutter something under her breath and go on with her business, or she'd perhaps recall someone close to her who'd died and recognise that someone in the form of the bird with the black and yellow feathers. That bird represents the spirit of the dead on our island and is never eaten.

So, somewhat reluctantly, I accompanied that friend of grandmother's to the south village. There were very few people there and, if it wasn't quite as desolate as we'd expected, the people who were there were very spread out, meaning there were lots of gaps in the village, gaps filled by the sorrow that extended over the island. Walking about the south village, you'd see a closed-up house, two sticks criss-crossed over the door at right angles. You'd pass that house and see another one just the same, with two sticks in the same position, and another, and another, and another. And because you knew the village you knew whose houses they were, and you knew that some of those houses would never be opened again, or at least not for many years, because their owners had perished, taken away by that wave of the cholera. Somewhere in the big village cemetery there would be a †, and most likely no other details, for whoever planted that cross probably didn't know how to write, not even a date. You'd see another house shut up with sticks and, outside it, you'd see the stone tripod of the fireside but no pot boiling with banana-leaf parcels. And beneath the house's *jambab'u* roof you'd see the stones the owners sat on when they were in the south village, and you'd see how the stones had become coloured with age, a sign that nobody had sat on them for a long time. And you passed another house, and another, and another, and in the next one a friend of yours used to live, a friend you'd never see again. They told you he died of the cholera and you couldn't go and see them bury him because you were only a child. And if you cried out in the south village, you heard an echo at the other end of the village, as if the emptiness dispersed your cry so that it might reach those who were no longer

there, those that might have been present in the form of
a black and yellow bird.

I went to the settlements with that friend of grandmother's
and in the south village I found a boy I'd met before. We
weren't exactly friends, because we didn't live near one
another in the big village, but in the south village any
company was welcome. That boy was a little older than
me and he'd gone with his mother to the village for the
same reasons I had, although in his case the woman he
was accompanying to make sure she wasn't lonely was
not his grandmother's friend but his own mother. It was
highly likely his father was in the place you went to by
boat. Being typical boys, we wanted to be like men and
act like men, men who'd been taught how by real men:
we wanted to fish. But back then, nobody had any nylon
in a strongbox. If our mothers had kept any hidden away,
they'd have given it to us, for they knew that the south
village was a place with beaches and that a little fishing
made life more agreeable in the solitude down there. As
we were only kids, nobody expected us to go out fishing
in canoes. And they didn't expect it because in the south
village the waves broke onto the beach with such ferocity that going out to sea was no easy thing. What's more,
where the waves broke was not even really a beach but
rather a rocky bay. The waves crashed against the rocks
with such ferocity they seemed angry about something,

about the place they'd been sent to die. So going out in a canoe from any of the south village shores was quite something. To fish at our age, we had to go and stand on the rocks and cliffs that jutted out to sea. There we'd throw out our bait, watchful of the waves that broke over the rocky headland, making sure we weren't dragged in by them. But as I said, we had nothing to throw out to sea to tempt the fish with. In previous years we'd tied together strips of plastic we found in leftover bits of rubbish. By tying them together carefully, strip by strip, we managed to get enough length to reach the depths the coastal fish liked to swim at. And on the end of our fragile fishing line we attached a hook, made out of a rusty bedspring from a mattress found at the rubbish dump. The rest came down to our fishing expertise. But the years went by and there was no more leftover rubbish to take strips of plastic and springs from. By then, not even the adults, not even the men who fished for a living, had anything to fish with. So in the southern settlements we longed for fish. We ate cassava, or whatever else was gathered from the plantations and given to us to eat, but we ate with little enthusiasm for we were unable to moisten whatever it was with sauce, the water that had boiled with something tasty. We had to do something about it. It would have shamed us not to do anything about it, little men that we were. So we weighed up our options. We could try and catch crayfish from the river or go out hunting and try and hit a bird with a stone mid-flight.

There were very few seabirds on that coastline and the chances of our hitting one of them with a stone were slim. Indeed the effort involved would probably have left us hungrier for fish than when we started. As for the cray-fish, there were not many people in the settlements but there was someone who threw stones at you whenever you went in the river. Whoever it was couldn't be seen, and it was frightening to expose yourself to the stone-throwing of a hidden stranger. Another option was a type of wild hen that could be found in certain clearings in the south of the island, but we'd never heard of anyone catching one by any means other than with a rifle. So there were things that could be boiled as a substitute for fish, but all of them were beyond our reach. And so our hunger for fish continued, until we saw a bird up in the mountains. The bird was large and it made its nest in the hollows of trees, but it could be reached by hand with relative ease. It may have been a kind of fowl, for it bore some resemblance to a duck, and although it nested in the mountains, mountains we could see from the south village, it fished in the sea, flying back to the nest with things it caught to feed its chicks. The more we watched the bird, the more encouraged we became, because although the bird was a good flyer and a high flyer, it seemed to have difficulty taking off. It made its nest wherever it found a hole but it had to build a ledge to launch itself from because it was too ungainly to take off directly from the ground. Which meant that if we snatched it from its nest and threw it to the ground, it wouldn't be able to escape. Another encouraging factor was that, although it was a wild bird, it didn't avoid human contact. In fact it was so unconcerned by humans you could go right up to its nest without it flying away. To catch that bird, that sea-hunting fowl, we wouldn't need sticks or stones or a rifle, just enough agility to climb up a tree with a hole in it, a hole with a feathered tail sticking out. The bird was white, completely white, and its tail was long, sometimes as long as the bird itself. What made the tail special was that it consisted of one single feather; one long white feather, poking out of the nest. Now that I think about it, I remember that bird was thought to be very nervous, so nervous that if you saw it flying over you and screamed, it would fall to the ground. I never saw this happen, but I remember screaming at it as a child, trying to make the bird that lived in the mountains and fished in the sea fall from the sky and land in my mother's cooking pot.

We longed for fish and we saw all those encouraging signs from that bird with the single-feather tail, a bird we could see flying about in the mountains from the south village. It became increasingly clear to us that the answer to our problems lay with the bird up there. And so one day, when that friend of grandmother's took the same path to the plantations as my friend's mother, we decided to make the most of the opportunity to look for the bird. We'd accompany our respective adults, his mother and my surrogate grandmother, and keep them company as required, but when the chance arose, we'd head up the mountain to see what we could do about our longing for something to eat that wasn't dry malanga or boiled banana. We'd whistle to one another from our respective plantations and assemble at an agreed meeting point. But we'd have to make sure we wouldn't be missed. The women we accompanied went there to work, but they wouldn't ask us to work, so if we waited until they were immersed in their tasks, we could sneak away and be up the mountain and back down again in time to put our loads on our heads and accompany the women home. We planned all this and we rubbed our hands in anticipation of the adventure that lay ahead and the result we hoped to achieve. In the bush, children can only communicate by whistling. The women emit a different sound, a sharp cry, something they've agreed on beforehand, or sometimes it's the call of a particular family and all the women in the family know the call. So me and the other boy whistled and assembled and started to climb up to where we'd seen the birds flying about, those birds that so whet our appetites. Lacking fish, lacking wild hens, lacking seabirds you threw stones at and river crayfish that meant stones were thrown at you, lacking anything at all that offered any flavour, we climbed the hill, excited by the prospect of the long-feathered bird. We didn't want the adults to miss us, so we hurried to get up there and we made quick progress. We soon found ourselves up in the clouds, the clouds that hover about the mountain-top, although we didn't realise it right away. It was very misty, and we thought it must have rained, or was about to. But then we saw the birds, flying in and out of their nests in the trees right in front of us. And we thought our luck was in. We looked around for trees that weren't too tall for our young bodies to climb, and we looked for white-feathered tails poking from holes. Eventually we found the perfect tree with the perfect tail, the tail of a beautiful specimen of that bird of our dreams. We were all set. He would go up, as he was the oldest and the more experienced. All he had to do was grab hold of the unsus-pecting bird, clip its wings or break them, and then throw the bird down to me on the ground. So my friend boldly set off up the tree, and he climbed up a considerable distance. Then he screamed. 'What's the matter?' I called. And he screamed again. His second scream was accom-panied by other signs that something was wrong, for he started to shake. But he couldn't move, meaning he couldn't carry on climbing or come back down. I was standing at the bottom of the tree, looking up, unable to understand what was going on. Frozen up there, half-way up the tree, he told me to look down. I didn't think there was anything to look down at, other than the path we'd come up. But he went on shaking and whimpering and he told me to look down the other way. I took a couple of steps forward and a great void suddenly rushed up at me. We were at the summit of one of the highest mountains on the island and we hadn't even realised it. My friend had only realised once he was halfway up the tree, and he immediately felt overwhelmed at being so high. And the thing was, that mountain had a precipice and the tree he'd been climbing was on the edge of the precipice, jutting out over it in fact, which was something we'd failed to appreciate, due to our desperate need for fish, or because of the clouds, or our simple youthfulness. You couldn't see the precipice from the south village as it was on the north face of the mountain; it would have only been possible to see from the settlements further east, on the mountain's other side. That explains why it's so misty, I said. But that was easy for me to say, for my feet were on firm ground and I could take a step back; he couldn't move at all, although on the other hand his body was moving rather exaggeratedly: like I said, he was shaking uncontrollably. The solution was for him to come back down, but he couldn't move, not now he'd seen where he was. And, although he was older than me, he was still just a boy, and so there he remained, stuck up the tree, shaking and crying. I became gripped with fear, convinced he was going to fall. And I saw that I too was in danger, so I moved further back. Had we really gone up so high? We'd reached the summit of the mountain without even realising it! I couldn't believe it. As he went on shaking, unable to look down because he couldn't bear the sight of the nothingness beneath him, I realised I had to do something. So I told him to hold on, I'd go and get help from the women further down. They were adults and they'd know what to do. I descended the mountain without looking where I was going. I have to say I ran, because I had two feet, indeed I still do. But really I flew, and I cried, for there was only one of us returning where two had set off, and that was a very bad thing. I got to my surrogate grandmother's plantation and saw my load waiting for me on the ground, the load she'd prepared for me to carry back to the house. And I knew that if she'd already prepared my load, she was either about to leave or had already set off. So I ran around the farm, making lots of noise so that she knew I was there. The woman was not my own grandmother so I was reluctant to call her by her name. On our island, children don't call adults by name unless they're family. But on the other hand, I'd gone to the south village with that woman, and we were living together in the same house, so it would have been equally disrespectful if I called her by the general term we use to address all female adults. I was in two minds because of this, so I went on making a noise, showing that I was back from the mountain, back with her, until finally she appeared. She knew something was wrong the moment she saw me. She put down whatever she had in her hands and came over to me with a look of alarm on her face, ready for me to tell her what had happened. Once I'd done so, her face filled with fear, and she made the call she'd agreed with the mother of my friend. As the woman was quite far away, I couldn't tell her what had happened until she reached us. And when she heard the call, she'd have understood it as the signal for departure, for it was in fact time to go home. My surrogate grandmother was too agitated to finish off the day's tasks. Unexpected developments had upset her plans. So we just waited and, as she was an older woman, she started talking to herself, muttering about what might happen. She was worried. A certain time passed and then my friend's mother appeared. Because her son had not come back in time to leave, and because her friend had called her, she knew something was wrong. She arrived looking worried, and it didn't require much from me to deliver the bad news, for she already feared the worst. And that was because so many awful things had already happened on the island, and everyone, especially the adults, were very affected by it. Well, something awful had happened again. She listened to me tell the story, but before I'd even finished, she put her hand on her head and set off, as if she knew the path we'd taken better than anyone, and up the mountain she went. I followed, along with my surrogate grandmother, both of us crying, until we all got to where I said the tree was. It was still misty, and the cloud cover had increased. This is it, I said, showing them the tree. And below . . . I didn't know whether to tell them that a few feet away from where we were standing was a giant void. I was certain we were in the right place, but there was no sign of our having been there, nothing we'd left behind, no item of clothing etc . . . So I began to have my doubts. But was there even anything we could have left behind? We'd set off without food, meaning there were no leftovers, no bones or peel; we'd not brought machetes to cut down branches and, as we were barefoot and had mainly been walking on fallen leaves, we'd hardly left any footprints. No, I was certain we were in the right place. The tree was unmistakable, the precipice too. But my friend was nowhere to be seen. The two women looked at me. They looked up, looked down and looked around, hoping to see the boy sitting there waiting for us. I looked up again and I saw one of the birds we'd come to catch approaching the tree, and any doubts vanished: that bird confirmed to me we were in the right place. I even thought I recognised the bird, that it was the exact same one that drew us to the tree in the first place. Never mind that those birds were all alike, I could just tell it was the one that enticed my friend up the tree. So I wasn't wrong; we were in the right place. But where was my friend? I told the women this was definitely the spot, and as there was no one up the tree, they felt their worst fears confirmed. But I didn't know what their worst fears were. All we really knew was that the boy wasn't up the tree any more. I had another look for him, going round all the trees nearby, until finally I gave up. And I passed the burden of the matter on to the two women. They had their hands on their heads but, before they wept, the boy's mother made the call their family used in the bush: *uuhu-huhu-huuuuuu . . . !*

There was no reply. She repeated the call, directing it over the precipice. Nothing. The boy wasn't there. We now knew he wasn't there because he hadn't answered the call, and so we had a catastrophe on our hands. The most likely scenario was that he'd slipped from the tree and either fallen to the ground or over the precipice. If he'd fallen over the precipice, he'd have landed in the trees below and come to serious injury in the branches. But if he'd fallen to the ground beneath the tree, his soul would have ripped out of his body on impact. That's what their worst fears were, what we all now feared. And we gave in to our sorrow. But first we had to get to the south village, to see if the boy hadn't made it back somehow. If there was no sign of him there, we'd wait for a little while longer before gathering our things and heading for the big village. The disappearance of a man, woman or child was not something the big village could remain uninformed about. Bad news for one family was bad news for the whole island, and the news had to be spread round the big village so that everyone was aware of it and suffered over it.

We put our loads on our heads and walked back to the south village, the village we'd originally gone to in search of food. With the disappearance of my friend, the son of my surrogate grandmother's friend, the circumstances had changed and our stay would be cut short. We'd go back to the big village where a decision would be made about what to do, whether to send out a search party to look for the boy, and if so, what sort of search party, whether the ministrants would be involved. And this was because on our Atlantic Ocean island, searches often failed when they were not led by the ministrants but by ordinary people. Or it might be decided simply to go back to the place where he'd been seen for the last time and place a † under the tree, on the understanding that his body had fallen to the ground and his innocent soul had ripped out of his body on impact. And that cross would have remained there forever, as a reminder to everyone that it was a dangerous place, so dangerous that somebody had lost their life there.

My friend and I had gone looking for that bird that fished in the sea and lived in the mountains, a bird with a long tail made of a single feather. I've already talked about the colour of the bird and spoken of the difficulty it had taking off from the ground. I've also said something about our motivations for going up to that misty and cloudy place, although we didn't know it would be misty and cloudy when we set out. Our motivations: we had a great hunger for fish and, in the houses where we slept, there were no adult males who knew how to fish, and we didn't know how, so we felt compelled to go to the mountains to catch a bird that wouldn't take flight when man approached it. The bird did tend to peck if anyone tried to touch it, but its peck wasn't so vicious that you couldn't grab hold of its neck. But we principally went to the mountain because of our lack of fish, that shouldn't be forgotten. If we'd had the means to throw a bit of nylon and an improvised hook into the sea, we would not have felt compelled to go to the mountain and put our lives at risk. Our duties in the south village should have been to accompany our respective mothers to their plantations so that they were not lonely, come back with them around midday, dump our loads in front of the house, follow the path to the nearest shore and return three hours later with a bundle of fish. I knew the shores of that part of the island well and I knew they were full of hungry fish. Indeed, I didn't know of a shore on the island that wasn't full of hungry fish. And I think that fact hurt us all the more, made our longing for fish that bit stronger. We could see fish right in front of our eyes and at the same time we had nothing to fill our mouths with. Or rather we had something to fill our mouths with, but it wasn't what we wanted to fill them with. What grew in most abundance in the south village was cassava, which could be made into a round, white bread. And that bread was much nicer to eat if accompanied by a piece of fish and the sauce the fish had been cooked in. So that the sauce could soften the cassava bread and . . . I think I've talked about it already. When there was no fish, there was nothing. At a certain hour of the evening, your mother, or your grandmother's friend, would shut the door, pulling it to from the inside with a stick, and you'd go to sleep on a noisy mattress of dried banana leaves. You'd go on hungering for fish, you'd have the cassava bread in your hand and you'd be in total darkness. Back then nobody in the south village had kerosene to light their lamps with. If there was any kerosene on the island at all, it would have been used to light lamps in the big village. So you'd be in total darkness in the south village, holding your hunk of cassava bread, waiting for sleep to take hold of you. Back then, all children slept right through. They slept right through whether they wet the bed or had grown out of the habit. Before going to bed you peed outside, two steps away from the door. In the south village, nothing gave off any light, and I think most people thought like me and preferred there not to be a moon, one of those bright full moons. Because they leave you exposed. I couldn't go anywhere on my own on moonlight nights, for I knew evil things could see me from far away. And in that south village there was no noise of any kind at night, other than the *cricri* of the crickets and a noise the bats made with their throats. It was unusual for there to be any cocks in the south village as the season wasn't right. So in that silence you heard the sea, the waves breaking against the rocks. The shores down there were rocky, in fact the whole southern coastline was rocky, and you heard the distant murmur of something pounding against the rocks. It was a frightening sound. In truth, everything was frightening at night. And before night had set in, you'd been hungry for fish, and you'd gone to bed in total darkness, so you'd been unsettled in the first place. And then you heard something pounding against the rocks in the distance, shaking the whole island.

We reached the south village, me, my surrogate grandmother and the mother of my friend, and told the few seasonal residents what had happened. The question of whether to begin an immediate search of the mountain was raised, whether to go to the big village right away or spend the night in the south village and go the next morning. Some people said there ought to be a search, that we ought to stop at nothing to find the boy, but that night was on the edge of the sky and the dying light, the crimson tide, would soon be upon us, so any search would be short-lived. Everyone would have to return to the village, for nothing could be done after nightfall, and it would be hard, very hard indeed on the poor mother to have to spend the night without her son. And this had become most evident because although everyone had come to help and offer support, the presence of the entire village in her house was what had saddened her most, for it felt like a wake, like her son had died, although nobody knew for sure. And it would have been a very hard night for her to get through with that heavy feeling in her heart. What's more, she was not in the big village, where she could have drawn comfort, understanding and courage from her people, from more people. But some of the south villagers said it was too late to set off for the big village, that she'd only get there after nightfall anyway, so very few people would learn of what had happened. They said that no matter what was decided, it was better to wait until morning, when news of the boy's disappearance could more easily be made known. But the woman was in a village where there was nothing to light the house with, and her son was lost in the bush. All the women of the village could come and keep her company, but nobody would say anything, for there was nothing to say. Everyone would sit outside the house until nightfall and then go inside to sleep on a big pile of dried banana leaves, people having brought them from their own homes, but still nobody in the big village would know what had happened.

Given all these considerations, it was decided the woman ought to go to the next village, a village not far from the south village, but on the other side of the mountain. The two villages are not so very far apart but they are divided by a mountain range that runs down the centre of the island, so anyone wishing to walk from one village to the next has to go up the mountain, the same mountain we'd climbed in search of the bird, cross one of its peaks and go back down the other side. With the sun half down, a group of us set off from the south village, a group that included me, my surrogate grandmother and the mother of my friend. We were going to that other village to ask its few seasonal residents if they knew anything about the boy lost in the bush, the boy who'd been hanging over the precipice. By the time we got there, it was dark and everyone had shut themselves in their homes. They didn't have anything to light their houses with either, so they'd gone inside to keep safe. Or if they weren't inside, they were sitting in their doorways, but it was impossible to see them in the darkness. And because the few inhabitants of that village were quite spread out, not all of them noticed our arrival. One of the women who'd accompanied us had a house in the village and we followed her, took the criss-crossed sticks from her doorway and went inside to sleep on a pile of old banana leaves. We shook them first, to check for snakes and rats that might have nested among them, then shut the door and went to sleep. I wasn't aware of anything else that happened that night, though things did happen. Walking through the bush at night had left me exhausted. It was something I'd never done before. In fact, other than when something serious happened, nobody ever went into the bush at night. No activity took place in the bush while darkness reigned over the island.

We slept as best we could and woke to find that most people hadn't slept a wink. Which was only to be expected given that we had a serious problem and nobody knew how it would turn out. But it was more than that, for something had happened in the night in that village on the other side of the mountain, something that had forced people out of their beds. A child who'd never been to the village before woke up in the middle of the night because someone was preventing him from sleeping. He screamed at the top of his voice because he felt like someone was squeezing his throat and he was choking. He thought he was dying. The adults in the house where he was sleeping realised he'd not spent a night in the village before and therefore probably hadn't been presented to the village's patron saint. And if he hadn't been presented to the village's patron saint, the patron saint wouldn't let him sleep, wouldn't let him remain in the settlement. The child went on screaming and they decided to go to the little church and make the presentation. But it wasn't as simple as that, and now I'll explain why. What we call being presented to the saint is a serious thing, though something we children never understood. In fact I still don't understand it. On our island all children are born in the big village. Only in the event of an unexpected birth or a miscalculation by the mother does a child come into the world on a planta-tion, or on the way to one. In fact, whenever this occurs, the child is immediately given the name of the place it landed after coming out of its mother. For example, a friend of mine's mother had put her load down to rest and quench her thirst at the river, a river where it was common for people on the island to stop for a rest and a drink, and that friend of mine thought it was a pleasant spot and pushed. And his mother had no choice but to let him out. When he was completely out, she bathed him in the river, tied him to her back and brought him home. And he took the name of that river. That friend of mine was very smart. His mother had just descended the steepest hill on the whole island. In fact, the hill was so steep that when the first white people came to the island and were faced with having to descend it, they turned right around and went back to the big village to get materials to build steps. Anyway, that boy's mother had been returning to the big village from the other end of the island, and she went down the steep steps and got to the river. She put her load on the ground, or on a rock, and sat down on another rock, with her feet in the water. And she drank the fresh water from the river, which still had a fair way to travel before it reached the sea. She too still had a fair way to travel, for after her rest she'd have to put her load back on her head and start climbing up the steep steps and on towards the big village. And it was a tough climb. The thing was, that freshwater river lay between two big bodies of rock, like a creek in a valley, and the only way to get from one side to the other was by going down and up again. There was no way round, no other path that accessed the south of the island. And so that friend of mine must have thought about all the effort his mother would have to make to climb back up to the top and he decided to come out and lighten her load. He timed it well, for carrying a child on the back is far easier than carrying a child in the belly, especially with all those rocks jutting out into the path.

Anyway, I was talking about being presented to the patron saint. It's compulsory. You're born in the big village and the first time you go to any smaller settlement on our Atlantic Ocean island, your mother has to take you to the little church before bedtime and present you to the patron saint. You go through the church door and your mother says a few words on your behalf, explaining that you've come to seek his protection. Then you go home and sleep in peace. If you don't do it, if an adult doesn't do it for you, it's unlikely you'll sleep at all that night. What's more, in this case, the patron saint of the village we'd travelled to in the middle of the night was San Xuan. I suppose it's like San Juan in Spanish. In any case, San Xuan is the most severe of all the patron saints on our island. He wears his severity on his face, if you look at the image of him that hangs in the little church. And so when that boy was choking and unable to sleep, they took him out of the house, thinking they'd take him to see San Xuan and ask for forgiveness, for it was too late for a presentation, that time had passed. But there were a number of factors working against them. First of all, the little church closed in the afternoon, and nobody on the island had ever seen anyone go into it or do anything inside it at night; there had never been a need to. And there was practically nothing on the island to make light with. There were a few seeds that burned with a flame, though finding them was another matter, and dry banana leaves were no good, for they flared as soon as you put a flame to them and the light they gave off would have burned out before being any use. So everyone knew that going into the church in the dark to speak to the saint was no easy thing, and nobody had ever done it before. For a start, few people would have the courage to. It's thought the saint also rests at night and no man or woman should disturb him without good cause. Another problem was that the child, the boy who was frightened and choking, did not belong to anyone in the village and the adults who were with him did not know his real name, so they couldn't speak to the saint, that very severe San Xuan, on his behalf. So, given the multiple problems of the night, the dark and his unknown name, it was decided that speaking to the saint to ask his forgiveness was an impossibility. But the child was choking, and he might die, and as far as they could tell from the crowing of the cocks, what few cocks there were in that little village, night had barely entered the small hours. So it was decided the boy must be taken to the big village by canoe. They found a man in the village who was willing to take him but, in order to do so, they'd first have to get the child to the nearest beach, and getting to the nearest beach from that village was one of the most difficult and hazardous tasks on the whole island. That's because the nearest beach from that village could only be reached by a treacherous pathway. Even to reach the path itself required navigating difficult slopes. And the whole trip was considered extremely hazardous by day, never mind at night, never mind at night carrying a child who was choking because he hadn't been presented to the patron saint, the very severe San Xuan! And there was more: the plan was to take the boy to the big village by sea, and this was the sea of the village of San Xuan! Only the very bravest canoemen lived in that village. Of all the island's canoemen, they were the ones who most risked their lives, for it was very unusual for the waves to be still on that beach, a beach full of rocks and projecting cliffs, like all beaches in the south, but here there were so many it was more like a cave. Everything about that little village was dictated by San Xuan's severity. At least that was my experience of the place as a child, and that's what I heard the adults say about the dangers of that coastline and the moods of the patron saint. But anyway, they decided to take that boy to the big village, for otherwise he might choke to death or die from some other sickness. They were adults and that's what they decided to do, though they knew it was a very difficult task. So they put that child on the back of one of the women and they started down the path, and the women said prayers behind them. This would have frightened me. Whenever there were prayers it was because there might be tears; that's to say, if there were prayers there was danger. What's more, those women prayed knowing that the whole drama was unfolding without the saint's knowledge or consent. I think deep down those prayers were for San Xuan, that he might show them mercy and not cause their journey to end in catastrophe.

I didn't go with the rest of them down to the beach, for I was a child and they wouldn't have let me, and anyway I was asleep, but I know they encountered many problems.

Many, many problems. It would have been a problematic journey if they'd done it by day and without the fury of the patron saint hanging over them. To be honest, I'd rather not say any more about that patron saint, for I've told you my religion and said that I'm a believer. Suffice to say, anything involving the patron saints filled me with fear as a child. Looking back, I see that everything filled me with fear as a child, even things that seemingly had nothing evil about them.

They went on saying prayers and they went on encountering many problems in getting that boy down to the shore and into a canoe, and in finding a moment of calm to push the canoe out into the water so that it might clear the rocks and other dangers. I know that beach well and I know you usually make several false starts before managing to launch out into the water, and to think they did it in the dark! And when I say dark, I'm not talking about any ordinary darkness. There was no moon and that beach was like a cave. I really think that to be an adult on our island back then was to live a life of extreme and constant danger.

They managed to get the canoe out into the water and the canoeman managed to paddle the child to the big village, the child who was choking because he hadn't been presented to the patron saint. When we arrived in the big village the next day, around noon and after many hours of walking, I found out that the boy they'd taken in the canoe was my friend, the one I'd left stuck up the tree, shaking uncontrollably because of the lack of firm ground beneath him. The boy I'd gone to get help for was now in the house of the bone healer and, when I saw my friend, he was covered in bandages from head to toe, as if he'd broken every bone in his body. He couldn't speak, but he heard my voice and he nodded his head. Only the inhabitants of San Xuan's village knew how he'd ended up spending the night there, or not, as it proved. Because we'd become friends, he told me what happened once he got better, what happened to him after I'd left him stuck up the tree, inches away from wringing the neck of that bird we'd gone in search of because of our lack of fish. But in fact he knew nothing, or very little, about what happened. This might be because most of what happened happened in the dark. Or it might be because he had his eyes closed. The dark. It was something that always had to be taken into account on our Atlantic Ocean island. It was like an extra person. One of my main memories of the dark is that sometimes we'd be eating at night and an adult would take away the lamp. I didn't like it because we carried on eating and by the time they brought it back I'd have nothing left on my plate. Eating in the dark wasn't as satisfying as eating in the light. So when the lamp came back, I was tempted to ask for more food, because the food I'd put in my mouth in the dark didn't count: it had been eaten in secret, or in hiding, and so I couldn't feel it in my belly. So I sometimes waited for the light to come back before I went on eating because when I ate without it I felt cheated. It had nothing to do with whether what I was eating had bones in, or whether I was able to pluck the bones out in the dark without choking on them. It was just that I wanted to be able to see what I was eating. As far as I was concerned, eating in the dark was like going down a path in the dark. If for some reason you had to move about in the dark, you did it on all fours, to avoid dangers. It's difficult to walk about upright in the dark, for there's no knowing what obstacles you'll encounter. You have to feel your way, keep touching the ground, reach out into the void. And it's very frightening, so if you have to walk anywhere in the dark, let's say down a deserted street, you put your hands wherever they make you feel safest. For example, by crossing your arms over your tummy and putting the palms of your hands on your sides, or by crossing your arms over your chest and putting the palms of your hands on your shoulders. This last one was the way we children felt most protected, the way we felt safest in the dark. The dark? We always thought something dangerous was lurking in the dark. Some of the littler children cried as soon as darkness fell. They screamed as if they'd been bitten. Bitten by the darkness. They felt they were in danger and they asked, they screamed, for the light to come back. And although we were afraid of the dark, we didn't like the excessive light of the full moon either. As I've already said, on moonlight nights you felt too exposed. Things could see you from far away. So with the dark, you couldn't see the danger, but with the moonlight you exposed yourself to the danger. Everything on the island brought fear. To be in the dark is to turn your back on life, for I don't think anyone can really understand life in all its detail if kept in the dark. It's like eating in the dark: you never get full, for you lose track of what's on your plate. I think that the darkness in a person's life is the darkest thing about living in hardship.

What that friend told me was that when I left him stuck up the tree to go and get help, he looked down and could no longer see anything. It was as if he were in the clouds; that's to say, up in the sky. I didn't believe him, but I'll carry on with his story. He said he was up there, looking out to see if help was coming, but no help came and he became increasingly nervous. He was nervous and he was holding on to the tree trunk, and he was looking out for help, for someone to come and tell him what to do. But like I said, according to him, he could no longer see the ground, only clouds . . . So what was stopping him from coming back down the tree? That's why I never believed his story. But anyway, he said he stayed up there and he started to hear the voices of the ministrants, many of their voices, although what he heard wasn't specifically their voices but rather their prayers, prayers only the ministrants knew how to say. So up in the tree, he heard their prayers, or songs, and they were getting closer and closer to where he was. He was afraid. I would have been too. You're alone in the bush, in some remote part of it full of mist, stuck up a tree, and suddenly you hear the songs of the ministrants: anyone would have been afraid. If it was me, and the songs got closer and closer, I'd throw myself over the precipice, if that was my only means of escape. I've already said how much the ministrants frightened me. If I'd been him, if the same thing had happened to me, what I would have thought when I heard the ministrants approaching with their mysterious songs was that there was an evil lurking nearby, the Devil even, and that was why they'd come, to drive the evil away. But then I'd have thought, and I don't know why, that the evil actually came from the ministrants and their songs, that they brought the evil with them. And I'd have jumped out over the precipice, if that was my only way out. Anyway, the boy was afraid and he said he tried to escape. For just because the ministrants were coming didn't mean they'd stop and help him down. We'd never heard of the ministrants stopping their singing and talking to anyone in a similar situation. Because as far as we understood it, from what the adults told us, whenever they were moving about in the bush they were guided by the *Maté Jachín*, and because the *Maté Jachín* wasn't a person, no ministrant was allowed to act like a person in its presence. So, you're in the tree and you sense the ministrants approaching, dressed in their white tunics. According to the number of voices in the singing, there are many of them, and you know they have the power to drive evil away, even if it's the Devil himself. But what if they found the Devil in the same tree as you and decided to put a curse on it? Obviously the curse would affect you too. So naturally my friend was afraid and he wanted to get down and escape, and that's just what he did. But after running for a while, he fell to the ground and couldn't go on. The ministrants reached him and sang their mysterious prayers over him. That's what he told me.

On the island I speak of, our island, when the ministrants went out in search of a lost person, they went to all corners of the island, and because the *Maté Jachín* was so powerful, they used it to find whoever was lost. Furthermore, it was the *Maté Jachín* that moved the ministrants' feet, and it made them follow the boy carrying the *Maté Jachín*, for anyone holding the *Maté Jachín* became filled with its power. No one moved of their own free will. That's what the adults said. The *Maté Jachín* was also taken out whenever it was felt something terrible was going to happen on the island, and so if you saw the ministrants out with the *Maté Jachín*, taking it, or being led by it, to all corners of the island, you knew a catastrophe was imminent. But because we'd been living in the south village at the time, a long way from the big village, we didn't know if anyone had been lost, be it in the bush or out at sea, although if it had been out at sea the songs of the ministrants wouldn't have been heard up in the mountains. Nor did we know if a catastrophe was imminent, and that's why the ministrants were covering all corners of the island. In truth, given all that happened with the fire and the woman and the cholera, there were plenty of reasons why the ministrants might have been out with the *Maté Jachín*. But anyway, no such news had reached us in the south village. My friend told me he heard them singing, fear swept through his body, he was already shaking, and in his fear he jumped out of the tree to escape them, and he ran until he could no longer run. That's what he told me. That's what he told me and told others, once he was well enough to speak.

We listened to him and we stared at him, covered in rags, scratches all over his face, barely able to move a muscle. He lay prone on the bed and people came out of the bone healer's house as if they'd seen a dead body. It was like visiting a wake. A deathplace. And before he was able to speak and tell us what had happened for himself, people talked about what they thought must have happened. Many repeated what they heard a woman say, a woman from the village of San Xuan, the very severe patron saint. And what that woman said was what she'd seen. On the way back from her plantation, which was at the foot of the mountain that separated San Xuan's village from the south village, she'd seen a boy on his hands and knees pulling up malanga plants from a farm that obviously wasn't his, for children don't plant on our island. At first she thought he was a thief, or rather a thiefess, for only women went to the plantations and only thieves pulled malangas out by their stems, being too hurried to dig into the ground underneath the tuber. But then she saw it was a boy and that he wasn't just pulling up the plants but sticking them into his mouth, indeed sticking anything into his mouth he could lay his hands on. She said the only way to describe it was that he was rabidly hungry, for he chewed frantically at whatever he put in his mouth, dry leaves, malangas covered in sand, small plants, anything at all. She'd never seen the like of it. She became afraid, for she thought it might be the Devil himself, but the boy became afraid too and tried to run away. Yet something stopped him: he couldn't run; he couldn't even walk. So how had he got there? That was the mystery. And who was he? After all the energy he'd used up ransacking the plantation, and after discovering he couldn't walk, never mind run, he collapsed where he was, mouth open, panting, a panting that gradually died down. The woman was shaking with fear, but she said an *Avemaría Purísima,* made the sign of the cross and approached. As she got closer, she saw the boy was in a terrible state. She saw he was at death's door, maybe even halfway through the door, given how strangely he was acting. It was the moment before death, she thought, and he'd lost his reason. But really she didn't know what was going on. She left him where he was and went to find other women on their way back from the plantations. When she told them what she'd seen, they didn't believe her. Word got round and people came from the little village to look at the boy and they all recognised him, all

knew which family he belonged to. Because everyone
lived in the big village most of the year, no child's face
was unfamiliar. And if it was to you, it wouldn't be to
someone else, to one of the people you'd called to come
and help you with the mysterious business you'd stum-
bled across; they'd confirm it was not an apparition, or a
living dead, rather that the boy was the son of so-and-so.
Female adults could always tell that we were from my
grandmother's house just by looking at us, and we never
understood what it was they saw so clearly.

They carried that boy as best they could to San Xuan's
village. They thought they'd let him sleep until his family
came to find him. It was all they could do: they didn't
know where his family was, and they didn't know what
circumstances he'd been lost in. They probably also tried
to send word of the boy to the other villages via anyone
who happened to be travelling to them. And they probably
found that no one happened to be travelling anywhere
at that time of day. The sleeping boy, or rather the semi-
conscious boy, would have woken up in the village the
next morning had it not been for the fact that he'd never
spent the night in San Xuan's village before and so he'd
never been presented to San Xuan. He'd never asked for
San Xuan's blessing nor sought his protection. And that
is why the very severe saint would not let him sleep
and woke him at midnight. After all he went through,
if my friend reached the big village alive it can only be
because *Dios* is great and because my friend's time had

not yet come. Or as the adults like to say, because he was still innocent. Although in fact the word in our language doesn't quite mean innocent, though that's the equivalent in Spanish. At least not innocent in the sense of not being guilty: when we say he was innocent we mean he was pure, because he was still a child. Well, that boy was utterly broken when he got to the big village, so the adults said. But he showed signs of pulling through and the ministrants were called to pray for him. From what that woman had said about how she'd found him, it was feared the boy would end up mad. So the ministrants sang their prayers to drive out the evil that had entered him. And bit by bit he began to recover, until finally he was cured. But he never fully regained his strength. In fact, for a long time he couldn't exert himself at all, which is why he never learned to fish, and he had to be taken to the small settlements by canoe because he couldn't get up and down the slopes. And he became quite mean, I don't know why. That meanness cost him his friends, and I eventually lost track of him too. He was probably taken by boat to wherever our fathers were, to finish off his recovery or start a new kind of life.

When the Pico burned and I saw my grandfather cry, my curiosity in him grew and I wondered about who he really was. And I thought about what we'd seen when we went into his room. What did we see in grandfather's room?

Well, after all those people were taken by the cholera, it was decided that we had to give food to the king of the sea. As a child, I never knew how news reached us of the things we had to do on the island, how the adults were told what needed doing. The ministrants took the *Maté Jachín* out and went round the island, three laps in a canoe. They took the *Maté Jachín* out and went through the bush, through all the streets and the surroundings of the big village. The *Maté Jachín* was carried at the front, followed by all the ministrants in their white tunics and then the women who accompanied them. First the order went out that everyone had to go and wash in the lake. Then that everyone had to go and give food to the king of the lake. And finally that we had to give food to the king of the sea. I never understood who it was that gave the orders to do these things, but what I do know, from what the adults said, the female adults, is that some women on the island talked to the deads. One such woman lived near our house and was called Sabina. Actually she wasn't just called Sabina, her full name was Maminda Zé Sabina, but anyway, she was one of the women who talked to the deads. And those women brought news of what we had to do and of what was going to happen in the future. This I know from my grandmother and other female adults. And from them I also know that most women who talked to the deads hardly believed a word the deads said. As I was only a child, this wasn't something I could easily understand and, indeed, I found the whole thing quite frightening. Like I said, I knew Sabina and I knew she was one of the women who brought the orders of what had to be done. Although in actual fact it wasn't quite like that: I knew Sabina talked to the deads, and that's all I knew. I don't remember ever speaking to her myself, but I remember she had a strange face, or at least I thought it was strange. Her face always looked as if it was about to laugh or cry, so when you saw her you thought she might burst out laughing or crying at any moment. And I say this not because I was an expert on faces and expressions but because when you're told a woman talks to the deads and you get a chance to look at her, you look. As far as I was concerned, a woman who talked to the deads was no ordinary woman. And Sabina's face made you think she was about to break down in tears or break out in a big smile. One or the other, at any moment. Was it because of the conversations she had with the deads? I don't know, but what I do know, from what my grandmother and the other female adults said, is that the women who talked to the deads suffered a lot. So was Sabina's face the face of a woman who would have been happy if it weren't for the constant strain of having to talk to the deads? That could be it. That's to say, if it hadn't been for the deads always bothering her with things they wanted to convey to the village, she'd have been a smiley woman. That could be it. From what I remember of Sabina, I'd also say she was a very beautiful woman. And again, I probably say this because I looked at her a lot, because she wasn't a she-devil. She-devils were no ordinary women either, but I wasn't brave enough to look at them. But I looked at Sabina a lot. There were other women on the island who spoke to the deads, but I only remember Sabina, because she was our neighbour.

So news reached us that we had to give food to the king of the sea, who ruled over the waves, the fish, the whole island in fact, for our island was out in the middle of the Atlantic Ocean. Was the king of the sea King Atlas? If only! What a discovery that would be! But anyway, we had to give food to the king of the sea, and during the offering ceremony there should be no one at sea, not a single canoe. And so it was announced that there'd be an offering the next day. A man went through the streets announcing what was going to take place and that everyone should assemble in the big village to witness the event. Really he announced it not so that people would attend but to make sure everyone gave something. You weren't obliged to give anything in particular, just some of whatever you had.

It so happened that around noon on the day of the offering, one of my mothers went out with a canoeman to collect a load from a place where there was a little church by a river. We had a plantation there and a few days earlier grandmother had gone there to harvest whatever was ripe and ready for eating, including two big bunches of palm dates. As the load was large, she thought she'd get a man with a canoe to come and pick it up. The place wasn't far from the big village and we could have walked there after school to fetch it, but grandmother thought it best to bring the load back by canoe. I mentioned school. Back then, the children in our house who were old enough went to school. There we did 'the junk', which was what the basic-level class was called. We learned the Spanish ideo-visual alphabet: *amapola, burro, cochino, dado, foca, gato, huevo; indio, jaula, kilo, lechuza, llama, molino, niño, oso* . . . that's as far as I can remember. Or rather I don't remember the 'p', so let's skip it and go on: *queso*, skip a few more letters, then *uva, vino, xilófono, yegua, zape*. We learned to count up to five hundred and also to do times tables. I remember the times tables because we learned them by singing and we enjoyed it: seven times one is seven, seven times two is fourteen and seven times three is twenty-one; seven times four is twenty-eight, etc . . . We did it all singing: five hundred and one, five hundred and two, five hundred and three, five hundred and four. In those days, I thought numbers stopped at five hundred; that five hundred and its add-ons, five hundred and one, five hundred and two, etc, were the highest numbers there were. We learned everything by heart, and I think that's why we did it singing. In fact, although we sometimes saw books with the letters and pictures, I didn't know that *amapola, burro, cochino* and *dado* were the Spanish words for poppy, donkey, hog and dice, or that poppy, donkey, hog and dice were things we were supposed to have heard of. I didn't know what any of them were, so I didn't know the words were supposed to represent the letters and I didn't associate the letters with the pictures in the books. It was only years later that I found out what an *amapola* or a *burro* was. But they sounded good. The other thing I remember about school is the whip. If you couldn't say *cochino* or *dado* properly, you got the whip. The whip was a cord made of I don't remember what, but it had several knots in it and was tied to a stick. The teacher held it in his hand when he gave class. Although we liked it when we sang, school was a place where we had to speak a language that was not our own and where we might get whipped, so it was a place we were afraid of. What's more, it was a place you went to but weren't allowed to leave unless the teacher said so, and sometimes he wouldn't even let you go to pee! Even if you went up to his table and asked in Spanish, a language that was not your own. I always wanted to be at home, with my mother, and I thought school was a terrible kind of punishment. For a while, I couldn't get the thought of being at home out of my head. Home and school were very different places, totally different. What's more, there were some wicked children in the school, children who would harass you and threaten to beat you after class if you weren't their friends. They were the same children who got the whip the most for not being able to point out *foca* or *gato* or 501 on the blackboard, and they took revenge on anyone who laughed by fighting them later. I didn't like any of this.

We had a break, a play time that we liked a lot because it was like being temporarily released from prison. And during play time we gathered in the yard and ran about. That was what most of us did, just ran about – I suppose because nobody had a ball or anything else round and soft we could run about after – but some boys refused to stay in the school grounds and went off into the bush. They tended to be the naughtiest kids. What did they go off into the bush for? To look for fruit, especially guava. If it was mango season, they came back to the schoolyard with huge quantities of mangoes, carried in their laps and pockets, and with their shirts mucky from everything they'd touched. The mango tree itself has a sticky sap that's impossible to get out. So yes, those boys went into the bush and had fun looking for guava and mango and sweetsop, but it wasn't easy to keep track of time in the bush and they couldn't hear the bell at the end of play time, so they'd get back to find the school in silence, a silence that really put the fear in you. And it put the fear in you because you realised you were the only one not in your seat. Some children even cried when it happened, for they knew what awaited them. And if you stayed outside until it was time for 'school break-out', which was what we called home-time in my language, you knew you'd get your comeuppance the next day. You'd probably have to spend the whole day on your knees, and this after getting the whip several times. And the red marks the whip left on hands and arms meant we all knew that getting the whip was no small thing. Besides being away from home and exposed to the threat of other boys, what I disliked most about school was the fact that I was expected to trust someone who might punish me with a furious beating, a beating from which there was no escape. That's to say, there was no way of avoiding punishment. I don't remember anything we learned in that school on our island, other than a class about Spanish words being divided into three categories, *aguda*, *llana* and *esdrújula*, depending on where the stress fell. It must have been a lesson after 'the junk', although it all merges into one in my memory. Anyway, the reason I remember the class about the three categories of Spanish words is because the teacher walked around the classroom with the whip in his hand, asking everyone how words are divided. Curiously, over half the class didn't know the answer. In fact, never mind half, not a single kid the teacher asked knew the answer, and he asked practically the whole class. I say curiously because the answer was only three words and they were three words we'd just been taught. So anyway, I used to sit towards the front of the class but the teacher started at the back, moving down the rows and asking every boy and girl the same question, and not one of them answered. Every one of them got the whip, be it on the hand or the head, and the less resilient started to cry. The girls sat on the left in class, the boys on the right. So he'd asked almost everyone in class by the time he got to my desk, and he asked the question to the children sitting around me, in desks of two. None of them knew the answer. He asked me the same question, wearily, for he no doubt expected the same non-answer, as no one in the entire class had replied, and I don't recall ever having shone at school before in anything. But without hesitation, for I knew the answer very well, I said words were divided into *agudas*, *llanas* and *esdrújulas*, and the teacher cried out, in joy and in anger, well at least one person in the entire room managed to remember one simple thing about the lesson. I swelled with pride. It was the single moment of acclaim of my whole school career.

Anyway, we had to give food to the king of the sea and one of the mothers from our house had gone to a nearby shore to collect food for our larder. I said we could have walked there after school, and that made me recall going to school and the things that happened there. But instead of having us walk there after school, grandmother thought it best if the load was brought back by canoe, that it would somehow be quicker. But people had already started taking their offerings for the king to the *vidjil*, which was where the ceremony would begin, and our mother and the canoeman had not got back yet, even though where they'd gone to was not very far away. So grandfather started to worry. Grandmother worried too, but I remember grandfather's worrying more. And this was because we hardly ever saw him, so when something happened involving him we were always aware of it. He was worried because, being an adult, he knew only too well that there should be no canoes in the water when the offering to the king of the sea was made, no canoes other than those involved in the ceremony itself. Nobody had ever broken with this custom, or rule, or whatever it was. And it was unusual for anyone to disregard any rule connected to popular beliefs on our Atlantic Ocean island. So my grandfather was worried and he left the house and set off for the shore, hoping to see them making their way back. But there was no sign of them from the beach where the *vidjil* was, so he thought he'd try a different vantage point, one where you could see further into the distance. So he headed south, increasingly concerned. It had been a long time since anyone had seen him on the beach, for he practically never came down from the upstairs where he lived. So for a lot of people it was the first time they'd seen him for a long time, and they could tell right away that he was worried. He walked all the way to the path that went up to the cemetery and went down to the little beach there, his eyes fixed on the sea, hoping the canoe might appear. If it had been low tide, he could have followed the coast all the way to the place our mother and the canoeman had gone to collect the food grandmother had left behind. On certain stretches he'd have had to come in from the shore, where the cliffs become very steep, and make a little detour into the bush, and if it had been high tide he could have done the same only with more detours. It was because of those detours that there was no coastal path that ran from the big village all the way to where the plantation was. But grandfather was down on the beach and he ran out of sand, by which I mean he got to the end of the small beach by the cemetery and he climbed up on the rocks. He went on walking, his gaze fixed south, anxious to see his daughter and the canoe. The time of the offering to the king was fast approaching and it was unheard-of for anyone to be out at sea who was not part of the ceremony. That offering was one of the most curious things on the island. I found it particularly strange, but although practically everything filled me with fear on the island, this didn't. I did, however, have my suspicions about it for, as a child, whenever fear didn't silence my doubts, I was very questioning. What happened when food was given to the king was the following: somebody said that the king of the sea had sent word, from wherever it was he lived, that he was hungry. That's what was said. Was it the women who talked to the deads who were told the king was hungry? Specifically, was Sabina the one who was told? However it happened, word reached the people of influence that the king was hungry and, at the end of the afternoon, when the sun was setting and everyone was at home, it was announced that on such-and-such a day food would be given to the Saltwater King. That's what we called the king of our sea on the Atlantic Ocean island: the Saltwater King. So whenever we heard mention of the 'Saltwater King', we knew people were talking about our king and not the king of some other sea. In the language of our island we have two ways of saying 'the sea' which are equivalent to the words for sea and saltwater in Spanish.

The offering ceremony began with many minutes, perhaps even hours, of orations from the ministrants. They got under way as soon as everyone had brought their offering, whatever they'd decided to pay homage to the king with: a bundle of firewood, a length of cloth, a litre of brandy, a bunch of bananas, a cooking pot, a pineapple, a radio set, a lamp, a small basket of cassava, a giant yam, a bottle of anis; whatever you wanted to give, or whatever you had. Although if what you wanted to give was a white man's product, then it had to be unopened. Who were we, on our little island, to give the king a half-used product? It was said he'd reject it, and I can't remember but there was probably some other threat connected to showing him such disrespect. All the offerings were left in the *vidjil* and then the orations began. And with just a few hours to go until that sombre ceremony got under-way, one of my grandmother's daughters, that's to say one of our mothers, for as far as we were concerned they were all mothers to us, was still out at sea, on her way back from a place that wasn't so very far from the big village. It would be the first time such a thing had ever happened. So all the adults in my house were worried and grandfather had gone down to the shore to try and find her. Finally, a long way from the cemetery, stand-ing out on some projecting rocks, he spotted the canoe.

He gestured to them and he called out to them, telling them to pull in to the first beach they came to rather than risk rousing the fury of the king. But I've already talked about my grandfather's lack of voice, so I doubt he was able to make himself heard like a man. In any case, if you were out at sea, it was practically impossible to hear what someone on land was saying to you, even if it didn't seem like you were very far apart. The sea wind simply stole the sound of the words. The person on land might be close enough for you to see them shouting to you, but all you could do was go, 'Huh?' for there was no way of hearing what was being said.

Grandfather saw his daughter and the canoeman who was transporting her and he called out to them, and he waved his hands, but they heard nothing. And he got increasingly worried. Was the canoeman about to paddle the canoe onto the main beach in front of everyone, showing himself to be the only person on the whole island who didn't understand there was an important ceremony taking place? What would happen to them then? On our island, if you ignore a rule or a custom, you're not given a penalty, in fact no one will say anything about it; they don't have to, for consequences will catch up with you by themselves: we're talking about an island where there's no shortage of catastrophes! Anyway, me and the other children of the household had followed grandfather and we stood on the beach near the cemetery. What could have happened for them to have been so delayed on a journey that ought to have taken less than an hour? Well, we didn't really deal in hours, but that's beside the point: there was nothing between the big village beach and the place with the plantation to justify such a delay; there were no big rocks to avoid, no projecting cliffs or especially turbulent stretches of water. What problem had they encountered to make them take so long? You couldn't even argue that the man had to beach his canoe, hide his paddle safe from the sea, gather his tools, climb up a palm tree with his axe and cut down the palm dates, because they'd already been cut; everything had already been piled up ready to load into the canoe. What had happened to cause them to be the first people in the island's history not to observe one of its most important customs? The man paddled, gestures were made, words shouted that he didn't hear. Grandfather was in a state of total despair. He was running out of time to make himself heard, running out of opportunities to get their attention, for there was an islet off the coast near the cemetery and, depending on the state of the sea and the canoeman's skill, he might go round the islet on the open side, the side that looked out to the horizon, or come through on the mainland side, the side closest to the shore. If the canoeman opted for the open side, grandfather wouldn't be able to call out to them again until it was too late, until it was too late to stop them from being seen by everyone on the main beach, too late to avoid ridicule and catastrophe. So granddad felt he had to do something to make himself heard before the canoeman reached the islet, had to do something to make the canoeman paddle in to the nearest shore. They'd return the canoe to where it was supposed to go afterwards, when everything was back to normal. The situation was further complicated by the fact that it was impossible to see the main beach from where we were standing, so grandfather didn't know how close the ceremony was to starting. How shameful it would be for his daughter to be the first person to disobey the rule, a rule of unknown consequences, and in front of everyone, everyone and their tremendous power for gossip!

When everything was assembled, the ministrants started their orations. I suppose they were some sort of blessing of the gifts for the king. They prayed, and prayed, and prayed, in that language that wasn't our island's language, for I didn't understand a word of it, and when they decided there'd been enough praying, they brought several canoes down to the sea's edge and started to load them up with the offerings. But only things that had been there when the ministrants had started their prayers; anything brought after they'd started had to be discounted. Then a few chosen men took to sea in the biggest canoe on the island, and they paddled out a certain distance from the shore, in front of the houses. What happened out there only those men knew, those men who'd been chosen for such an important mission. Sometimes there were great piles of things to give to the Saltwater King and more than one canoe had to go out, but no matter how many there were, everything was carefully monitored by the ministrants. What people said – what those who'd been chosen for the mission reported – is that you had to close your eyes when you threw the offerings out for the king. Or you stood in the canoe with your back to the sea and threw the offerings out behind you. I always thought I could never be one of the chosen ones. I'd have suddenly sprouted an eye in the back of my neck, for there's no way I would have been able to not look to see who took the things from the water. But you were forbidden from looking and naturally there was a punishment if you failed to observe the rule: you'd be taken away by the king and never seen again. When I was a bit older, I found it hard to believe that no man was ever curious enough to sneak a look at that phenomenon. For that's what it was: a phenomenon. I was never told anything to make me think otherwise. I've already told you what was tipped into the sea. And although I find it phenomenal that no one looked, I appreciate it's each to their own as regards wanting to know about life and what surrounds you. So the real phenomenon was not that they didn't look but that the sea king accepted everything he was offered, which was a great quantity of things. And he really did take everything, every last thing, and it all took place not very far away from the big village, so nobody could claim there was any trickery. But was there any proof that the king accepted all he was offered, any proof that he took everything for his larder? The proof was that, of the great quantity of things tipped into the water for him, not a single item made its way back to the island. Never. Not to any of the island's shores, not even with all the strong sea currents. What's more, and this is why I first wanted to mention the things that were offered, while you may well question whether the king really accepted a tin plate, a lump of coal, a bottle of brandy or a padlock, for they would sink to the sea bed in seconds anyway, lots of objects wouldn't sink even in the stormiest of seas. Bundles of firewood, bunches of bananas, a length of cloth, linen to tie about the head, packets of cigarettes, more firewood, more bananas, more cloth for the king's robes, cloth for the robes of the king's daughters, things that everyone knew would ordinarily float forever, come what may. None of these things came back to shore. Not that day, not the next, not ever, nor did anyone come across them out fishing in the furthermost parts of the horizon, and this in times of terrible shortage. Was it not a miracle? To be honest, I never experienced the ceremony at close quarters. I experienced it from the beach, like most of the islanders, and by helping to load the canoes when it was my turn to do so, but I never stopped considering it the single biggest mystery on the island. And like I said, of all the mysterious things on the island, it was the one I was least afraid of, for I felt confident that if the king didn't like something, he'd make his feelings known. The whole thing was incredible, from start to finish. There's a beach on the south of the island that's known as The Beach of Riches, because so many things wash up on it from other shores, from other countries. One thing that's never lacking down there is tar. The tar is good for nothing at all, except staining the beach, although men sometimes use it to fill in holes in their canoes, for although the wood they are made of won't sink, it does sometimes have other defects. But aside from that, all the tar does is arrive from who knows where and stick to people's feet when they walk on the beach. Wooden boards also wash up on that beach, boards with words written in foreign languages, bottles and cans too, and lots of tree trunks from trees that don't grow on the island. And men make the most of them and build canoes out of the alien woods. But they have to be strong to do so, for the wood can be tough. Anyway, I mention that beach because you'd have thought anything rejected at the gates of the king's palace would end up there. But nothing was ever found that was thought to be an item rejected by the Saltwater King. Never. What if someone found something but said nothing? But why would they say nothing? Nobody on the island doubted the ceremony but me! And I was young, so young that I worried that if I went on living on the island then I'd inevitably one day be chosen to go and give food to the king, and I knew my curiosity would get the better of me. I'd go, I wouldn't be able to resist looking and that'd be the end of me. I wouldn't be telling this story now. And just so you don't think I'm exaggerating, I was so convinced this would

207

happen and spent so much time imagining what life would be like there, I formed a mental image of what the king's palace looked like. It was said that if you looked, you'd be swallowed by the waters and dumped at the bottom of the steps to the king's palace, and I knew I wouldn't be able to resist looking. That's how you entered the palace, by going up some steps. I could draw a picture of it for you now, as if it were right there in front of me.

Grandfather made one last big effort, and he went very close to the cliff edge and made wild gestures and roared in a voice nobody had heard before, and somehow he made himself heard by the man who was paddling, paddling one of grandmother's daughters back from collecting food piled up at the plantation. The canoeman saw grandfather and knew something must be seriously amiss for him to have left the upstairs where he lived. That he'd left the upstairs was enough on its own, but grandfather had also gone down to the beach, the one by the cemetery, a beach used for practically nothing. Well, nothing I care to mention. Some things are best left unsaid. Although the beach was also used for something else, something I can mention, because a bit further out, in front of the islet, the waves broke and boys who were grown-up and daring went out on chest boards or in canoes to glide on them. They paddled out to the islet, either on chest boards, which were the remains of broken canoes, or in canoes themselves, although without actually getting inside them. They paddled out to the mightiest waves and then waited for one to break and glided in on them, fast, all the way in to the beach. They did this at low tide. And because of those breaking waves, anyone there not for gliding usually went round the islet on the open side, and this was what grandfather wanted to avoid. Which was why he had to get the canoeman, who might have been his son-in-law, to hear him. And grandfather managed to make himself heard and managed to avoid the canoeman paddling around the open side, but then there were the waves to contend with. As I said, the waves broke in front of that islet and only the most skilled and experienced canoemen dared paddle through them in a canoe with a load, never mind a canoe with a woman sitting in it. Of those skilled and experienced canoemen there was one who stood out in particular, one who went further than all the rest in his daring. I remember his name, but what's the point in me telling you his name if I haven't even told you my grandfather's name? So anyway, there was a situation that my grandfather wanted to avoid at all costs and that was his daughter and the canoeman interrupting the ceremony in front of everyone. And when the canoeman saw grandfather on the shore, so very far from the upstairs where he lived, the canoeman knew something must be seriously amiss. Grandfather made gestures for them to come in from the water right away, and the canoeman, who might have been his son-in-law, obeyed. The canoeman may well have been aware of the ceremony taking place on the island that day after all, for as I said, the announcement had been made to everyone. Either way, grandfather called him in and, because he knew what the bay was like there, knew about the waves breaking one after the other as they rolled in to shore, he was worried about what could happen to his daughter, the canoeman, the canoe and its load. And so by the time we'd reached him, grandfather had taken his trousers off and gone a little way into the water to wait for the canoe. Imagine how worried he must have been to have done that. It was the first time any of us had seen him so much as splash in the water. The first time in our lives, which although we were young was still a long time given that we lived on an island in the middle of the Atlantic Ocean surrounded by sea. Furthermore, it was very dangerous to enter the sea when a canoe was coming in on a beach where the waves were so wild. It was very dangerous because the canoe could easily smash into him, for the whole operation depended on whether the canoeman, who may have been grandfather's son-in-law, could master a canoe in the waves. In order to glide a canoe in on those waves and keep the boat upright, the canoeman had to be very skilled with his paddle. And in this situation, gliding a canoe in on the waves was especially inadvisable, because the canoe had a full load and a woman sitting in it, and the woman would have a terrible time if the canoeman lost control and fell in the water. If that were to happen, the woman would be in serious trouble because on our island women didn't know how to paddle canoes, nor did girls ever go out to glide in the waves on chest boards. Grandmother's daughter, one of our mothers, was therefore in great danger. Which was why grandfather took his trousers off and waded out into the water, to try and slow down the rapid approach of the canoe as it glided in on the waves. This was also very dangerous, but anyway, into the water he went, and by the time we'd reached him, he was in up to his knees. We could have shouted for him to come back but he was worried and determined to deal with the situation. The waves became more frequent and some of them came in very high, so from time to time grandfather had to backtrack to avoid getting soaked. As he moved further out, the water grew deeper and reached to higher parts of his body, and so he had to hitch up his shirt to avoid it getting wet. I thought he might as well have taken it off, as he was practically naked without his trousers on anyway. Our hearts raced, for we knew something terrible could happen. We were only little and so we couldn't help, at least we couldn't help the canoe reach the sand without coming to any harm. And our grandfather, having hoisted up his shirt so as not to get it wet, revealed something plastic he had strapped to one of his sides. The right side, I think. Yes, something strapped there, which wasn't a part of his clothing and wasn't part of his body. It was something that seemed to be covering a hole. We saw it clearly. We were surprised to see it, for we knew hardly anything about the man. What was it?

Out in the waves the canoeman was worried too. He knew that if he lost control, the waves could flip the canoe over, sending the woman overboard, and that in the speedy approach to the sand, the canoe could smash into her father and something serious could then happen to either of them. To the woman, for she wasn't used to how the sea behaved, and to the old man, because of his age, because he wasn't used to the water and because, as we could all now see, he was sick. So, quite close to the shore, the canoeman lay his paddle down, jumped into the water and grabbed hold of the back of the canoe. He wasn't heavy enough to halt the canoe or stop it being violently pulled in to the beach, but his efforts had some effect. The canoe came rushing in onto the sand and the canoeman told the woman to get out right away, something women can't really do at speed. But our mother was already soaked, so there was no need for her to take care, and she got out as fast as she could. The next thing was to try and keep the canoe upright so that the waves would help push it up the beach, even if just a bit. Then our hands and the hands of our mother were needed, for while the two men held the canoe steady, we had to unload it as quickly as possible and take everything as far away from the water as possible. Everything, no matter how heavy it was. We gave it our all, and we dripped with sweat, even though we were in the water, and we managed to get the canoe unloaded. Mission accomplished. But then we had to move everything again, further up the sand, for the tide was coming in fast. So we did that too. When it was all done, grandfather told our mother, the one who had been in the canoe, to take us home. He hoped it wasn't too late to contribute to the offering to the king, so he said to tell grandmother to take the water filter that was on the table in his room. He said all this in a voice that was so low we couldn't make it out. We only knew what he said because our mother told us afterwards. And because she was being honest with us, we dared ask her about what grandfather had strapped to his side, or stomach. What was it?

We did as grandfather said and carried the load home on our heads, and when we got there grandmother brought the water filter down to take for the king. It was a sort of bottle, like a vase, and I knew of it because it was one of the things we'd seen in grandfather's room when he'd gone out, which happened so very, very rarely. I liked that filter a lot and considered it a precious item. It had a tap on the front, in the bottom corner. I thought the filter was the most beautiful object in the whole house, certainly the most beautiful thing I'd seen upstairs, and it made me sad to see grandmother taking it away. That afternoon I didn't go down to where they performed the orations. I wanted to watch the canoes from the shore nearest to the house. I didn't want to be around other people while I was busy questioning whether the king took what was tipped in the water for him. I wanted to be on my own, able to take it all in and keep my doubts to myself, my doubts about the people in the canoes not looking. Not looking to see who took the things, out of fear of what might happen to them. Practically the entire island was gathered by the *vidjil*, filling the beach from one end to the other. I think the only people not to watch the ceremony were grandfather and the canoeman. When we left the beach with our loads on our heads, I was at the rear, behind my other brothers and sisters, and I looked back to see grandfather and the canoeman sitting on the beach talking. It was one of the very few times I saw grandfather talk and that canoeman was one of very few people to hear his voice. What did they talk about? What did grandfather say to him? Interesting things no doubt, so interesting that a few months later, the following thing happened.

One day, in the middle of the night, when we were already in bed, we heard adult voices. In truth, adults were the only ones allowed to speak at night. What was going on? Well, a young man had come running from his house crying because he'd gone to live with a woman and the woman wasn't intact. Not intact? He cried, because this evidently pained him a great deal. It turned out the woman was my grandmother's niece and she'd been raised in our house. The man? The very same canoeman we'd left talking to grandfather on the beach by the cemetery. Over time he'd been through all the formalities required to marry a woman from the family, and I guess one of the things he'd had to do to earn the right was go to the plantation to bring that load back by sea. Why did they take so long? Was he trying to convince that mother of ours to do something? Do what? Whatever it was, there was nearly a catastrophe because of it. So anyway, one night the canoeman came to the house crying and complaining that his woman wasn't intact. It was their first night together, but what was he hoping to do on their first night? He was most aggrieved because she wasn't intact and so he cried all the way from his house, on the other side of the village, to our house. Or so I was told. In fact, the word used in our language is not quite the same as intact, but it can be translated like that. It was only later, when I was more grown-up, that I properly understood what he was upset about. The man had expected to be the first man in the girl's life. He wanted her to be a virgin, and it had been believed, or at least the man believed, that she was. But somehow he found out she wasn't and this pained him; in fact, it pained him so much he cried all the way from his house to our house. When I understood the real 'flesh' of the story, I laughed a lot. What had he been planning to do with her that he could not do now that he'd found her as she was? Some people even said he arrived practically naked as well as crying. I'm not sure I believe that, although I consider both to be equally over-the-top reactions. Is the disappointment at finding out your woman is not a virgin really so great? I couldn't believe it. I don't know how they resolved that case, and I hope it didn't cause trouble for grandfather, as he was probably the one who arranged the relationship, otherwise what were they talking about on the beach by the cemetery? As I said, they stayed behind on the beach, and I don't know whether that young man already knew about the bag grandfather had strapped to his stomach or whether he saw it then for the first time. But either way, they likely exchanged confidences, for that young man knew of grandfather's troubles, that's to say he knew grandfather suffered from an illness that required a bag being strapped to his side. And from that day forth I began to understand my grandfather a little better. When I asked what that bag was, I did so with tears in my eyes. And the tears came because of how I felt. I felt sorry for him, and I thought about how his life had seemed so strange to us that we'd even gone into his sleeping room to see what he had in there. And so now I should tell you what we saw. But after we'd been in there, when we came out, we made the sign for silence with fingers on lips. We were the only ones who knew what we'd seen, and we decided not to tell anyone. We decided not to tell anyone because they might tell our mothers, or our grandmother, and then our grandfather would find out that we'd been looking at his things in his absence, and this could lead to severe punishment. Yes, what we saw made us afraid, but with that gesture of fingers on lips, we promised not to tell anyone. And we kept our mouths shut forever. Which is why even now, I can't really tell you what we saw.

That bag. Grandfather had no anus and he had that
bag to collect what could not come out of him in a natural
way. How long had he suffered from such a thing? The
illness probably caused him to lose his job on the boat
he worked on. All this makes me feel very uncomfortable, and has done ever since I first found out about it.
It must have been awful to live back then with an illness
like that. What happened to him? How did the illness
start? Where did he put the bag? How many people knew
about it? The illness was probably also the reason why he
lived separate from the rest of us, why he didn't go to the
vidjil, why he didn't fish. I now view the way he conducted
his life as entirely reasonable. And let me repeat what
I said before: I never saw him eat. I never saw him eat
anything at all. And I guess that was because he couldn't
eat just anything. I say this because I don't think it was a
simple matter of that bag filling up from time to time and
having to be emptied. I'd find it very hard to live with an
illness like that. Not being able to lead a normal life on
an island where life was hard enough as it was, for the
island had nothing! When I found out, I decided grandfather had actually been a hero. But even so, his illness
didn't explain everything. What did the haircut have to
do with it? Was it some kind of pledge? A ritual of some
sort? I know it was often said that men who worked on
boats kept many secrets and made many pacts. A lot of
things were said about men who worked on boats. But I
just don't know, for he was gone before I had the chance

to find out about that terribly ugly haircut. Half his head shaved, and he took care to keep it like that. Was it not something that people really ought to have asked him about? I once drew a picture of my grandfather, of when I saw him on the sand with half his body in the water, not wearing any trousers, on the beach by the cemetery. He was as thin as a thread, naturally, for he didn't eat anything because he had no anus to expel what wasn't needed. But you didn't notice he was skin and bone when he was dressed. My grandfather.

Speaking of that man who came crying to our house because his woman wasn't intact, or wasn't as he expected to find her, makes me think of what it was like as a boy growing up with girls. I've already said that when we learned the ideo-visual Spanish alphabet the boys sat separately from the girls. And when you went to *Misa* on Sunday, if you were a boy or a man you sat on the left, and if you were a girl or a woman you sat on the right, as you went into the church. The *Padre* never mentioned this during *Misa*, but it was instilled in us from an early age that males and females shouldn't intermingle. We were told this to keep us away from the girls. And the girls were told the same thing. But we boys and girls also knew there were certain things you did without telling the adults. For example, playing at mummy and daddy. When our parents were out, and before we were old enough to go to school, we played at kitchen, dividing ourselves up as mummy, daddy and children. Those given the role of children ran errands and might get a smack. Whoever played mummy went away and brought back firewood and food; she'd been to the plantation. Whoever played daddy went away and brought back fish he'd caught at sea. The mummy cooked, we all ate and then it was bedtime. All of this was pretend, acted out as if we were giving a performance, though the smacks were real enough. At bedtime, the children curled up wherever, but the mummy and daddy slept together. We knew daddy had to sleep with mummy, even though it was something we'd never seen before. The children from our house, and indeed the children from most houses, knew that was the way it was meant to be – only there were no daddies to sleep with the mummies where we lived. And we didn't know whether grandmother slept with grandfather as she was always the last one to go to bed. I never asked her where she slept. But anyway, we played at mummy and daddy and the two people playing the mummy and daddy roles slept together. And at our age, that was as far as it went. But I knew a girl and a boy could go and play mummy and daddy elsewhere, on their own, and do things they couldn't do in front of the rest of the 'family', things that couldn't be done in front of the children. Even though we lived in a house where we'd never seen our mothers do anything with men, for there were no men, or practically none, we knew you could go and play mummy and daddy

on your own. From what I remember, nothing happened
other than you went away and found a hiding place and
then the game broke up because the 'children' didn't like
being abandoned by the 'parents', who'd gone away to
play at being parents on their own. So all the 'children'
got up and either tried to find the hiding place or said
they didn't want to play any more and went home. Like
I said, nothing happened, but it was still something you
couldn't tell the adults you'd done. And even though
nothing happened, when we grew older and wanted to
take the game further than we had back then, we still
called it playing mummy and daddy. We still thought
it was a game. And we still didn't tell the adults. But it
might so happen that 'mummy' got upset, or one of the
'children' got jealous, and then tongues began to wag.
Then the real parents found out and took drastic action.
The girl could end up with chilli burning inside her, all
for a sin she hadn't committed, or had merely thought
about committing, or had committed only a little bit,
kids' stuff. They used chillies to punish girls who'd done
things with boys that they wouldn't confess to. The chilli
was put down there and they cried for hours. I think the
Padre, the parents, the teacher and all the adults were
worried about what we might get up to. And I think
their vigilance was effective and most children became
adults knowing you could play mummy and daddy but
you couldn't actually do it. In fact, any young man who'd
reached the age of taking drinks to the house of a girl

he wanted to marry might expect, as the canoeman who talked to grandfather on the beach did, that the girl he wanted to marry would be 'intact'. That's to say, that games of mummy and daddy had gone no further than rolling around on the ground with your eyes closed. But of course some children weren't afraid of chillies, or they knew good hiding places – a house being built, your own house while the adults were out, or underneath an upturned canoe, for example. I think we must have been quite good at hiding, as I don't remember many cases of chilli being applied, or tears from other such punishments. All of which is why I thought the man was overreacting when he came crying because the girl whose house he'd taken drinks to was not intact. He cried like a child, and everyone saw him cross the village with woe pouring from his heart. He'd overreacted. And what if he was lying when he said the girl wasn't intact? What's more, was it really something he couldn't put up with? Was it really an insurmountable problem? In any case, I was born on the island and I grew up on the island and became a man on the island, and nobody ever told me anything about what to expect of a girl whose house you took drinks to because you wanted to start something serious. Or maybe these things were usually taught to you by the man of the house, and we didn't have one. I grew up not knowing what to expect of a girl you spoke to with serious intentions. I didn't know what being intact was, nor why it should make a man run crying through the village in the middle of the night feeling sorry for himself. How did people learn such things? Who taught that young man? If it was an important piece of knowledge, I grew up without it. Maybe you did need some special preparation before taking drinks to the house of the girl who'd won your heart, but I was never told about it. Oh, and I never saw chilli applied to a boy either, though I did hear of it happening.

I mention all this about boys and girls, infants really, to show how we lived in the big village, and in the other villages of our Atlantic Ocean island, and grew up believing whatever we understood or thought to be the truth. And of course there's nothing remarkable about that, nothing special about boys and girls having eyes to see and hearts to feel with. As a general rule, all boys and girls who were at or below the age of first Communion were considered innocents, or 'pures'. Everyone was pure up to that age, and I don't remember any example of an evil happening that stopped them from being considered pure. Which meant that if for some reason you needed a 'pure', any child would serve the purpose. In the same way that men couldn't be visited at night by a mysterious being that made them feel hot and want to bathe in the saltwater, as happened with the she-devils, children couldn't become infected by evil. Be they boy or girl. Other than the usual illnesses, children were immune to evil. They were pure. And as I already said, they were used whenever pures were required. For example, in our village there was an illness that was treated using urine, but not anyone's urine, only a pure's urine, only a child's. It was said that people suffering from that illness should be given a pure's urine to drink, and if the doctor was dealing with such a case you'd see the doctor's helpers going through the streets with bottles asking children to pee in them, as many bottles and children as it took. Only the urine of pures, boys or girls, but of course it wasn't as easy for girls to pee into a bottle, though they did the best they could. I know the name of the sickness you treat using urine, but I only know it in my language, the language of our island. Looking back, I suppose if you really could treat that illness using urine, then surely anyone's urine would do. By which I mean it would make no difference whether it was a child's or an adult's, though I see why they only asked pures to pee in bottles, the innocent. It's fairly obvious why, but it does change what was meant by innocence.

Time went by on our island and there was no news of our fathers, who were somewhere you went to by boat. The sun rose and set, it rained, we experienced the rain in the big village and then went to the settlements with our mothers when the dry season came. On our island, everyone went to the settlements where they had plantations. Almost everyone went, except for my grandfather and a few others who had reason to stay in the big village. Something must have happened with my grandfather, circumstances that I was never made aware of, because I have the feeling I never saw him again after leaving him on the beach by the cemetery. I left him sitting there, talking to the canoeman who had been transporting grandmother's daughter, and I have the feeling I never saw him again, although when that man came crying to the house my grandfather must surely have been there and said something. But I don't remember. As far as my memory is concerned, I left him there on the beach, the day we gave food to the Saltwater King. That was the last I knew of him, though in truth it probably wasn't. That time and place is doubtless engraved on my memory because of the special circumstances. Besides, that was the day I discovered that grandfather was sick, and that perhaps because of his sickness he'd lost his job on the boat where he was captain, and was brought to the big village for someone to take care of him. He had a bag strapped to his stomach to put his leftovers in, his excrement. I don't want to talk about it any more. But through grandfather I learned that such a thing could happen to a human being. And I think he was the only person on the island who suffered from it. So it gives me a funny feeling when I think about it. In any case, life went on and as far as I'm concerned I left him sitting there on the cemetery beach, and that was the last I knew of him until he died. When he died, on the very day of his death, they burned a lot of things from his room, things we'd seen when we went in there in his absence. But I'd rather not talk about it. I've said why.

So in the dry season everyone who could went to the settlements to work on the plantations and to harvest what they'd planted at the start of the rainy season. Those who couldn't make the journey, for whatever reason, stayed in the big village, including the *Padre*. He never went to the settlements, not once. I'd have liked him to have gone to the village whose patron saint is San Xuan. I'd have liked him to have spent the night there. But there was no *Misión* house there, and if there had been, he'd have had to sleep on a bed of dry banana leaves. On a bed of dry banana leaves on the floor under a *jambab'u* roof. If the priest had gone to San Xuan's settlement, he'd have been given a chamber pot to pee in at night. And if he'd had bigger needs, he'd have had to do them in that chamber pot and give it to one of the villagers in the morning to empty out somewhere, somewhere on the outskirts of the village. I think it was because of all these things that the *Padre* never went to the settlements and always stayed in the big village, at the *Misión*. But I'd have liked him to have spent a night in the village of San Xuan, the very severe patron saint of that place that has a beach like a cave. I'd have liked to have seen what happened between the *Padre* and the patron, whether the patron would have allowed the *Padre* to sleep.

We went to the settlements with our mothers, and those children who were old enough to walk walked and those who were too young were carried on backs. And almost everyone who went to the villages had to go down the steep hill that had drinking water at the bottom. That was the only way to get to almost all the settlements, unless you went by canoe. But woe betide anyone who tried to paddle their canoe into the cave at San Xuan's village. The waves there were . . . Anyway, you got there somehow: there were too many things to do in the settlements not to go; you couldn't just stay in the big village for the dry season because of the waves or the steep hill. For whoever stayed in the big village ran the risk of having nothing to eat in the rainy season. Or not having enough to eat: having too little to see them through the rainy spell. Eating fish was a different business. It was very hard to get fish to eat in the big village during the dry season. And there were two reasons for that: firstly, there were not many men around to go fishing; secondly, the sea was very different from the way it was when fishing was easy, for the water became cold. So to eat fish again, you had to wait until everyone came back to the big village and the weather turned. You led a different life in the settlements. Part of that life, something that happened when we were in the south village during the dry season, became etched on my memory forever. It was something that caused great sorrow, in me and in everyone else who witnessed it, and I will tell of it now.

That friend of grandfather's, the one who came to speak to him the day they went to the cemetery, was in the south village, and someone asked him to build a canoe. As I said earlier, he was a maestro. A maestro in canoe building and in other things. For example, he knew how to speak to the Calabarians, and to dance like them. Anyway, he agreed to the request, went to wherever the chosen tree was, felled it and without further ado got down to hollowing out the trunk. The hollowing out stage is the hardest stage and so sometimes the maestro is helped by a younger man. In this case he and the younger man had made good progress, and they were working away when a woman came to see them with a child on her back. Who was the woman? She was the maestro's goddaughter, a woman who'd lost her father when she was very young, then lost her mother too and was left all alone, all alone except for a sister. She'd gone to where the maestro was working to ask him a favour. She asked the maestro, her godfather, to take her to the big village because her son was sick. Her son had only just started crawling, so he was not many months old. And who was her son? Well in fact it was Luis Mari. She went to where her godfather worked to ask a favour of him. She was all alone in that village and her child was sick, her only child, a child she'd had after visiting the boat of the sailors who stole our fish. She spoke with a tearful voice and said that the white child was burning up with fever and there was no medicine in the south village, as everyone knew, so she thought she should take him to the big village, in case the man in charge of the hospital, or anyone else for that matter, had anything to give the boy. The maestro didn't so much as look at the child, who was on the woman's back with his eyes closed, sleeping; he accepted what she said and didn't doubt her need. But the child's sickness had come at a bad time, for all the men in the south village had already been told their help would be required that very afternoon to carry the half-built canoe to the shore where the final work on it would be done. And the canoe owner's female relatives had been told to prepare malanga soup for everyone who took part in that arduous task. Everything was ready and everyone was all set, so the job of moving the canoe couldn't not take place. That's what he told her, but as she was his goddaughter, he promised he'd help her as soon as the half-built canoe had reached its final destination. He said that as soon as the canoe was on the sand he'd ask the canoe's owner to take her to the big village to find medicine for her sick child, the child with the foreign father. The child whose father was from a friendly nation, albeit one that stole our fish. The young man who was the future owner of the canoe could not refuse such a favour, given his obligations to the maestro. And the maestro himself was old and he found certain tasks onerous, and he'd have found it onerous to paddle, with some haste, to the big village in a canoe that carried his goddaughter and her child. They agreed to do as the maestro said and the woman went home to wait until it was time for her and the child to leave. Hours went by and everyone gathered around the half-built canoe. The rope was tied, the rollers were cut, smaller branches and tree trunks were collected. They waited for the last people to arrive for, as everyone lived in different places, it took more of an effort for some to get there than others, so not everyone arrived at the same time. And then the mother of the sick child appeared. That woman, who had only one living family member, a sister, knew there could never be too many hands when it came to pulling a canoe to its final destination. She knew her strength ought not be wasted, for until it was time for them to leave with her sick child, she'd be doing nothing, nothing other than waiting. So she went to help and she carried her sick son on her back.

The last people arrived and all the preparations were in place. The maestro checked over everything, looked at everyone, made the sign of the cross and announced that the long journey to the shore was about to commence. And then he sang that song which, as I said, is the most beautiful song I've ever heard:

Aaale, toma suguewa,

Alewa!

Aaaalee, toma suguewa,

Alewa!

And the transporting of the canoe to the shore began. Everyone pulled and sweated, and they took care to avoid accidents, to which end a thin rope was tied to the back of the canoe and held by a man who walked behind everyone else. He watched to make sure the canoe didn't veer off the path and he pulled on the rope whenever it had to be stopped.

Aaale, toma suguewa,
Alewa!
Aaaalee, toma suguewa,
Alewa!

And they advanced a stretch. The men sweated, the women sweated, and that goddaughter of the maestro sweated even more, for besides pulling the canoe, she had a sick child to carry on her back. She'd worn a worried look when she'd gone to ask her godfather the favour and she still wore it, for the child's sickness was serious. But nothing more could be done, for the plans were set and she just had to wait. She knew she just had to wait, and therefore she knew she ought to help, regardless of the seriousness of the baby's sickness. The maestro also knew the child was very sick, although he hadn't looked at the boy when his mother had come to ask the favour. He must have sensed it by some other way old people have of knowing things.

Aaale, toma suguewa,
Alewa!
Aaaalee, toma suguewa,
Alewa!

And they advanced another stretch on that journey to the sea. The men sweated, the maestro sweated and his goddaughter sweated with her sick child on her back. The path to the sea went downhill and the maestro had to shout warnings to the people pulling to make sure there were no catastrophes, for if the canoe slipped and they couldn't get out of the way in time they could be crushed or knocked over. The maestro sang, the men pulled, the women pulled and so too did the woman with the child on her back. And if their hearts beat hard with all the effort they were making, her heart beat harder, for she was making the same effort as them but with the added heartache of her child's sickness. The maestro sang and that song echoed through every corner of the south village. Anyone anywhere nearby heard that simple but meaningful song:

Aaale, toma suguewa,

Alewa!

Aaaalee, toma suguewa,

Alewa!

And they sweated, they took care, they moved out of the way when they were told to, so that the propulsion of their combined strength didn't lead to a catastrophe. And they sang unceasingly:

Maestro: *Aaale, toma suguewa,*

All: *Alewa!*

Maestro: *Aaaalee, toma suguewa,*

All: *Alewa!*

And that song echoed around the bush and through every corner of the south village. And the men, the women and the woman with the child on her back went on pulling whenever the maestro said 'pull'.

They all gave their energy to get that canoe to the shore. They stopped to rest several times over the course of the journey, and each time they did so the woman moved a little bit away from the others and took the sick child off her back. She perhaps did this to suckle it and also to relieve the weight. And although she took part in the pulling of the canoe just as much as the men did, she had to move a little bit away from them to suckle her child, for suckling wasn't something men did and she couldn't do it in front of them. They rested, then the maestro looked at them and started the song again:

Aaale, toma suguewa,
Alewa!
Aaaalee, toma suguewa,
Alewa!
Aaale, toma suguewa,
Alewa!
Aaaalee, toma suguewa,
Alewa!
Aaale, toma suguewa,
Alewa!
Aaaalee, toma suguewa,
Alewa!
'Will you give it a pull?'
'We'll PUll!'
'Will you give it a pull?'
'We'll PUll!'
'Will you give it a pull?'
'We'll PUll!'

I ought to mention that *alewa* is not actually a word in my language. I've only ever heard it used for pulling a canoe to the shore, not for anything else. Like the ho of heave-ho.

Those men and women pulled to the limits of their strength, they were tired, they asked the maestro to let them rest, he let them rest, and then they took hold of the ropes and pulled again to the sound of the song:

Aaale, toma suguewa,

Alewa!

Aaaalee, toma suguewa,

Alewa!

Aaale, toma suguewa,

Alewa!

Aaaalee, toma suguewa,

Alewa!

The woman was at the limit of her strength, but she didn't give up, she couldn't give up. She had the sick child on her back, but she had to keep pushing herself, giving her energy to help get that canoe to the shore where the maestro would finish working on it. If she'd had an older son, or if the son on her back had learned to paddle, he'd have been one of the boys asked to take the canoe out when it was ready. New canoes are given to children to 'treat'. Treating a canoe means paddling it for the first time and for several days, long enough to find out how it handles. Once the canoe is in the water and given over to children to paddle, no further refinements are made, but it has to be treated, whereby the sap in the wood seeps out and saltwater seeps in. The canoe gets used to being paddled in the shallow waters before being taken out and paddled in the deep, and that's why it's a job undertaken by children, for they can only paddle in shallow waters. But the maestro's goddaughter had no older sons; her only boy had not learned to paddle, for he was so little she carried him on her back; and he was sick. The maestro sang, the choir responded, the maestro sang, the chant came back, and everyone gave their energy to get the canoe to where it needed to be, on the south village beach. The patron saint of that place was cross-eyed but not especially severe. When they got to the beach, they rested a little and then went up to the village to eat the malanga soup that the women had prepared. They gathered around the cooking pot, but first they went home to fetch a bowl, for no family had enough bowls for so many people. They fetched their own bowls and then sat around on stones waiting to be served, and while they did this three people remained on the beach, three people unable to go up to the village to eat the malanga soup: the maestro, the goddaughter and the man who would take her to the big village. The young man gathered his paddling kit and put it in the canoe, which would have been a borrowed canoe, perhaps the maestro's own. They dragged the borrowed canoe down the beach and left it at the water's edge. In all villages with rocky beaches the sea demands your attention and you should never turn your back on it, no living being should. With the canoe at the water's edge, it was time for the woman and child to get in. The banana leaves the woman would sit on had already been laid down in the canoe, but for her to get in she would have to take the child off her back. She did so, and in order to climb in and sit down, she handed the child to her godfather for a brief moment. The child was wrapped in the cloth she tied around her back and it was asleep, suffering from the sickness they were hoping to find medicine for in the big village. She sat down and her godfather handed the child back. She laid the child in her lap and they were now ready to launch the canoe into the water. From then on, it would be down to the seafaring skills of that young canoeman, down to his ability to guide them smoothly out of that bay full of black rocks and jutting cliffs. He quickened his hands and took hold of his heart, as we say on our island, and he pushed off out to sea. In almost all the bays of the settlements, a canoeman requires someone to push him off and watch to make sure a wave doesn't come in and immediately knock the canoe back, even send it careering into the rocks. That's what the maestro was there for, and he watched them make their way out of the rocky bay. If something happened and an angry wave came rolling in to send them back from whence they came, the maestro would be their only hope. He'd have to throw himself into the water, grab hold of the canoe and try and keep it afloat, for he knew terrible things could happen if the canoeman lost control and the canoe was sent careering into the rocks. And there was a woman on board, a woman with a sick child asleep in her arms, so the canoe simply couldn't capsize. But nothing untoward did happen: from the moment that young man jumped out of the water and into the canoe, he did as all men of the island did: he proved his skills with hand and paddle. It was important to leave the shore behind as quickly as possible, for it was a bay of unpredictable currents. And he was a skilful canoeman, as were all men in the south, and he steered the canoe clear of hazards. By the time he'd done this, the maestro had moved away from the beach and was standing further up, on a small mound from where he could see them better. When he saw they were clear of the bay and out of harm's way, he shook his head, as if in disbelief at the situation, and he turned his back on them and the sea and went up to the village. The other men, who were by now eating malanga soup, had already taken away all the equipment that had been used to pull the canoe to the beach. You didn't make the maestro carry unnecessary loads, because of his age and because he was a maestro.

The canoeman steered them clear of any hazards and then he sat down. A canoeman doesn't sit down until he's sure he's clear of any waves that might knock the canoe back. He made himself comfortable, for going from the south village to the big village meant going from one end of the island to the other, but in a canoe, and travelling through waters that demanded attention and respect. In fact, the sea route between the two villages included a stretch of water that was so turbulent there was a folk song about it. The song said that only a man could cross those waters and, as only men had canoes on our island anyway, what the song meant was that only a real man could cross those waters. Anyone else should turn back and avoid the worst. But what was strange about those waters was that they were quite close to the shore, and you don't usually get turbulent waters so close to the shore. It was difficult to tell, but the water was very deep there and if you stood on the cliffs to fish you needed many yards of nylon. And no ordinary nylon either, it had to be thick nylon, because deep-water fish were big. That cape had a fearsome name, though I only know it in our island's language. Above the cliff there was a mountain and on that mountain there was an area where it was said the deads lived. All the deads on the island apparently went there, though I never understood why as I thought dead people were buried in the cemetery. But anyway, everyone knew the deads lived on that mountain, which was a little in from the coast, and so no woman should ever plant there. I never knew how they found out that mountain was where the deads went, nor for how long the deads had been going there, but anyway, the deads living there had nothing to do with the sea being so ferocious. The water was a long way from the mountain, way down below, and, besides, the sea had its own reasons for being ferocious, different reasons; the deads living on the mountain was a different matter.

The canoeman sat down and mentally planned the journey to the big village. That way he could work out how long it would take and what rhythm he ought to paddle at. There was a woman with a sick child in his canoe, so there was a certain urgency, but the sea would dictate things. The young man knew that anything could happen when travelling from the south village to the big village. Getting there sooner or later wouldn't depend solely on how he handled his paddle; there would be other factors too, circumstances beyond his control and impossible to foresee. Nevertheless, he faced up to the challenge and determined to get there as quickly as circumstances would allow. Like most canoemen, he'd made the sign of the cross before getting in the canoe, and now they were out of the bay and clear of the waves that might have knocked them back, he repeated the gesture. But, like all canoemen, he knew the journey only really began now. The young man started to paddle. He paddled, and paddled, and paddled, and he shook his head. Crossing the turbulent waters that only a real man could cross was proving very difficult. He paddled with all his might, but he barely made any progress. Despite its fearsome name and ferocious waters, crossing those waters was really only a matter of paddling hard and leaving the south village coastline behind. The man went on paddling, for he had no other option. He could not turn back. The big village was the objective of his every stroke: he couldn't not get there, for that was where the medicine was, or so they liked to think, for the big village was big, hence its name. He paddled with all his might; he paddled, and paddled, and paddled, and finally he showed that he was a man: he rounded the infamous cape with the turbulent waters. The place was well known for its waters, and also because of the crosswinds that whipped around the headland. So it might be that you managed to pass the infamous cape but then the crosswinds wouldn't let you go a stroke further. They might even threaten to capsize your canoe – such a calamity was suffered by many a canoeman, but *gracias a Dios*, before learning to paddle on our island, you're taught to swim. However in this case there was a woman with a baby at the breast, a sick child who had never been in a canoe before, so the canoe simply couldn't capsize. And with great effort and determination, the canoeman paddled them clear of the worst of the crosswinds. Yet they were still not advancing as quickly as they should have been. Something was wrong. It wasn't normal that no matter how hard he paddled, the canoe stayed in the same spot: it was as if someone was pulling the canoe back, preventing its progress. The man couldn't understand the canoe's sluggishness. It was as if the canoe were new, as if the wood were full of sap, yet to be treated. But it wasn't new, so what was the problem? He didn't stop paddling, for you couldn't stop paddling at any moment when journeying from the south village to the big village. He went on paddling, but he was getting increasingly frustrated at the lack of progress: as a native of the south village, as someone who'd made the journey several times before, he knew what progress he should be making, given the load he was carrying. It was as if he were carrying a different load, a load that was a good deal heavier than a woman with a small child. Someone's preventing us from advancing, he said to himself, but he went on paddling. He refused to accept defeat, and the situation wasn't so bad that they didn't advance at all, and eventually they rounded another headland and left the turbulent, ferocious waters behind. Even so, he knew they were still not advancing enough. It felt as if he was carrying more than the load he could see in his canoe. Was there a problem with the canoe? he wondered. For the canoe wasn't his but rather the maestro's, who had lent it to him to take the woman, the maestro's goddaughter, to the big village in search of medicine for her sick child. So it might have been that the canoe had an extra thick base, that for some reason the maestro preferred a canoe with very little wood removed from the bottom, and that was why it weighed so much. But if that were the case, the maestro would surely have told him about it, or the canoeman would have realised when he had the canoe at the water's edge. That couldn't be it. So what was it?

The man went on paddling, and he advanced enough for the headland of a village that was halfway between the south village and the big village to come into view.

It was a small village with calm shores. That halfway village's canoemen were spared the worst vagaries of the sea. They could paddle out of their bay with their eyes closed. The man paddled, confident he'd soon be leaving the calm waters of the halfway village behind. But he went on feeling like he wasn't advancing properly. Either he had a huge invisible load in the canoe or someone was pulling him back, preventing his progress. This had never happened to him before. One woman with a baby could not weigh so much, he thought. He went on paddling and, just to say something to distract himself from his travails, he asked the mother whether she shouldn't suckle the child. The child wasn't asking to be suckled, but it was a long time since she'd suckled it and, if it was sick, that couldn't be a good thing. And the mother said she hadn't suckled it because the child was asleep and she didn't want to wake it. That was the end of the matter, although a little later, the woman took out her breast and put the child to suckle. The man didn't look and, as the child was wrapped in cloth, he couldn't see whether it suckled or not, though he presumed it did. That she hadn't suckled the child hadn't been bothering him: he'd only said it to distract himself from what was puzzling him so. Which was why they were not advancing properly. Something was obstructing them, though he couldn't think what. And it was beginning to anger him.

It was common on the island for a canoeman paddling from one village to another to throw a fish hook and bait out and to have a length of nylon at his lips. That's how he held on to the line, by curling his lips. Anyone who's not been a fisherman on our island might imagine this being troublesome or difficult, but it's not, and there are two things I ought to make clear: one, the canoeman never stops paddling, and two, the nylon is not really nylon but rather a thicker type of thread used to fish larger specimens, fish of the shark variety. If a fish tugs on the nylon, the line of thread falls away from the canoeman's lips and only then does he stop paddling, to deal with developments. If he's in luck, he'll be able to haul in the thread, pull the fish into the canoe and kill it with his baton. This is easier said than done, and struggling with a large specimen can be dangerous, but anyway, assuming he kills the fish, there might not be enough room for it in the canoe. In which case the canoeman puts it back in the water and tows it to the big village. In such circumstances, he'd be justified in feeling an extra weight as he paddled, because of the drag caused by the large specimen, a shark, a swordfish, a tuna, etc . . . But no such thing had happened that day. Given the child's sickness, the canoeman hadn't wanted to lose any time, so he hadn't thrown out a fishing line. He wanted to get to the big village as quickly as possible, to seek out the medicine. That being the case, what was the problem? What was hindering their progress? He paddled, he paddled, he paddled, but they didn't advance as much as they should have. What a tremendous weight, this really isn't normal. Something's happening that I'm unaware of. Is someone preventing me from reaching my destination? I never expected an old canoe to weigh so much. I can't understand it. That's what the canoeman said to himself. He even thought about pulling up on a beach to see if there was anything stuck to the underside of the canoe, something that was preventing it from advancing properly. But what could it be? Sometimes little fish, the sort that follow bigger ones and travel in pairs, accidentally get stuck to a canoe. They fix on to the canoe using their suckers, though nobody knows why. But they are tiny fish and barely weigh a thing. And besides, they're found much further out at sea where they follow the bigger fish, fish that are so big they don't notice a couple of tiddlers stuck to their underbelly, until the fishermen pull them off and throw them back into the water.

The man knew all this, and he knew it couldn't be the cause of the problem. So he didn't pull up on a little beach to check whether anything was stuck to the canoe and obstructing it. But it was exasperating and it was making him angry. He was having to make much more effort than he ought to, and they hadn't got to where they were going yet and he started to worry, for he was getting tired. What was it? He was a long way from guessing what the problem was, but he was right to think there was a reason the canoe felt so heavy, much heavier than there being just a woman and a sick child in it. To understand what it was, we have to go back to when they were pulling the half-built canoe to the beach. Back to the south village, to when the half-built canoe was still a long way from the shore, to when the women who had received the call were peeling malangas to prepare the soup that those pulling the canoe would eat later.

Aaale, toma suguewa,

Alewa!

Aaaalee, toma suguewa,

Alewa!

Maestro: *Aaale, toma suguewa,*

All: *Alewa!*

Maestro: *Aaaalee, toma suguewa,*

All: *Alewa!*

And the canoe advanced as the men and women cried out in unison. And in among those men and women there was a particular woman, who had gone to see the maestro to ask a favour without knowing a canoe was being pulled that day. She'd gone to see the maestro, who was her godfather, to ask him to take her to the big village because her child was very sick. But there are lots of things you do collectively on our island, and to bring people together collectively you have to give them prior warning. And once people have readied themselves for whatever collective exercise you've called them for, you can't just tell them to go home and come back another day, for those people have volunteered their help out of goodwill, even though they've been asked to do an arduous task. Which is why the maestro told the woman she'd have to wait, that they'd deal with her matter as soon as this other matter had been taken care of. Furthermore, because of the way these things are done, the maestro had to be there. He was the only one who had to be there, despite the fact that the song seemed simple, despite the fact that in terms of pulling the canoe, what you might call the actual pulling, he'd do very little. But he was the maestro, and on our island there are many things that seem simple but that are only done when the right person is present. Nobody takes someone else's place on our island without being publicly invited to do so. And that was the case here. The woman had to wait and she understood this. And although she had a child on her back burning with fever, she joined the men and women who had volunteered to pull the canoe from the bush to the water's edge, where the maestro would finish his work. He'd earn nothing for the work, because back then people didn't charge for such things.

As I've already said, that woman was an orphan: her parents had died and she'd been left with nobody but a sister. She had nobody else in the world. She was a woman, that's to say an adult, but she felt like an orphan, for she'd grown up without anybody. With the terrible shortages we suffered on the island, she'd been taken to the boat and she talked to the fish thieves and was given something to help relieve our hardship. And after the visit she was left with a child, a baby boy, and the boy's fathers came to visit him. But it seemed that we were condemned to

Juan Tomás Ávila Laurel

go without and we were soon back to living without matches, kerosene, soap, tobacco, clothing, needles or sewing thread. And after seeing so many people die, people began to return to the settlements, in order to get away from the reminder of the cemetery in the big village. That woman went to the south village and she took her white child with her, the boy she'd got after going on board the boat. As the boy was so little, she put him on her back and took him with her to the plantations. Then she left him to sleep on some lengths of cloth, while she went round harvesting and weeding. She covered him up to protect him from the sun and from any creatures that might come along. If the boy cried, she got up and went over to suckle him. On our island it's said that a mother who doesn't eat fish is a mother without milk in her breast. And because she was an orphan, she ate very little fish. She only ever ate fish when she was given some by a neighbour whose husband had come back with a big catch. Otherwise she closed the door when night fell and went to sleep with her child in the dark. They slept on dry banana leaves, over which she'd lain lengths of cloth and old bedspreads. If she came across a coconut tree on her plantation, and if it was in season and she was able to climb it, she took coconuts for herself and her child, for the baby liked coconut milk and she could make a mash with the pulp that saw her through times of hardship. She threw a little cassava flower in with the coconut mash and ate well enough. But I'm not sure that woman always had the strength to climb coconut trees. And when she didn't, she'd look up at the coconuts and sigh, and suckle her child as best she could.

That was the way things were until the child got sick. The sickness could have been caused by any number of things: a hard life, the sun, mosquitoes, the fact that the child's mother had no one in the world but a sister. What's more, the child was white and I don't think white people are born to lead such hard lives. And so the child's mother sought medicine. She knew she could not stay in the south village with a sick child. But she had to wait. And when she held the rope and heard *Alewa!* she added her strength to the strength of the others, and anyone who looked at her would have seen thick beads of sweat pouring down her face. She had the child on her back. *Alewa!* – the canoe advanced a little, and anyone who looked at her would have seen her face covered with perspiration. She added her strength to the strength of the other men and women from the village, in order to get that canoe where it needed to be. It was a long journey. As she carried a double load, she tired quicker than the others, but she couldn't give up. She had to be where the rest of the village was. She knew that the sort of help she needed came about because of these collective exercises. And so she went on pulling when it was her turn to pull on the rope. Hours later, when the canoe had reached its final destination and there were only a few hours left before sunset, she put her child in her godfather's arms, sat down in the middle of the canoe, on the dry banana leaves, and took her child back in her lap. She was ready to cross a stretch of water so turbulent there was a folk song about it, in order to get medicine for her sick child. The water in the bay went calm for a moment and they pushed off into the sea. The woman's godfather climbed up onto a mound and watched them leave the bay, and from there he shook his head in pity. He knew what had happened. He knew her secret. Her secret was that when she'd gone to see him to ask his help, the child was already dead. He'd seen it from a foot poking out of the cloth in which the child was tied to her back. He could tell from the child's little face, and he could tell from the woman's face and from her words. And he could tell because he was old. And because of this he knew that it made no difference whether the child was attended to sooner rather than later, for what they wanted to avoid happening had already happened. But he kept quiet, just as the woman kept quiet. He knew the woman had nobody and that she'd need to be strong to get to where she had to go: the big village. If everyone knew of her misfortune, she probably wouldn't have found the strength to get there of her own free will, she'd have had to be carried there. And he knew there was only one cemetery on the island, the one in the big village, so he acted in such a way as to keep her secret safe. And he told her what he told her, said what he felt he ought to say. The rest of what happened is something I'll never know how to explain. The woman pulled the half-built canoe with the dead child on her back, and anyone who saw her face thought she was sweating from the pulling, for they didn't know her story. What they took for beads of sweat were mostly tears, tears that poured from her eyes, tears of hurt, tears for her terrible misfortune. She cried, but she refused to give up. She didn't like to ignore customs, nor did she think it necessary to do so now. And she held it all in until, out of necessity, she placed her dead child in her godfather's hands, so that he might share her secret: the child was dead. And she didn't cry until the canoeman asked her whether she shouldn't suckle the child, for a long time had passed since she'd last done so. She took out her breast and put the child to suckle, to satisfy the canoeman, who still didn't know he was transporting a dead child. She suckled the dead child, though it could no longer suck. It had been dead for some time. And she did this to make the man paddling think the child was alive, so that he wouldn't worry. But he was worried, for due to something he was unaware of, they were advancing much more slowly than they ought to. Only the woman knew the reason. She knew what was obstructing them, what made him feel as though his hands were tied, which is how it felt, for the fact of the matter was there was a dead person aboard the canoe. And it was no ordinary thing to transport a dead person, even if, as on that occasion, the dead person was an infant. Everybody knew deads weighed more than alives. Some people think what weighs is the sadness, the pain, the immense darkness of their closed eyes. In death, you have to cross a strange, dark wall. You stop being. You're destined for the blackness, and you let yourself be taken there. You sleep more deeply than a normal person. And all of this weighs. Other people say no one knows what weighs or why death weighs. It just does. Any man transporting a dead should therefore be forewarned, even if, as in this case, the dead person is a small child. Such journeys are special and the canoeman should be mentally prepared, even though he won't do anything special himself. But on this occasion, the canoeman was not informed. He went on paddling and asking himself why there was such a great weight all the way to the big village, specifically to the big village's beach. The bay at the big village was rarely plagued by turbulent or troublesome waves. Indeed, rarely were the waves that broke on its tranquil shores worthy of comment. The canoeman paddled in to the shore and guided the front part of the canoe onto the sand. Does anyone know what time it was? First of all, I ought to say that it's unlikely anyone on the whole island had a watch. That said, the hours of the clock did sound in the church belfry, although nobody paid them much attention. What time could it have been? The cocks were crowing, the sun had long since set. Darkness reigned over the island, for it was not a moonlight night. The canoeman got out of the canoe and pulled it onto the sand, and as the waves were gentle, the woman could get out easily enough. But she'd have to pass her sick child to someone again, and the canoeman offered her his arms. She'd been sitting down for a long time and so had a little trouble standing up and stretching her legs. And she was carrying a child. So the man came to her aid; he took the child in his arms for a brief moment, while the woman got out of the canoe. Then he returned the child to her and they bid each other farewell, as if they'd been in each other's company for only a few moments. The woman turned her back. It was night and, although she moved away into the darkness, she could still be seen. The man watched her walk away, he looked briefly out to sea and when he looked back again he couldn't see her. He thought it strange she could no longer be seen walking up the beach. Had she disappeared in a puff of smoke? There was no way she could have reached the first houses of the big village yet. She'd vanished into thin air! The canoeman gave a start, and he moved forward to investigate the mystery. It was impossible! he thought. But after a few steps he saw what had happened. He was alone on the beach, for the men typically leave the *vidjil* along with the last of the day's light, except on moonlight nights, when men go out at sunset to fish under the full moon. A few men then stay at the *vidjil* to help bring the canoes in and because they know they won't go home empty-handed. A fisherman's cheer tends to be the cheer of the men at the *vidjil* too. So the canoeman was all alone on the beach and, because he planned to wait a few hours before heading back to the south village, he'd made sure to leave the canoe in the middle part of the beach. This he did by taking hold of the back end and dragging it round, spinning the front end as if on a pivot. After the first pull, the back of the canoe pointed up the beach to the nearest houses, the front end out to sea. He then picked up the front end and repeated the process, and so on, until the canoe was a safe distance from the waves. A safe distance meant calculating the height of high tide; no fisherman on our island could ignore whether it was high or low tide. What the man planned to do was go home to his house in the big village and sleep for a few hours before heading back to the beach, launching the canoe into the water and fishing all the way back to the dark and shiny rocks of the south village, which he'd reach by the time the sun was at its highest point over the island.

But before he'd had a chance to do any of that, he'd stood at the water's edge in the big village, looked out to sea, then back at the woman walking away with a child in her arms, and she'd disappeared. What had happened to her? There had never been talk on our island of people having the ability to disappear, or even that such things had ever happened. There had been talk of people having the ability to fly. And of apparitions: people materialising on the island without anybody knowing where they'd been born or come from. But these weren't things the island's inhabitants had experienced themselves; they were stories from long ago, when the islanders believed that the people who just appeared must be very powerful, for they came from a place where magic was possible. Back then, the island's inhabitants could point to particular families and say that such-and-such a man had appeared just like that, without anyone knowing where he'd come from. But all of this, the apparitions and the pointing, had happened long ago and many years had passed, many, many years, since the men who appeared just like that had died. What I mean to say is that people on our island did talk of people who appeared, and of people who could fly from one place to another, or to places that were far away and out of sight, but only of it happening long ago. When we lived through that period of hardship, nobody flew or appeared out of nowhere. Rather people got lost in the bush, or went out fishing, or out to sea for some other reason, and were never seen again.

So I was talking about a man who'd been looking at a woman he'd just left on the big village beach, a man who briefly turned his eyes away and, when he looked back, could no longer see her, as if she'd disappeared. And then I said that nobody actually disappeared on the island back then, rather that they got lost in the bush or at sea. It wasn't very common but it did happen, and I can't go on without telling you of a time when it did happen. I was just a child, as I was when everything I've been talking about happened, but I knew a man who was going to go to hell. Everyone knew he was. All the adults on the island knew that man would not be granted salvation. I never knew whether the man had a wife, a mother, children, brothers or sisters. It's quite possible he did not. In any case, he was a man who was openly wicked. You could accuse him of any wicked thing you could think of and people would believe you. He was afraid of nobody, though I was very afraid of him. And the reason I was afraid of him was that I knew he would not be saved, that he was going to go to hell. I was afraid of him because he said things that nobody should ever say. He said, for example, very wicked things about *Dios* and the *Virgen María*. He was capable of saying things like *Dios* is jealous or the *Virgen María* is an epileptic, things as bad as that. And he didn't say it playfully, but deadly serious. On the other hand, although he had no mother, wife, children or siblings, he had no physical defects; he was even rather handsome, quite light-skinned. So maybe he acted the way he did because he had nobody and he hadn't been able to stand being an orphan. He was wicked because he was free to say and do whatever he liked. He was also a very good fisherman, and he was one of the best at gliding over the waves that broke on the beach by the cemetery. That man, who was still young, might have been paddling a canoe laden down with a precious load, but if he went past the shore by the cemetery and the waves were breaking from far out at sea and might be glided over, he paddled his laden-down canoe right into the waves and played in them. And nothing ever happened to him! In truth, I never knew specifically of any wicked things he did, although I did hear him say awful things about the *Santos*, the *Virgen* and *Dios*. And he didn't respect other adults. He wasn't very talkative but he tended to argue with people when he did exchange words or when there was something he decided to speak up about. That man was known throughout the island, because of the way he behaved and because he ended up being mentioned in a folk song.

Well it so happened that one day, during a period of great hardship, Sabina went out into the street crying because the deads wouldn't leave her alone. She even said that this time it wasn't just the deads talking to her, but that she could see clearly what was going to happen, as if it were right there before her eyes. Sabina, who as I've said was very pretty, although I knew her only when she was old, said that whenever she was on the path to the plantations, whether she was coming or going from them, she would be approached from behind by a group of men, and they smelled strongly of sea water, she even said they were soaking wet. They were men, lots of them, and going in the same direction as her, so she had to move to one side of the path to let them pass. But before they reached her, she always smelled them first, the smell of men soaking with saltwater. She said she even recognised one of them and that it was the man who said awful things about *Dios* and the *Virgen*, the man who was free to say and do whatever he liked. Of course, Sabina saw what other people could not see, and so people doubted her. Ordinary people couldn't see or smell men coming from behind their backs. And so Sabina suffered alone, suffered for what was going to happen and for those men, because she knew the deads were telling her to warn everyone that something bad was going to happen on the island, and furthermore she knew the man who would not be granted salvation was going to be involved. We lived in our usual hardship and Sabina went on crying about what was going to happen. She also cried because nobody would believe her, and because nobody believed her she was punished by the deads. Or so we understood it. It went on like this until the hardship on the island became unbearable. It had been unbearable for years but hardship gets worse as the years go by, and the years went by without offering any respite. That was the situation we found ourselves in when, during a month when most people were in the settlements, the men in the village of San Xuan saw a light on the horizon. Back then, anything appearing on the horizon looked very far away, so far away that having anything on the horizon seemed an impossibility. And if you saw a light on any of the four points of the horizon, it would be as small as a speck of light in a person's eye. Those men saw a light and they imagined what it might be: a boat bearing all that we lacked on the island. It was night but those men thought it better to go out and meet that light than to go on suffering because of what we didn't have: soap and kerosene, clothing, medicine, nylon, tobacco, firewater, matches. Can anyone believe that I grew up thinking tobacco was a product of primary necessity? I've already mentioned this. Well, those men said they had to try, and they got together and talked and then went down to the beach, a beach shaped like a cave. They put their benches, paddles and scoops in their canoes and dragged the canoes down to the water's edge. They waited to see if the furious waves would let them out onto the open sea, and they were in luck and the waves let them out. It was a moonless night and there was no light anywhere on the island except for the stars and some lights you saw in the bush, at the tops of trees. Nobody knew what those lights were and we were afraid of them. The men went out into the dark open sea and set off towards the bright speck on the horizon. They paddled, and paddled, and paddled, and paddled, and paddled. I could say it a hundred times and still not come close to describing how much they paddled to get towards what they thought was a boat full of all that we needed. They paddled, and paddled, and paddled, and paddled, and paddled, and paddled, and they got tired, but they didn't get nearer to the light. They hadn't realised the light was so far away. But they didn't stop paddling. They paddled, and paddled, and paddled, and paddled, and when they looked back, they could no longer see the island. But they were no nearer the boat; they were still very far away from it. They could no longer see the island, which was a significant thing, and I think that's why they didn't stop paddling. How could they see the island if there was no source of light anywhere on the island? No source other than something frightening that shone in the tree-tops, and which anyway would have stopped shining by that time of night or would have been too far away to be seen? By now, their salvation depended on the boat, for if they reached it, they would be taken back to the island after they'd been attended to. It had happened before, and the sailors on the boat couldn't believe the canoemen they'd taken on board had come from the island they said they'd come from. They put their hands on their heads in disbelief when our men told them where they were from. The sailors looked at a map and said that if our men really had paddled from there, they were lucky to be alive to tell the tale. They set off for our island with the sailors still not really believing the canoemen. But history didn't repeat itself. This time our men didn't reach the boat. And nor could they return to the island, for they could no longer see it, paddling as they were in total darkness. They went on paddling, knowing they couldn't stop paddling, and then nobody knows what happened. I ought to say that there were eight of them, eight men, and that they were in several canoes, most likely two to a canoe. Of the eight men, the sea returned only one of them to land. Not two.

At least not as far as I remember. In fact I'm sure it was only one. The sea returning that one man was a sign that the rest of them had perished, that nothing could be done for them, and we never heard anything about them ever again, not ever. If not one man had been washed back, we might have thought they'd reached the boat and the captain had decided to take them all to a different land, to one of the countries that lay somewhere way back behind our island, countries none of us had ever seen before, and that they were all now living there in better circumstances, albeit without their wives, their sons and their daughters. But we know this didn't happen; they all died, except one. What we know of the story we know from the sole survivor, the one the sea brought back. And that's not all that happened to him. The only one of the eight canoemen who was saved from an anonymous death spoke of things that nobody would have thought possible. For he'd been to a place that, once there, few people come back from. He'd been to the other world, albeit in his canoe. He said it was something he started to experience when he'd given up all hope of returning to the island alive, to the extent that he'd even given up paddling. There were things . . . Things that nobody had seen before, nor ever would see unless they lived through a similar experience. He said he'd experienced being in two different worlds at the same time. A man who does a lot of fishing and goes out to sea a great deal sees many things, but even such a man would never see the things that sole surviving canoeman saw. They were things you could only see with one foot in the next world – though he came back, he didn't stay in the next world. But even after they'd pulled him ashore and he'd recovered his health, even after he'd told us what had happened to the other canoemen that he'd set off with in pursuit of the boat, one foot remained in the next world. That's right: he was never himself again after that, not his full self. Besides, to bring him back to this world, he had to be given special cures. This was something that was only done on our island to people with special sicknesses, sicknesses that weren't known to us but that people with special eyes could detect and could tell were life-threatening.

The men who died in that pursuit of the light were Sambachita Ánkene, who I think was the tallest man on the island, Ze Gutín Pêndê, Fidel Gañía, Pudul Jodán, Ze Fingui, Zancus'u Gueg'a, Ze Jandjía Teix, Menembofi Sugalía and that man who everyone knew would not be going to the *Señor*'s paradise, because he said such awful things about *Jesucristo* and the *Virgen*. And once again, Sabina's premonitions had come true. For she had said she'd been met by many soaking men who smelled of saltwater, and she'd seen a face among the men that had been so familiar she hadn't been able to keep quiet about who it was, and so she'd told everyone that something bad was going to happen and that it would involve that man who was not going to be granted salvation, that something bad was going to happen at sea, and that was why those men looked soaking wet and smelled of saltwater, at least to Sabina's eyes and nose. But nobody had listened to her, maybe because nobody was willing to accept that yet another catastrophe was going to befall the island. And in fact that had a lot to do with why Sabina went around crying; she didn't want to be the bearer of bad news, to have to tell people that more misfortune lay ahead. But there was no escaping it. When I got older and started to listen to adult conversations, the deads would make me very angry. Up until then, I'd understood that deads could help alives avoid catastrophes. But once these things came out of Sabina's mouth, or out of the mouths of any of the other clairvoyants, the catastrophes happened without anybody being able to do anything about them. I said to myself: What's the point of the deads? I thought they were meant to protect us? I found it hard to believe that they were so powerful they could bother Sabina by telling her a catastrophe was going to happen, but they couldn't do anything to prevent the catastrophe from happening. I thought of all this because it was what I heard the old people say, and they knew the most about everything.

The whole island cried a lot, a tremendous amount. They were eight men with wives and children, families who'd start to have it bad now that the man of the house was gone. To have it bad even in the context of the hardship we had anyway. The whole island cried a lot and for several days. It was said, based on what the sole survivor said, once he could finally speak, that the light they saw

261

on the horizon wasn't real, that it had been a trick. That's to say, a light that led them to their deaths. It led them far out to sea and, when they were so far out they could no longer see the island, the light disappeared, as if it had never shone in the first place. They realised they'd been tricked, but there was nothing they could do other than go on paddling; from then on, and until midday the next day, they paddled non-stop, searching for the lost island. That's why I said I could say it a hundred times and still not come close to describing how much they paddled. They paddled, and paddled, and paddled, and paddled, and paddled, and paddled, and paddled, and paddled, and paddled, and paddled, until they could paddle no more. And that's when they saw land with mountains and trees. But it wasn't real. There were trees and mountains that they could see right before their eyes, as if they could reach out and touch them with their hands, but when they rubbed their eyes to look closer, the mountains and trees were gone, and all they saw were the four points of the horizon again. They hadn't eaten since leaving the village of San Xuan, and they'd taken nothing to drink with them either, for they had set off thinking that on that boat, from whatever nation it was, they'd be given food and drink, even that they'd smoke. But it didn't turn out like that.

One thing I know, for I've heard it said by adults many times, is that the last thing a lost canoeman does is stop paddling. When he lays his paddle down in his canoe, it's because he's handing his life over to destiny. Even if there's no land in sight, you paddle until your last breath. What I also know, or think, is that not even the adults who went out in canoes knew how many countries there were close to our island, nor how near to us any of them were. So doubtless they did paddle until their last breath, but without knowing which direction to go in, until they were swept up by a current, and nobody can escape from a current, you just have to wait until it lets you be and deposits you wherever. The phenomenon of being swept up by currents has a fearsome name in my language. It only occurs way out at sea, in waters that know nothing of our Atlantic Ocean island. If any of those canoes ended up in one of those currents, they were doubtless taken to die somewhere very far from our island, somewhere no one returns from. They disappeared. We cried a lot, but they were never heard of again, except for one of them, who told the story of having been to the other side. The others were never heard of again. They disappeared from our lives.

That was the terrible case of the men who got lost at sea. But I was talking about the young canoeman who left a woman on the shore of the big village and then she disappeared from sight. So what happened to her? The man knew she was in a hurry because her child was sick, but even so, she couldn't have got up the beach in such a short time. Something had happened to her. The man became worried and set off to investigate, to find out what had happened to the woman with the sick child in her arms. And what had happened was this. On our island, children go to the sandy beach of the big village during the day. They go there because the sand is fine and fun to play in. And part of the fun, or the play, consists of digging big holes in the sand with your hands, climbing into the hole and hiding from other children. The adults know about this game and make sure the children fill in the holes before leaving the beach. But sometimes night might start spreading its dark cloak over the island and the children, hiding in their holes or running from one hole to another, are having too much fun to notice. Then their mothers appear to tell them it's time to leave the beach and come home. And in their haste, brought on by the impending gloom and their mothers' anxious calls, the children leave the holes they've dug and run home. Most children run home without even brushing the sand off themselves, never mind filling the holes in. And because most children are afraid of going near the water at night, they go to bed with sand all over their bodies, feet and face. *Gracias a Dios*, sand doesn't stain or irritate the skin. I know this from experience. And considering how deeply we slept, a few grains of sand in the sheets obviously didn't bother us. Just think: even with a bed full of sand we slept so deeply we wet the bed without realising it.

Anyway, what's significant about all this is that holes are left without being filled in, and anyone walking on the beach in the dark, like that woman with the sick child, could easily fall into one and hurt themselves. And that's exactly what happened when the man laid down his paddle after travelling many hours from the south village. The woman fell into one of those holes and disappeared from the canoeman's sight. And as he knew nobody on the island had ever disappeared before, the man became worried, became alarmed even, and so he took a few steps forward, for he'd have a story to tell the next day. If you were with someone and they disappeared, you'd be the first person on the island to tell of someone having the ability to disappear. And if that someone was a woman, she might be a she-devil. So you had to be alert. He went to see what had happened to the woman and, after taking a few steps, he saw what it was. It was night and the whole island was in darkness. The woman had stepped forward, met with no ground and been swallowed up by the hole. Furthermore, she'd toppled forward and landed face-first against the side of the hole, and sand had got up her nose and into her mouth. And because she didn't know where she was stepping, and then stepped on nothing, the impact when her foot hit the bottom of the hole had jolted through her leg and sprained her ankle. The woman wasn't expecting to come across a hole in the middle of the night, and when you put your weight down on something that ends up being nothing, you tend to get injured. That's how the man found her. Her face ached from banging into the side of the hole, she'd swallowed a mouthful of sand and her ankle hurt from the jolt it got when her foot hit the bottom of the hole. The injury to her ankle caused her more pain than her nose and mouth. She could no longer walk. And what about the child she'd had in her arms? The child had come loose as she fell and landed a few feet away from the hole, still wrapped in cloth.

The man got to where she was, found the woman whimpering and realised what had happened. He could make out the shape of the child lying a few feet away from the hole, although it wasn't crying, it remained silent. The canoeman climbed into the hole and pulled the woman out. It wasn't easy, for the hole was deep. It had been dug by several children at once. He sat the woman down on the sand and turned his attention to the baby boy, who the man understood was sick. And because the boy was sick and still only very little, he'd not moved from where he'd fallen after coming loose from his mother's arms. Darkness reigned over the island. There was no light on the beach and they could see only what was close enough for them to make out. The man picked up the shape he assumed was the child and handed it to the woman, who was still whimpering because of her sore ankle. Did the man not notice that the child hadn't whimpered at all, that it hadn't cried once during the whole journey? He probably did notice, but the way things had happened there wasn't much time to think, and the woman was still in need of assistance.

Having established what had happened, he now needed to go for help. The woman had a sick child, but she could no longer walk. If she'd been on her own, without the sick child, the canoeman would have carried her home on his back, but he couldn't carry her if she had to carry a child, for she wouldn't have been able to hold on to his shoulders. So he needed to get help. There was no other option. In other circumstances, he would not have left a woman on her own on the beach with a sick child in the middle of the night. In other circumstances, the woman would not have let him leave her on her own in the dark at the water's edge holding on to a dead child, for that's what her boy was. Any unknown being might emerge from the sea, and she was a woman, and it was night. There wasn't another soul on the beach, for no one was expecting anyone to arrive from one of the settlements. But they had arrived, and in painful circumstances. They had no choice. The canoeman would knock at the door of the first house he found open, or else at the closed door of the house of an acquaintance, and ask for help. Given the situation, the man probably didn't know where the woman with the sick child lived, so he could not go to her house to seek help there. And in any case, the woman had only one sister, and if the sister were away in another village, that house would be empty and shut. There'd be no sign of life in it and not just because of the dark.

The big village wasn't totally empty and the man found some people and explained what had happened:

he had brought a woman from the south village with her sick child; they'd had a problem advancing in the canoe, but they'd got there in the end; the woman had climbed out of the canoe, taken her child and set off for home, but a few feet away from the water's edge she'd fallen down a hole, and now she couldn't walk. He said he needed help to get her off the dark shore, and that they needed to act right away. She'd be very frightened on her own at the water's edge. As I've said before, everyone on the island knew each other, although not everyone knew the particular circumstances of everyone else. The people he told the story to showed their concern and a few minutes later they were all down on the beach, at the exact spot where the man had left the mother and her sick child, near the hole into which she'd fallen and hurt her ankle. They went with a lantern, and with people pitying that poor woman's plight, but she wasn't where the man had left her. She couldn't walk, so how could she have moved? Did the woman have strange powers after all? The hole was there, but there was no sign of the woman. The lantern they had didn't produce much light, and it made them nervous being on the beach at that time of night. Although if the lantern had made a lot of light, they'd have been nervous too, for they'd have been combating the darkness but exposing themselves to who knows what – for it was the middle of the night. Where had the woman gone? The man had assured the people who'd come to help that she couldn't walk, and surely he would not have lied to make them leave home in the middle of the night. They looked at one another, they looked around, but they didn't dare call out. Had yet another misfortune befallen her? Just as they started to doubt what they were doing there, they heard a whimper from a few feet away. A whimper like someone blowing their nose. A little fearful of what it might be, they approached with the lantern, the canoeman in front, and, in among the beached canoes, he found the woman. She lay sprawled out in the sand, her child held to her chest, though because of the way she was turned, the boy was also laid out in the sand. What had happened was that she'd felt very exposed out there in the middle of the beach, so she'd managed to drag herself, or crawl, with her child under one arm, to the beached canoes, where she'd squeezed in between two of them. The canoes were beached very close together with just enough room for a man to walk between them, so as not to take up too much space. She felt safer there. Lying in the dark, she'd thought about how all she had in life was one sister, that they'd had a hard life and that, although it had gone on being hard with a child she'd got after going to talk to the white men on the boat, she now felt devastated, for in a few hours' time her child would be buried in the ground, because some sickness, or hardship itself even, had taken the child's life away. That's why she held the child to her breast, as if her son were still alive, and she cried for all that her life had been, culminating with

269

breaking an ankle on the beach in the dark in the middle of the night. She cried in silence but you could still hear her sniffling, the sound of her nose. She lay sprawled out in the sand, something an adult rarely did. Sprawled out in the darkness, at the water's edge, on an island in the middle of the Atlantic Ocean.

I'm not a writer, or a teacher, or a priest. I don't know anyone on the island who could be described as a writer. It's an occupation, or a state, that none of us knew anything about. We'd never heard of it before. The only people who ever knew how to write on the island were the teacher, the priest and the functionaries who worked in the governor's office, though we never knew what they came to do. What I have spoken of is what I experienced, heard and saw when I was a child. It has never been put down in writing before, because, as I said, I am not a writer; nobody on the island is. If this story becomes known, it will be because of some white people. They came to our island and wanted to know our folk tales, the stories we tell at night before going to sleep. Or that we used to tell, or that we remember being told by others as we gathered round, ears at the ready. They asked me to tell them a folk tale, or several, and I thought the best thing to do was to tell them the story of my childhood, for I couldn't remember any folk tales from back then. The white people said they had come to recover our oral storytelling tradition, and their leader, a man named Manuel, said I could tell him whatever story I liked, because childhood memories would likely hold some significance too. I told him what I remembered of those years, and I closed my mouth when I considered the story finished. It took us two days; that's to say, we met twice, on two different days. I hope the contraption he used to capture my words captured them properly . . . If I'd been good at writing myself, I wouldn't have required someone else to put down in writing what I myself experienced. But after learning to count up to five hundred and something, after learning to add, subtract, multiply and divide numbers with two figures, and after learning that Spanish words are divided into *aguda*, *llana* and *esdrújula*, I couldn't take my studies any further. For many reasons. So the white people's interest is my opportunity. I hope Manuel manages to find a way to get my story written down, so that anyone who experienced it, anyone from our island who was the same age as me when I experienced these things, is able to recall what happened in their lives. I know you can't cover everything in a story told over just a few hours. But I thank Manuel for allowing my story, which is also the story of many people on the island, to take the place of the folk tales he wanted for his work.

They found that woman drowning in tears, her child held close to her chest, sprawled out in the sand. She could no longer contain herself. She'd held it all in for the whole journey, and even a good while before that, but she could no longer contain her grief; she could no longer bear to wait until she got home, as she'd planned to do. Before getting home, yet another misfortune had befallen her, another misfortune to add to her living on that island in total hardship, to her never having lived with her parents and to the only child *Dios* had seen fit to give her having died. Her sorrow was tremendous, and she cried for herself, and they let her cry. And she'd broken her ankle, or at least could no longer use it, and could not take her dead child home. Few people have experienced such things. Her misfortune seemed to be particularly great, for ending up without the use of your foot just when you need it most is no small thing, not something that happens every day on the island.

The people who had come to help the canoeman picked up the dead child, or the sick child, depending on how much of the story they knew, and the canoeman put the woman on his back. Then they went to the house the woman told them was hers, or that some of them already knew was hers. By midday the next day, a little coffin to bury the dead child in was ready. And because the boy was from his land, or at least half of him was, the *Padre* came down from the *Misión* and sprinkled holy water on his coffin. Then a man hoisted the coffin onto his shoulders and they took it away to be buried. Only a few people followed, people who knew the young woman, her only sister for example. The woman herself was not there. She could not attend her son's funeral. She could not walk and there was no one strong enough to carry her on their back all the way to the cemetery. Besides, the adults on our island say that a person with broken bones should not enter a cemetery. If they do, the bones might heal wrong or not at all. And so she could not follow behind the tiny coffin of her son, Luis Mari. And while her son was taken away in that small, narrow coffin, she sat in her house crying about everything that had happened. No one stayed behind to console her. She cried in a low murmur, as if she hadn't the strength to show the magnitude of her pain. But her tears were plentiful, so abundant that you feared for her. She cried for herself, for her solitude, for her many years of hardship, and because she'd been abandoned by Luis Mari, the only child she had.

They came back from the cemetery and waited for night to come before recalling all that had happened; to recall it, but only after dark. Because of her misfortune, someone would have given her a little kerosene to light her sad house. Then again maybe nobody had any to give, in which case her tears ran down her face and splashed on the floor in the dark. And without any light, her heart would have ached with sorrow all the more. She'd have cried for hours on end, until she fell asleep. She'd have woken up in the morning and started crying again, and the first person to talk to her would have heard a voice that was hoarse, spent and pained.

A few hours after the funeral, the canoeman who'd transported the woman and her child from the south village went back to the beach and pulled his boat to the water's edge. When he'd mentally planned the journey, he hadn't imagined it ending in the cemetery. Luis Mari had been laid to rest, but life had to go on. He picked up his fishing tackle, put the canoe to float and jumped in. Behind him he left much pain, but life had to go on. There was no other option. With a few strokes of the paddle he moved away from the shore, whistling out of the corner of his mouth. Any canoeman on our island, any fisherman going out to sea, respected the island custom of whistling out on the open sea. Anyone walking close to the shore, even high above sea level, would hear his whistle. They would hear him even though it was difficult to call out to land from at sea. The wind carried words off to other parts, perhaps to the mountains up above.

The canoeman planned to paddle as far out from the coast as he could and then cast out his fishing hook. He would fish until around midday and then paddle on to the south village. If during that journey he saw a little stick on the thin line of the horizon, a little stick that indicated the presence of a boat, he would change course and launch himself after it, no matter what time of day it was. If no little stick appeared on the horizon, he'd paddle on to the black stones of the south beach, pull his canoe up the beach and clean the fish he'd caught. There might not be anyone there to help him pull the

274

canoe in, but he knew how to make a good go of it on his own and leave it beyond the scourge of the waves. Then he'd pick up his basket and go up the hill to the south village. There he'd select the best specimens and prepare a bundle of fish for the maestro. This was his duty. This way he informed the maestro of his return and allowed the maestro to share in the fish caught in his canoe.

But if a little stick appeared on the horizon confirming a boat was nearby, or far away, that young man would have pointed the maestro's canoe towards it and set off in hope of getting something to relieve the hardship. It didn't matter that he hadn't rested properly after such a long night. And it didn't matter how slim the thing was on the horizon. He would set off after it, and whether that decision proved the right one or the wrong one would depend on destiny, and it would be destiny that decided whether he ever set foot on our Atlantic Ocean island again.

Malabo, Equatorial Guinea
11th August 2008

Dear readers,

We rely on subscriptions from people like you to tell these other stories – the types of stories most publishers consider too risky to take on.

Our subscribers don't just make the books physically happen. They also help us approach booksellers, because we can demonstrate that our books already have readers and fans. And they give us the security to publish in line with our values, which are collaborative, imaginative and 'shamelessly literary'.

All of our subscribers:

- receive a first-edition copy of each of the books they subscribe to
- are thanked by name at the end of these books
- are warmly invited to contribute to our plans and choice of future books

BECOME A SUBSCRIBER, OR GIVE A SUBSCRIPTION TO A FRIEND

Visit andotherstories.org/subscribe to become part of an alternative approach to publishing.

Subscriptions are:

£20 for two books per year

£35 for four books per year

£50 for six books per year

OTHER WAYS TO GET INVOLVED

If you'd like to know about upcoming events and reading groups (our foreign-language reading groups help us choose books to publish, for example) you can:

- join the mailing list at: andotherstories.org/join-us
- follow us on Twitter: @andothertweets
- join us on Facebook: facebook.com/AndOtherStoriesBooks
- follow our blog: Ampersand

This book was made possible thanks to the support of:

AG Hughes
Abigail Miller
Adam Butler
Adam Lenson
Aidan
    Cottrell-Boyce
Ajay Sharma
Alan Ramsey
Alannah Hopkin
Alastair Gillespie
Alastair Laing
Alec Begley
Alex Martin
Alex Ramsey
Alex Sutcliffe
Alexandra Buchler
Alexandra de
    Verseg-Roesch
Ali Smith
Alice Nightingale
Alisa Brookes
Alison Hughes
Alison Winston
Allison Graham
Alyse Ceirante
Amanda Anderson
Amanda Banham
Amanda Dalton
Amelia Dowe
Amy Rushton

Amy Webster
Andrea Reinacher
Andrew Marston
Andrew Nairn
Andrew Pattison
Andy Burfield
Andy Paterson
Angela Thirlwell
Angharad Eyre
Angus MacDonald
Angus Walker
Ann Van Dyck
Anna Demming
Anna Holmwood
Anna Milsom
Anna Vinegrad
Anna-Karin Palm
Annabel Hagg
Anne Carus
Anne
    Claydon-Wallace
Anne Maguire
Anne Meadows
Anne Waugh
Anne Marie Jackson
Annie McDermott
Anonymous
Antonio de Swift
Antony Pearce
Aoife Boyd

Archie Davies
Asher Norris

Barbara Mellor
Barbara Thanni
Barry Norton
Bartolomiej Tyszka
Belinda Farrell
Ben Schofield
Ben Smith
Ben Thornton
Benjamin Judge
Benjamin Morris
Bettina Debon
Blanka Stoltz
Bob Hill
Brenda Scott
Brendan McIntyre
Briallen Hopper
Brian Rogers
Bruce Ackers
Bruce & Maggie
    Holmes

C Baker
C Mieville
Candy Says Juju
    Sophie
Cara & Bali Haque
Carole JS Russo

Caroline Adie
Caroline
    Mildenhall
Caroline Rigby
Carolyn A
    Schroeder
Cath Drummond
Catherine
    Mansfield
Cecily Maude
Charles Lambert
Charles Rowley
Charlotte Baines
Charlotte Holtam
Chris Day
Chris Elcock
Chris Hancox
Chris Radley
Chris Stevenson
Chris Wood
Christina Baum
Christina
    MacSweeney
Christina Scholz
Christine Luker
Christopher Allen
Christopher
    Marlow
Ciara Ní Riain
Ciarín Oman
Claire Fuller
Claire Mitchell

Claire Tranah
Clare Fisher
Clare Keates
Clare Lucas
Clarissa Botsford
Clifford Posner
Clive Bellingham
Colin Burrow
Collette Eales
Courtney Lilly
Craig Barney

Dan Pope
Daniel Carpenter
Daniel Gillespie
Daniel Hahn
Daniel Hugill
Daniel Lipscombe
Daniel Venn
Daniela Steierberg
Dave Lander
David Archer
David Breuer
David Eales
David Gould
David Hedges
David
    Johnson-Davies
David Smith
David Wardrop
Dawn Mazarakis
Debbie Pinfold

Deborah Jacob
Deborah Smith
Delia Cowley
Denis Stillewagt &
    Anca Fronescu
Denise Muir
Diana Brighouse
Dimitris Melicertes
Dominique Brocard

EJ Baker
Ed Tallent
Edward Baggs
Eileen Buttle
Elaine Rassaby
Eleanor Maier
Elena Traina
Eliza O'Toole
Elizabeth Draper
Emily Jeremiah
Emily Taylor
Emily Williams
Emily Yaewon Lee
    & Gregory
    Limpens
Emma Bielecki
Emma Kenneally
Eva
    Tobler-Zumstein
Evgenia Loginova
Ewan Tant

Fawzia Kane
Fi McMillan
Fiona Doepel
Fiona Graham
Fiona Powlett
	Smith
Fran Sanderson
Frances Chapman
Francesca Bray
Francis Taylor
Francisco Vilhena
Friederike Knabe

G Thrower
Gale Pryor
Garry Wilson
Gary Debus
Gavin Collins
Gawain Espley
Gemma Tipton
Genevra
	Richardson
Geoffrey Fletcher
George Wilkinson
George Sandison &
	Daniela Laterza
Geraldine Brodie
Gill Boag-Munroe
Gillian Doherty
Gillian Spencer
Gillian Stern
Giselle Maynard

Gloria Sully
Glyn Ridgley
Gordon Cameron
Gordon Campbell
Graham & Steph
	Parslow
Graham R Foster
Gwyn Wallace

Harriet Gamper
Harriet Mossop
Harriet Owles
Harriet Sayer
Harriet Spencer
Helen Asquith
Helen Brady
Helen Buck
Helen Weir
Helen Wormald
Helena Taylor
Helene Walters
Henrike
	Laehnemann
Holly Johnson
	& Pat Merloe
Howdy Reisdorf

Ian Barnett
Ian Kirkwood
Ian McMillan
Irene Mansfield
Isabella Garment

J Collins
JC Sutcliffe
Jack Brown
Jacky Oughton
Jacqueline Crooks
Jacqueline Haskell
Jacqueline
	Lademann
Jacqueline Taylor
Jacquie Goacher
Jade Maitre
James & Mapi
James Clark
James Cubbon
James Huddie
James Portlock
James Scudamore
James Tierney
Jane Brandon
Jane Whiteley
Jane Woollard
Janet Bolam
Janette Ryan
Jasmine Dee
	Cooper
Jasmine Gideon
Jason Spencer
Jeff Collins
Jen Grainger
Jen
	Hamilton-Emery
Jenifer Logie

Jennifer Higgins
Jennifer Hurstfield
Jennifer O'Brien
Jennifer Watson
Jenny Diski
Jenny Newton
Jess Wood
Jethro Soutar
Jillian Jones
Jo Elvery
Jo Harding
Jo Hope
Joan Clinch
Joanne Hart
Jocelyn English
Jodie Free
Joel Love
Johan Forsell
Johannes Georg
    Zipp
John Allison
John Conway
John Fisher
John Gent
John Hodgson
John Kelly
John McGill
John Nicholson
John Stephen
    Grainger
John William
    Fallowfield

Jon Gower
Jon Iglesias
Jonathan Ruppin
Jonathan Watkiss
Joseph Cooney
Judith Heneghan
Judith Norton
Judy Kendall
Julian Duplain
Julian Lomas
Juliane Jarke
Julie Gibson
Julie Van Pelt
Juraj Janik

KL Ee
Kaarina Hollo
Kaitlin Olson
Kalbinder Dayal
Kapka Kassabova
Karan Deep
    Singh
Kari Dickson
Karla Fonesca
Kate Pullinger
Kate Rhind
Kate Wild
Katharine Freeman
Katharine Robbins
Kathryn Lewis
Katie Smith
Kay Elmy

Keith Dunnett
Ken Walsh
Kevin Brockmeier
Kevin Pino
Koen Van
    Bockstal
Krystalli
    Glyniadakis

Lana Selby
Lander Hawes
Laura Clarke
Laura Solon
Lauren Cerand
Lauren Ellemore
Leanne Bass
Leonie Schwab
Lesley Lawn
Lesley Murphey
Lesley Watters
Leslie Rose
Linda Harte
Lindsay Brammer
Lindsey Ford
Liz Clifford
Loretta Platts
Louise Bongiovanni
Louise Rogers
Louise S Smith
Lu
Lucie Donahue
Lucie Harris

Lucy Luke
Lynda Graham
Lynn Martin

M Manfre
Maeve Lambe
Maggie Peel
Maisie &
    Nick Carter
Marella
    Oppenheim
Mareta &
    Conor Doyle
Marina Castledine
Marina Lomunno
Marion Cole
Marion England
Marion Tricoire
Mark Ainsbury
Mark Blacklock
Mark Waters
Marta Muntasell
Martha Gifford
Martha Nicholson
Martin
    Hollywood
Mary Hall
Mary Nash
Mary Wang
Matt Oldfield
Matthew Francis
Matthew Todd

Maxime
    Dargaud-Fons
Michael Harrison
Michael Johnston
Michael Kitto
Michael &
    Christine
    Thompson
Monika Olsen
Moshi Moshi
    Records

Nan Craig
Nan Haberman
Nasser Hashmi
Natalie Smith
Natalie Wardle
Natasha
    Soobramanien
Nathalie Adams
Nathaniel Barber
Nick James
Nick Judd
Nick Nelson &
    Rachel Eley
Nick Sidwell
Nick Williams
Nicola Balkind
Nicola Hart
Nicola Hughes
Nina Alexandersen

PM Goodman
Pat Crowe
Patrick Owen
Paul Bailey
Paul Brand
Paul Hollands
Paul Jones
Paul M Cray
Paul Miller
Paul Munday
Paula McGrath
Penelope Price
Peter Armstrong
Peter Burns
Peter Lawton
Peter Murray
Peter Rowland
Peter Vos
Philip Warren
Philippe Royer
Phyllis Reeve
Piet Van Bockstal
Pipa Clements

Rachael Williams
Rachel Kennedy
Rachel Lasserson
Rachel Van Riel
Rachel Watkins
Read MAW
    Books
Rebecca Atkinson

Rebecca Braun
Rebecca Moss
Rebecca Rosenthal
Réjane Collard
Renata Larkin
Rhian Jones
Rhodri Jones
Richard Ellis
Richard Jackson
Richard Smith
Rishi Dastidar
Rob Jefferson-
    Brown
Robert Gillett
Robert Saunders
Robin Patterson
Rodolfo Barradas
Rory Sullivan
Ros Schwartz
Rose Cole
Ross Macpherson
Roz Simpson
Russell Logan
Ruth Stokes

SE Guine
SJ Bradley
SJ Naudé
Sabine Griffiths
Sally Baker
Sam Gallivan
Sam Ruddock

Samantha
    Sabbarton-
    Wright
Samantha Schnee
Sandra Hall
Sandy Derbyshire
Sarah Benson
Sarah Butler
Sarah Duguid
Sarah Fakray
Sarah Pybus
Sarah Salmon
Sarah Salway
Sascha Feuchert
Sasha Dugdale
Saskia Restorick
Sean Malone
Sean McGivern
Sharon Evans
Sheridan Marshall
Sherine El-Sayed
Shirley Harwood
Sigrun Hodne
Simon Armstrong
Simon John Harvey
Simon Pare
Simon Pennington
Simona Constantin
Sinead Rippington
Siobhan Higgins
Sophie Eustace
Sophie Johnstone

Sophie North
Stefano D'Orilia
Stephen Abbott
Stephen Bass
Stephen H Oakey
Stephen Pearsall
Stephen Walker
Stewart McAbney
Stuart Condie
Sue & Ed Aldred
Susan Ferguson
Susan Murray
Susan Tomaselli
Susanna Jones
Susie Roberson
Suzanne White

Tammy Watchorn
Tania Hershman
The Mighty Douche
    Softball Team
Thomas Bell
Thomas Fritz
Thomas JD Gray
Tim Gray
Tim Jackson
Tim Robins
Tim Theroux
Timothy Harris
Tina Rotherham-
    Winqvist
Tom Bowden

Tom Darby
Tom Franklin
Tony & Joy
    Molyneaux
Tony Messenger
Tony Roa
Torna Russell-Hills
Trevor Lewis
Trilby Humphryes
Tristan Burke

Val Challen
Vanessa Garden
Vanessa Nolan
Vasco Dones
Victoria Adams
Visaly Muthusamy
Vivien
    Doornekamp-
    Glass

Walter Prando
Wendy Irvine
Wendy Langridge
Wendy Toole
Wenna Price
William G Dennehy

Yukiko Hiranuma

Zoe Brasier

Current & Upcoming Books

Title: *By Night the Mountain Burns*
Author: Juan Tomás Ávila Laurel
Translator: Jethro Soutar
Editor: Sophie Lewis
Typesetting & Proofreading: Tetragon, London
Cover Design: Hannah Naughton
Format: Trade paperback with French flaps
Paper: Munken LP Opaque 70/15 FSC
Printer: TJ International Ltd, Padstow, Cornwall, UK